Beautiful WILD

Also by Anna Godbersen

The Luxe
Rumors
Envy
Splendor

Bright Young Things
Beautiful Days
The Lucky Ones

When We Caught Fire

ANNA GODBERSEN

An Imprint of HarperCollinsPublishers

alloyentertainment

For Francesca,
and all the wild girls

PART
ONE

The Maiden Voyage of the <u>Princess</u>
by Dame Edna Sackville

You have all heard by now of the <u>Princess of the Pacific</u>, the Farrar Line's newest and most impressive ship. But only I, dearest readers, can give you the full story of her maiden voyage, for today I sail on the celebrated ship into the open ocean, that vast and magical field of water—a landscape by turns starkly brilliant under the rays of a fierce sun, or dizzying, changeable, windswept. Who cares about all that, you may wonder, when there are three formal dining rooms, a Turkish bath, and a ladies' couturier on board? Fear not, I will give every detail, my sweet ones, the landscape and the parties. It is sure to be a romance to thrill the heart and elevate the soul, this voyage to the very edge of the world. But, like many a sea voyage, the plot began to thicken while still on land. . . .

The land in question is the farthest west you can

go in our country, a backwater called San Francisco (named by the Spanish, who tromped through in one or another of the previous centuries), where a fortune of two generations is considered old money. This is a town where you always smell the sawdust, not to mention the low tide. I descended upon the place along with many of the fine people you are familiar with from my columns—the Misses Van Huysen, Emma and Lucille, resplendent in the couture they acquired over the summer in Paris; the Marquis and Marquise of Brenn; members of the most eminent families of New York, Philadelphia, and Boston; and descendants of the grand old lines of Europe. The first voyage of the <u>Princess</u> is one of those events that bring all the best people together, for it promises lavish parties and gossip galore. (I suffer for you reader; I do; I do.)

The Farrar Line, which has been responsible for moving stylish people across the Atlantic for over fifty years now, spared no expense in publicizing the <u>Princess</u>. It is well known that she has a swimming pool and tailor and wireless on board. That there is an indoor tennis court and a top-deck observatory. Over the summer it was a kind of competition amongst the sporting set to get on the passenger list.

And for no one more so than the unattached ladies of the best families. . . .

The scions of the Farrar fortune will be making the trip, too, you see. The elder Farrar son, Carlton (first in line to succeed his father, that eminent businessman and philanthropist Winthrop Farrar II, as head of the family concern), is here with his wife, the renowned beauty Camilla née Jones. But more exciting to the rest of us: the younger son, the one the columnists call Fitz (just as dashing as he sounds, I can assure you!). He is popular among the gents for his legendary explorations (serialized by my competitor The Evening Phoenix, but we forgive him) and with the ladies for cutting such a fine figure and for being such a riotous good time. These young men are thought to be one of the main attractions on a ship that boasts many unheard-of luxuries and entertainments. The charter is San Francisco–Honolulu–Sydney, and as has been much reported, the young Fitz will be leading an expedition into the interior of Australia upon arrival.

The night before the ship's departure, a grand fete was held at the Palace Hotel for all the first-class passengers, and while it was at first a staid affair, soon well-dressed people who were not on the guest list began to arrive and I got to witness firsthand the spirit of this barbarous coast. San Francisco society is not at all as formal as we are back East, and certainly not as sophisticated as in the grand houses of Europe. Even among this rather raucous group of young millionaires, one young woman stood out. Not on account of her stature—she was rather slight—but because she seemed entirely indifferent to the rules of decorum usually observed in such rooms. She was dressed impeccably—I could not fault her there—but she talked loudly, ordered champagne rather than waiting to have it brought to her, moved around the room to whomever she found interesting, expressed frank opinions, and was generally conspicuous.

And yet Fitzhugh Farrar could not take his eyes away.

Presently, Fitz and this wild girl began to dance together, and with such energy that many saw not only the lady's stockings but also her underskirts. It must be admitted that the heir to the shipping fortune drank more than his older brother thought proper. It was a true "scene," as we say, though nothing compared with what I expect shall come next.

For Vidalia Marin Hazzard—that is the peculiar name this rogue of a girl's parents gave her—has just been added to the passenger list of the _Princess_, having taken a very fine suite on the promenade deck. I wondered, as any reasonable person might, if there was a story in this sudden thirst for travel. . . .

ONE

For Vidalia Marin Hazzard—age seventeen years and four months, height five feet one, with eyes a color as shifting as fool's gold—the ocean possessed no special romance. To be certain, the silver, shining sea was a perfectly beautiful backdrop to a picnic in the Presidio, or an evening's entertainment at the Cliff House, but she was a girl with feet firmly planted on the earth and had never thought anything much of the vast waterway that was her own backyard. But now, in the hustle of the Embarcadero, seeing the gleaming side of the ship that rose from the gray-green surface of the San Francisco Bay like a monument, like a towering city unto itself, she felt her breath snatched and her spine tingling and she had to admit that maybe it was impressive enough to merit so much frenzied anticipation.

"Vida!" cried one of the scrum of reporters gathered at the waterfront to document an event that had been the talk of the town for some months already. He had to shout to be heard over the brass band and the confetti shooter and the ubiquitous exclamations of wonderment. "Miss Hazzard!"

His shouting cut into the fog that resided somewhere between her forehead and the backs of her eyes, and she remembered what a hideous quantity of champagne she had drunk the night before. But a headache was no excuse not to leave a winning final impression on the people of her hometown. She turned in her artful way and by the time she met the young man's eye her mouth had assumed a magnificent smile. She clutched a fistful of her opulently tiered ivory skirt (*White for sailing,* she had decided that morning, after her parents had told her to board the famous ship or settle quickly on a local boy to marry before she ruined her reputation once and for all) and placed her other hand on the narrow of her waist. A camera's flash went *poof.* "Yes?" she said to no member of the assembled in particular.

"What do you make of it?"

"It's a little small, don't you think?" The young man laughed and she shrugged and went on in a confessional tone: "Oh well, I guess it *is* a little wonderful after all."

"Not more wonderful than you."

"You know very well that *I* would never say any such thing—I am never immodest," she replied, and winked. For it was one of her charms that she knew who she was, and never tried to hide that she wasn't really very modest at all. The reporter, who had been with the *Chronicle* almost a year now, and whose favor she had bought with little favors like opera tickets and baskets of big ripe strawberries from the Salinas Valley, knew it, too. He had been crucial in keeping certain stories about her out of the press, and getting others into print—which was one of the reasons it had taken until this morning for her parents to become fully aware what a wild kind of life she had managed to live right under their noses.

Her immodesty had nothing whatsoever to do with beauty, however. She was not a beauty, as she was quite aware. Her chin was an imprecise proposition and her nose was broad and she was too short to stand out in a crowd. But she had a gift for putting herself together so as to bring attention to her best features. That, and how to let the light of her spirit shine through the pale skin of her face so that everyone who met her came away with the impression that she was the loveliest girl in all of California.

Why try to stand out in a crowd, when you could rise above like a shining star?

That was Vida Hazzard's personal philosophy, and on a fine, late-October day, which had dawned bright and a little misty and was now absolutely blue, her way of doing things was on display to a rather dizzying degree. Her late-night adventures had appeared in the early edition of the paper, and her parents had fretted and paced, and she had lain on a chaise longue with a cold compress on her fore-head wishing very much that they would shut up. It was hard enough, without their pacing and fretting, to decide if it was better to marry the most malleable boy she knew (and carry on as she had been, albeit with a new ring and a new name) or leave town and try to save her reputation that way.

In the end it hadn't really been much of a choice. She wasn't interested in the ocean, but she *was* interested in all the places she had not yet seen. The world was big—so she had been told—and she had never been content to sit still long.

Leave town it was.

The papers had been calling the *Princess* the "Million-aire's Ship of the West," to rival the White Star Line's grand floating worlds that moved every sort of person and pack-age between Boston and New York and the ports of the Mediterranean and the British Isles. The people her parents socialized with had talked of little else all summer, which had stoked her contrariness. She had taken every opportu-nity to insist that this going on about a boat was enough hot air to fly a balloon. The notion became quite fixed with her, and she insisted to her parents—who were perfectly nice in their way, but were prone to put too much stock in the general prattle—that she would never set foot on such a grand lie. Yet she had a weakness for parties—the party she could not resist. She insisted they go to the party for the *Princess*'s inaugural passengers at the Palace Hotel, the night before the ship sailed, just to see all their acquaintances who'd been taken in by this Farrar Line racket behaving like suckers.

"All right," her father had agreed. This was yesterday afternoon. He told his butler to go steam his white tie and tails. Her father didn't follow the news unless it pertained to his business, but he, like his daughter, enjoyed a party. "Where, by the way, does this ship of fools go?"

Yesterday it hadn't mattered, and Vida had told him so. Today it did.

Her parents, Mr. and Mrs. Arnold Hazzard—whose family holdings originated with bitumen, but were now comprised of all sorts of industry—had purchased the tickets that morning. They had been in a high tizzy over the swirling stories of what a scene their daughter had made the night before. "She's ruined, she's ruined," her mother had wailed into her cocoa, and her father had patted his wife's shoulder and told her that all could be solved by a swift engagement. They sent cards to several friends to say they planned to only go so far as Hawaii, where they did have a few business interests to see to. But they told Vida to pack for a longer trip—if everything went according to plan, she would be engaged by Honolulu, and it would be only logical for all three Hazzards to travel on to Australia with her intended.

If Vida became engaged to Fitzhugh Farrar, they reasoned, the stories of her wildness the night before would soon be forgotten. If she did not become engaged soon, however, she risked dying an old maid. The whole brouhaha seemed rather humorous to Vida, but if it assuaged her parents' anxieties she would go along with it, and have a little adventure in the name of getting respectable.

"Will you remember me on your voyage?"

Vida had almost forgotten the young man from the *Chronicle*, so digressive and flighty were her thoughts. It really had been a very late night. "You know I will," she said. "Don't you go forgetting me, either."

"Come back soon. It will be a boring town without you."

She didn't want to agree too readily and so gave him an oblique little smile and a lazy wink, and let her gaze roam over the gathered crowd, many of whom she knew from the early days of her much-remarked-upon social career. There, with elbows on the rail of the promenade, was Theodore Grass—the first boy to propose marriage to her. His father was a newspaper publisher, and Theodore had been educated back East, but he possessed an unwavering love for his hometown, and though he was as adoring of Vida as a girl might rightly hope, she knew he could not keep up with her. He was perfectly content where he was, and there was so much she yearned to see. And there, sitting on the second-floor terrace of a saloon, was Bill Halliday, the author of her third proposal, with a stormy quality in his eyes. She winced a little at the memory of Bill, with whom she'd had some fun—he drove his horses fast, and was on speaking terms with parts of the city that fine people like them were not supposed to visit. But his adventuring had only left her with a taste for more, and anyway, she had seen how his father's same proclivity had dwindled the Halliday family fortune. And there too, leaning against a ticket agent's kiosk, was Whiting de Young, who only last month she had warned with a flash of the eyes that he should not humiliate himself by trying to propose at all. He watched her now with a sad little smile, and she could see in his eyes that he half expected her to change her mind and come running to him. For Whit was all things: rich, jocular, adoring, and descended from two of the most prosperous and prominent families in San Francisco. If he had come to her father with a ring, she knew that she would have had to marry him. Her parents would have insisted.

There was absolutely nothing wrong with him, and she was even rather fond of him.

And that was how she knew.

That was how she knew for sure that marrying well in San Francisco was not enough for her, and that she would always be vaguely dissatisfied with her lot, always wondering if there was something better going on elsewhere. That she would have nothing to do about it but to stay out too late and get boring people to tell gossipy stories about her the next day. She was a huntress—her hunting grounds were drawing rooms and polo fields, it was true; but that did not make her any less a huntress. Now, standing alongside the sheer cliff of the *Princess* (which she had derided for months as not worth talking about), she shuddered with some presentiment of the future.

For a moment she saw clearly that her fate and the fate of this ship were entwined.

After all, if she had not bothered to argue about its worthiness, she would not have made a spectacle of herself, and would not be here now.

"You can come aboard," said a familiar voice at her ear. "It's almost time."

Vida squeezed the hand of her maid, Nora. Nora was a tall, bright-eyed girl with an upturned nose who had been her ally in all her stratagems since she had begun training for cotillion five years ago. They moved together toward the plank. It had a fancy rope gate for a railing, and was made of handsome wood, but it was still a plank. As Nora guided Vida upward toward the little door in the side of the ship several stories above the pier, Vida felt how it swayed with the wind, and her heart bounced with a thrilling fear.

"Wobbly, isn't it?" said Nora, who had been this way already to escort Vida's several suitcases.

"Well, yes," Vida replied drily. "Though I may be wobbly for other reasons."

Upward they went through the decks, past uniformed sailors and early-boarding travelers, past vast quantities of starched sheets and pillows, glassware and dinnerware, past salons, past dining rooms and observation decks, up interior and exterior stairways, all that brass and oak and freshly painted white iron, all of it brand new and gleaming and as suitable for a grand ball as any millionaire's house. Nora was urging her on and on until suddenly they were outside again, on the polished planks of the top deck of the *Princess*, with all the city spread out beneath them.

When she had been a part of it, Vida had sensed the largeness of the crowd, but she hadn't really understood until she looked down on it from above. Beyond the piers that jutted from the Embarcadero was San Francisco, looking very much like a diorama city constructed by a child out of pastel blocks of Turkish delight. As Vida strode toward the rail, Nora placed the scarlet scarf in her hand; it was half unfurled by the time she reached the edge. For a moment, Vida forgot to breathe. She was farther up from the pier than she could have imagined, and had not been prepared for the dizzy feeling that overcame her when she looked down from on high. Then she remembered herself, and gazed out at the crowd, all of her friends and acquaintances reduced by distance to miniatures.

"There he is," said Mrs. Redford Flynn to her daughter—they were standing close to the rail a few feet away, both in enormous fur coats.

Vida's skin prickled at the word "he." She knew who *he* was.

Down on the pier was the young man that Mrs. and Miss Flynn had been referring to. Unlike the other men, he had forgone a navy or white suit for a khaki getup, and he was talking to a number of reporters and curious crowd members who had formed a circle around him. He cut a trim and rakish figure, and even at a distance Vida recognized the playful darting of his smile and the aristocratic line of his jaw. She had observed both quite a bit last night, at much closer range. As anyone who read the papers knew, this was Fitzhugh Farrar, the second and handsomer son of Winthrop Farrar, who controlled the Farrar shipping conglomerate.

Fitzhugh, the notorious bachelor.

Fitzhugh, the famous adventurer.

In all Vida's late nights, it suddenly occurred to her, she had never met a young man to match her own high spirit. She took a last glance at her city and wondered if she finally had.

TWO

A flurry of pastel streamers arced through the thin blue atmosphere as the *Princess* drew away from the pier. Champagne bottles popped as she moved showily along the city's shore. Cheers erupted, on land and on deck, as she traveled at last through the mouth of the San Francisco Bay—which some poet had bestowed with the moniker the "Golden Gate"—and was finally out to sea.

Vida saw none of it.

She was ensconced in her carpeted and chandeliered cabin, and only emerged onto her private little deck to blow a kiss to the receding jut of rocky green land, before hurrying back inside to resume a rather busy schedule of glamorizing. That was when she encountered the gaze of

Nora, her lady's maid; a mixture of disapproval and knowing amusement. She had come back into the cabin with
the welcome gift of a champagne bottle and two coupes
on a golden platter. Not for the first time, Vida marveled
at Nora's loveliness, which was somehow or other only
enhanced by the plainness of her black dress. Her hair was a
titian cloud above her heart-shaped face, with its dark lashes
and pink bow of a mouth. Nora was three years older than
Vida, and had taught her everything there was to know
about how to be a woman of style and grace.

"Afraid they'll forget you?" Nora asked as she crossed
the carpet, put the platter down on a mahogany sideboard,
and began to adjust Vida's evening gown, a fitted cascade
of pale red ruffles, beading, and lace, with a square neckline and a petite train that followed the fanning of the
mermaid-like skirt. "That's just the dress for tonight," she
remarked.

"Thank you." Vida did a twirl, though she didn't really
need confirmation that the dress was made to flatter her
form in particular and that it struck an alluring balance
somewhere between attention-getting and high-class,
which was precisely what she needed for the game she
would be playing this evening.

It was after all a game and not a pleasure cruise. Though
she wasn't sure if she would do as her parents wished and
return engaged, she knew that she was being talked of, and

would not have it said that she, Vida Hazzard, had gone off chasing a boy and been ignored.

"But you missed it all," Nora was saying, with her usual chiding affection. "The fanfare and all that, of course. This ship, it's a maze—I got lost twice. But—oh! You should have seen how big the ocean is when you leave the bay and are truly out to sea."

"Yes, that does sound nice. But you know we can't all be you."

"I don't know what you mean," Nora replied so that Vida's insides sloshed a little in regret. For all Nora's confidence in matters of dress and manners, she was a tender being, easily embarrassed, and when anyone drew attention to her remarkable beauty, she felt uncomfortable and went looking for a closet to hide in.

"Oh, Nora, my darlingest, don't be like that! Don't make me say it. We can't all be so effortlessly beautiful as you. Most of us have to try a little bit to get noticed, you know."

"Well, to me you are the most beautiful girl on the *Princess of the Pacific*."

"I am grateful you think so, but I don't have time for your flattery—my hair is a disaster, and we are running out of time."

"But cocktails aren't for another hour, silly. It's only four. We have plenty of time."

Vida gasped in anguish. "Is it that late?" And though she knew that widows, and gullible children, and the sweet-hearted and capable, and all those who do good in the world rather than seeking after their own pleasures, deserve the patience of everybody else, she couldn't help but feel a little irritated at Nora, whose hair went up quite easily into a bright, hazy pouf, for not understanding what a trial it was to have hair that waved and frizzed and could not at all be trusted with a change in the weather.

"Here," said Nora. She poured a glass of champagne for Vida and assumed the place behind her at the vanity to see what needed to be done. The area was already overpopulated by divers hair tonics and perfumes, lash blackeners, lip tints, rouges, jewel boxes and hairpins, arrayed over a detailed map of all the levels and rooms, public and private, of the *Princess*, as well as an embossed card listing the evening entertainments for the first-class passengers.

"Lord, Nora, please don't let me drink alone," Vida said, and before Nora could begin her work, she had poured her maid a glass, and clinked it with her own.

"What are you up to, I wonder," Nora mused, as she pinned and looped Vida's hair—of a middling brown color, nothing special, and prone to unruliness without the taking of extreme civilizing measures—into a high, romantic pile.

"Oh, you'll see," Vida replied, and handed Nora the golden, pearl-dotted strand to pin into her coiffure.

Nora smiled vaguely and let it be. Then her skillful fingers went to work on the final touches.

There, Vida thought with satisfaction as she gazed at the girl in the vanity mirror—her eyes were bright, and the high line of her cheekbones were accented with shimmering powder so no one would notice her lack of a chin, or the wideness of her nose, or her total lack of a bust. It didn't matter if she wasn't the most beautiful—she had done it again, with a little makeup and some sparkly things, and the ray of confidence that shone through her when it was a big, important night, with crowds and parties and people to impress. Miss Vida Hazzard, the most remarkable girl onboard the *Princess,* beamed back at her. Then she remembered Nora, and took her hand. "I'm glad you came with me," she whispered. She knew that Nora had wanted her to stay in San Francisco and marry Whit, for she had been pining after one of the footmen employed by his family. Vida knew this, but disapproved. The footman was almost thirty, and never smiled. He was not in the least good enough for her Nora.

"Well, now, how else would I see the world if you did not drag me along with you?" Nora asked with a little shimmer of melancholy in her eyes.

"Maybe you were meant to come on this journey," Vida gushed. "Maybe you will meet your true love tonight!"

"Oh, come now." Nora smoothed her hands over her skirt. "Do you need anything? What can I do?"

Nora's nervous palaver was cut short by a rapping of knuckles on the door, and the sight of Vida's father's big head inclining inward from the hall. A little panic sped Vida's pulse. She had a plan, and the plan was quite time-specific, and his interruption might scuttle the whole business. But, luckily, he was wearing exactly what he'd worn when he arrived on the pier. She saw an opportunity.

"Oh Papa, you aren't dressed for an evening at all!"

"I thought this was some sort of adventure," he replied good-naturedly. "And you mean to tell me that I have to be as dandified as ever?"

"*Daddy,*" she said in the exaggerated and girlish tone that he could never refuse, "have you read the first-class passenger list? It's all kinds of fancy gentlemen and ladies who travel everywhere, from castle to villa to first-class cabin on their way to safari or grand tour or what have you; they are always on the move and always dressed correctly, and they don't know who you are, or that they ought to be impressed."

Her father grinned and mimed a knife entering his heart.

"I mean they don't know *yet*, of course. I thought you *wanted* me to get myself a husband, and look at you—you're no help at all."

"If you insist, my dearest, I will go put on something to please these fancy types you want to be friends with. I just wanted to see how you were getting on. Come to our suite in half an hour? Your mother and I will be having cocktails before cocktails, and if you promise to be good, you can have a tipple of champagne."

A little late, Nora moved so as to obscure the bottle of champagne on the golden tray.

"Oh Daddy, no. I have much too much to do."

"As you wish, but promise me you won't be dancing with these East Coast bores every dance. Save one for your old dad," he said with a sigh, and kissed her forehead, and gave Nora a pat on her shoulder. "Tell our girl to be demure this evening," he said in a stage whisper. "Her mother is too nervous to even leave her cabin just now. . . . She's taking smelling salts, and wringing her hands over Vida ending up an old maid."

"Yes, sir," Nora replied with a very grave face, and showed him to the door.

"Oh thank God," Vida said, and held her breath until the retreat of his footfalls confirmed he had disappeared into his own realm. "Make sure he's gone?" she asked Nora.

While Nora leaned out of the cracked door, Vida checked her reflection once more, to assure herself that every lash and strand and bead was in place. Satisfied that she had the high gloss of a painted doll, she folded her deck plan into the invisible pocket of her gown, grabbed the bottle of champagne that Nora had procured, and moved on to the door.

Don't do anything ridiculous, Nora's face said as Vida crossed into the hall.

You know I will, Vida's impish smile replied.

Then she was off through corridors and up and down little stairways, past uniformed crewmembers of every kind, and at last into a particularly masculine hallway—all dark wood from floor to ceiling and oil paintings of seascapes with brave captains and that sort of thing. At an imposing, carved door with a little brass decal above to label it *The Map Room* she came to a halt and blew an errant strand of hair out of her eyes.

A sudden nervousness prickled Vida's skin. She glanced around. She was ever a creature of instinct, and this operation required the kind of flair that she'd possessed even as a child. But she had the uncharacteristic sense that she was about to do something that she could not take back. She felt so cold and so hot at once, and rather weighed down by the ponderousness of it all. And, oddly, she was afraid that she might not be able to go through with what she'd planned to do. . . .

Which was more or less to rap on Fitzhugh's door, and hold aloft the champagne bottle, and say something rakish like "Fancy a little hair of the dog?" or maybe just

"Remember me?" Both of those sounded foolish to her now, though, and she could not for the life of her summon something clever.

Was she, Vida Hazzard, nervous? Through the hurly-burly of the morning and afternoon she had told herself that she had only been going along with her parents to get Fitzhugh Farrar to be interested in her and thus dispel the rumor that she was the sort of girl who had wild nights with one boy after another. But she was taken aback by these sudden flutters at the prospect of seeing him again.

Oh damn it, just go on, before he finds you standing out here like an idiot, she told herself. *Just put on a coy smile and don't say anything—that always seems clever.*

Yes, she went on to herself. *Right. Go on now.*

An inner light suffused her face. She stepped boldly forward, fist raised. And just then, as she was about to knock, her new high-heeled slippers lost their traction on the polished wood floor, and momentum—and then gravity—had her, and she went sailing through the air. She heard her own voice sing out in surprise, and felt the planks hit her hard on her left side as she landed. The floor was wet. There had been a puddle on the floor, and she had slipped on it, and now that puddle of wetness was seeping through her skirt. And meanwhile her champagne bottle rolled away from her, and the door under the brass map room sign swung open, and Vida could see there was nothing to stop Fitzhugh Farrar, with whom she had been so arch and charming the night before, from seeing her in this abject position.

She did her utmost to effect a smile.

But the smile did not hold.

The young man who filled the frame was not Fitzhugh. He was nobody.

Vida propped herself on her elbow, wincing at the pain spreading over her left flank, while the nobody in the door-frame did not move to help her up.

"Hello," she said hotly when it became obvious that he was not going to say anything at all.

But he did not reply in kind. "Comfortable down there?" he asked in a tone that did not seem exactly curious about her well-being. He leaned the long whip of his body against the frame and crossed his arms, neither moving to help her nor closing the door, so the humiliation that had already begun to rise in Vida's throat began to heat, and swirl, and become anger. Unlike nearly every other man on the boat, who, rich or poor, had chosen either their best for the occasion or a starched uniform, this man was wearing a threadbare shirt that was neither white nor brown but somewhere in between, and rolled trousers, and a wool cap. His arms, where they were not covered by his old shirt, were sun-dark, and his eyes were so black that she could not read them. He had long eyelashes, and a long face in which his big features were somewhat askew.

"What is it?" called a voice within. The same commanding and precise voice that had told her many tales last night and then shut up to hang on her every word.

"Same puddle, different girl with a twisted ankle," the nobody called over his shoulder. Several seconds passed and she did not hear the commanding voice again. "Want to see her? I don't think it's anything you need trouble yourself with."

Well, this Vida could not have. She could not have anyone going around implying that she was like the nitwits who apparently risked life and limb just to have a few moments with Fitzhugh. *She* had had his attention for most of the previous evening, and was herself the sort of creature that men were often making fools of themselves just to meet. With little grace but much determination she arrived on her feet so that the nobody could see that her ankle was just fine. Her pride ached, but she would not let this nobody see that.

"You're a real gentleman," she said aridly.

"I am sorry," he said, and extended a hand—to what purpose, she had no idea, as she was already on her feet— and, when she did not accept it, his fingers did a graceful little flourish through the air. "Girls are always slipping and falling here, you see—I've gotten a little used to it, and sometimes forget the rules. How you're supposed to act when it happens for real."

Vida drew herself up at this accusation. "How could girls 'always' be slipping and falling here? I thought this ship was brand new."

If Vida had expected the nobody to crumble at her brilliant logic, she was destined for disappointment. He only grinned at her and maintained his amused silence.

"I am a first-class passenger on the *Princess*," Vida went on. Though she let her anger show in her eyes, she brought her voice down to a hoarse whisper so Fitzhugh would not know it was she who was having this stupid spat with a nobody, "And I was merely curious to see its famous map room—there is a puddle here, as you can plainly see, so why don't you go get a mop and do something about it?"

And with her chin high she grabbed fistfuls of her skirt and walked with as much dignity as she could summon from the site of her failure. She (*she!*) had failed to suavely run into the man whose interest she had believed herself to already have. She kicked the champagne bottle out of her path, but this too was a mistake. Pain bloomed in her toe and it was all she could do to not cry out before she reached the next corridor.

THREE

"Oh dear," said Miss Rosa de Hastings, one of the girls who Vida had traded dance partners with in the ballrooms of San Francisco, as she arrived at Vida's side, and together they joined the stream of first-class passengers from the salon into the grand dining room. "If *you* are looking wistful, then we are all in a grave and terrible danger."

Vida accepted Rosa's arm. "I know," she replied in a little voice. "Wistful is not at all my best color."

They were surrounded by the throng, by the high shine of black tuxedo jackets and the pastel ruffles of ladies who, much like Vida, appeared to have spent the first hours of their journey attending to their dress and coiffure. A gloom had settled in Vida since her failed encounter with Fitzhugh Farrar, and though she tried to shake it off, she found she could not. She followed instead the well-heeled crowd, hoping their enthusiasm for light fixtures and fine carpets and each other's silks and jewels was catching.

The ship's social director, a Mr. Selvedge, greeted Vida and Rosa and made all the usual compliments regarding their loveliness and what an honor it was to have them on the maiden voyage of the *Princess*, et cetera, et cetera, and asked solicitously after their accommodations, and mentioned—in what he perhaps considered a subtle way, but which rankled Vida's already wounded pride—the names of bachelors that he could introduce them to. She was not the kind of girl who needed help meeting young men! But apparently her fame in this regard did not extend beyond the borders of San Francisco.

"What a bore," Vida muttered when at last he departed and they found themselves seated at one of several long tables, immaculately cluttered with crystal, silver, china, and hyacinth. Beyond the rows of tables, beyond curtains of velvet and gilt-encrusted columns, beyond potted palms and silken fainting couches, were windows that framed an unfathomable seascape of deepest midnight blue. "I thought he'd never leave."

"Me too," said Rosa, craning her lovely pink neck. Her

blond hair fell in sweet ringlets, but her eyes had a steely quality. "As though any of us are interested in meeting anyone but Fitzhugh."

After the stinging humiliation of that afternoon, this statement didn't exactly shock Vida. Still, it wasn't good news that Rosa considered Fitzhugh fair game. Vida regarded Rosa, who was not exactly a friend (though they'd known each other all their lives), and wondered if she could truly have missed the report of Vida's wild night with the Farrar heir. Maybe Rosa had been too busy dressing for a run-in with him—for some kind of slip in front of the map room—to know that he and Vida had been attached in print. "Well," Vida replied, not hiding her irritation, "you should have asked Selvedge for an introduction."

"To whom?" This from a voice Vida had never heard before, female and British, a voice that resounded high in the nasal cavity. The owner of the voice was practically skeletal and encased in emerald green satin. Peacock feathers were wound into her high, pinned hair. Her age was impossible to determine—she might have been a few years older than Nora and lived a hard life, or was otherwise a perfectly preserved seventy-nine.

Rosa and Vida must have appeared confused enough by this interjection, for the lady quickly went on: "What I meant, my pretties, was *to whom* do you want an introduction?"

The woman sat down beside Vida, ignoring the little brass name tag that claimed the seat for Mr. Arnold Hazzard, and lit a slender cigarette, although there were no ashtrays and smoking was generally not done in mixed company. She put her pointy elbow on the table without the slightest notice of how this rattled the crystal, the china, and the silver. Before Vida could think of a clever way to avoid the question, the woman was talking again.

"I can introduce you to absolutely anybody you'd like. I know them all. I have a little something on all of them, you know. Don't blame me. It's that kind of world. Myself, I am an old libertine, and cannot be shamed. But all of these types"—she made a conductor-like flourish at the assembled—"well, really, I think you could shame any one of them for sneezing audibly, so it's not difficult at all, and if you ask me, entirely their own fault. There's Lady Narcissa of Ghent, who was born Lydia Astor. And Charlotte Coburg, who married a duke, making her a duchess of course."

For the first time since her slip by the map room Vida felt interested in the evening, and she liked this lady who didn't seem to believe that any of the first-class passengers were to be idolized at all. Vida's eyes roamed the room for someone interesting enough that she'd want to learn their secrets. But her gaze became fixed and her bottom lip dropped at the sight of someone not fancy at all.

"Now, darlings, tell me, whom do you most want to meet?"

"Who is that?" Vida asked. She would not ordinarily have spoken so impulsively, but her anger had returned, heating her blood and bringing color to her face. The nobody from the map room had caught her eye. He was lingering near the grand doorway with that same easy posture and insolent face. She was glad to feel angry, actually. She much preferred anger to mortification.

"Who?" The woman squinted.

"There." Vida pointed, and then remembered that that was the sort of thing that got a girl like her in trouble, and bent her arm back into her lap. Too late, though. The nobody, even all that way across the room, noticed, and his mouth slipped into a grin.

"Oh . . . *no.*" The word dropped right out of the lady's mouth and she was violent in getting another cigarette lit. "And here I thought you were sharp. He's a nobody, dear girl."

"Oh yes. I *know.* I'm not desirous of meeting him—he was rude to me, that's all, and I was curious where he got his gall."

"He probably works for one of these gents with egalitarian ideals," the woman went on, as though gents with ideals were an unfortunate but unavoidable part of life in these modern times. "Anyway, I see Mr. Selvedge has been through and done all the complimenting I was going to do, so I won't bore you ladies with your qualifications, your stunning wit, and your fine dress and all that rot. But here's what I do. I try my best to know all the pretty things, for that is where the stories are. My name is Dame Edna—Edna Sackville. I am sure you have read my column in *The Daily Chimera*." Here she paused significantly, and met Vida's eye.

So this was the lady who had written about her little spree of the night before! Vida knew she should be cross with this woman who had publicized her unladylike behavior, whose column had forced her to pack her bags in the fog of the morning and to find herself on the open ocean now. But in fact she was delighted. The way for a girl to have an adventure, as she had long known, was to make herself seem exciting to people so that she is invited absolutely everywhere. The social columnists were the most useful in making oneself seem exciting. And Vida chastised herself inwardly for having pursued Fitzhugh so artlessly, when the person whose connection she should have really been after was here before her. "Oh," Vida said. "I've heard of it."

"Yes, I'm sure you have. It's all about the shiny young people like you."

"Like *me*?" Vida asked, and gave Dame Edna a little smile to show she wasn't shy of the attention.

"Exactly. I know a good story when I see one, and you're it, dear. Anybody you would like to meet, just ask old Edna. They may not like me, dears, but they fear me. And that is better."

She brandished a card of fine emerald-colored stock with her name printed in gold, and then she shook her arm so that a little gold pen, attached to her wrist by a gold chain, fell out, and she wrote on the back the number of her cabin. "Come any time, day or night, with whatever story you have to tell," she said. "I will always listen, and I will repay you in kind."

"Is this woman bothering you?"

For a marvelous stretch of minutes Vida had forgotten her failure of that afternoon, and had become absorbed instead in the juicy promises of Dame Edna. She had idly draped her fingertips on the edge of an empty crystal champagne glass, and allowed herself to imagine other adventures. But then the young man interrupted them, and it occurred to her that she had heard his voice before, that commanding yet unperturbed voice asking if she were bothered.

She glanced up at the face of Fitzhugh Farrar. Last night she'd seen it plenty, though that all seemed a bit fuzzy and faraway now. Somehow he was handsomer than she remembered. His sandy hair was neatly slicked up and away from his square forehead and cornflower blue eyes. His strong jawline was more or less parallel to his high white starched collar. His tie was very black, and his teeth were very white, and his cuff links were very, very gold. Here was a man who stood out in any crowd. He wasn't smiling, and there was a bright intensity in his expression. Vida couldn't be certain if Dame Edna actually whispered in her ear that she should say something, or if the moment was of such world-shifting consequence that the dame was briefly capable of reading minds.

"Hello" was the best Vida could do, being uncharacteristically tongue-tied. But she said it archly, with just a smidge of drama, and an extra-subtle raising of her shaped eyebrows, so that that single word had the energy of a brilliant witticism. "I *am* sorry," she went on, "have we met?"

"Last night, though I suppose it was quite a well-attended party, and you certainly may have talked to several young men who own ocean liners."

"I usually do," Vida replied coolly, though she was experiencing an odd and overwhelming sensation, as though a flock of cherubim were fanning her with heavenly air. The humiliation of the last few hours lifted, and she felt curiously light-headed, just the way that lucky, lovely girl addressed by the most eligible man on the ship was supposed to feel. "But, now that you mention it, you do look a *little* familiar."

"Strange," he said, matching her ironic tone. "You don't seem like the kind of girl who forgets easily."

Vida fought the urge to smile at his knowing this about her. Yes, it was true, she remembered all the details of parties and stories. She remembered when she was insulted, too. But she resisted showing him how much she liked having this part of herself recognized, and kept her gaze quite steadily upon him. She allowed her smile to fade away and lifted her hand so that her fingers dangled in the vicinity of his. "I don't," she said evenly. "Where is Mr. Selvedge when you need him? Oh, well, why be formal about it. I am Vida Hazzard, in case *you* forgot."

"I did not. Fitzhugh Farrar, at your service. My family owns this ship, if your memory is weak on that point," he went on, as though he knew she knew all about it and he was not at all uncomfortable with the fact, "so if you have any complaints, I'm the one at fault."

"That's good to know, Mr. Farrar. It is a pleasure to meet you formally."

"Oh, but the pleasure is all mine." And then, when she was sure he was about to make a little bow and move on to meet other people, so that she could finally turn and look at Rosa in triumph—when she felt that her coup was complete, that she could rest easy knowing she still held his interest—he instead gripped her hand yet tighter, and bowed yet deeper, and said, in a voice so low it seemed at risk of breaking, "Miss Hazzard, would you dance with me?"

She had not noticed the music before. But now she heard the cascade of strings and the gentle swelling of melody in her belly and in her toes. Already they were moving across the floor, already his arms had made a structure around her body that led her into the rise and fall of a waltz and on into the center of the room under the great winking drape of the chandelier. Little murmurs escaped the crowd, and a thousand eyes seemed to be on them. But Vida—her lips pressed together to keep herself from smiling *too* much—was looking up into the face of the man her parents wanted her to marry, thinking that maybe for once they did know best, after all.

The moment was so perfect, so complete, that she could see it in the eyes of a bystander, could see the sweep of her red skirt, and the chandelier light dappling her bare arms, could see the brilliance of Fitzhugh's smile, the neat black line of his tuxedo as he waltzed her across the floor. She thought that she could hear Rosa's jealous murmur, could hear the scratch of Dame Edna's little golden pen, recording this moment so that it could be serialized in the dozens of newspapers that ran her column around the world. It was as though she could hold this moment of gem-like perfection in her palm and have it always. She permitted herself one errant glance—across the room, in the direction of the grand door where that nobody had stood laughing at her, so that she could have the satisfaction of seeing his face at the precise second when he came to understand how entirely wrong he had been about Vida Hazzard.

But her heart dropped, and her limbs went slack with disappointment.

The nobody was gone—he had disappeared into the ship too soon to witness her triumph—and there was just the hole of an open doorway where he had been.

FOUR

By the morning of the *Princess*'s second day at sea, the humiliating incident by the map room was to Vida nothing more than an amusing anecdote. By the second evening it seemed an odd aberration in an otherwise thrilling journey. And by the third morning it had become for her a neat lesson in never doubting oneself. She was on a quest, and any quest comes with little ups and downs. Perhaps her parents were still nervous about the propriety of her behavior, about her reputation being ruined. But they could not argue with the proof of Fitzhugh's interest. By the third afternoon of their journey, Vida had collected the following evidence that she was well on her way to a proposal:

ONE note from the famous Fitzhugh Farrar, on a gold-embossed card that bore the logo of the Farrar Shipping Line and a little illustration of the *Princess* herself, and upon which was written in elegant script what a pleasure it was to have danced with her. (How giddily she and Nora had discussed it when it arrived! She did hope the couple in the next cabin didn't hear them, as that sort of girlish enthusiasm really was not the image Vida was trying to project.)

TWO invitations to dance, on the second night after dinner. One might have been taken as an obligatory gesture, since their names had been associated in the columns. But two, Vida thought her parents and everyone else would surely understand, meant that she had become a fixture in his thoughts, that by the third evening he would dance with no one else, unless not doing so would make him seem rude. And the two dances didn't really convey the attention he had lavished on her. For all last night, from across the ballroom, his eyes had searched for her with such intensity that she forgot the other girls who (as that mysterious nobody had truthfully pointed out) were always trying to throw themselves in his way from every corner.

THREE minutes of thrilling conversation, that morning after breakfast, when he was passing through on his way to meet with the ship's captain—not thrilling precisely because of anything that was said, but rather because of the way he looked at her, as though there was nowhere else he would ever want to look.

And lastly, and most crucially:

FOUR more days on board the ship in which to make Fitzhugh Farrar fall so madly in love with her that he would not tolerate the prospect of continuing on to Australia without her. She wanted to be at his side when Honolulu came into view, and for Dame Edna and everybody else to remark how quickly she had won this supposedly unattainable bachelor.

But just now, on the third afternoon of their voyage, there was only the endless expanse of ocean, and the cool whip of wind on her face as their floating fortress moved steadily in the direction of that grand (and very socially acceptable) future. Vida had gone with her parents to the lido deck on the very top of the ship, where on warmer days the first-class passengers sunbathed and swam in the swimming pool, to tally all these proofs of Fitzhugh's affection. Once they were convinced, Mother and Father's conversation pivoted to prattle about the ship's amenities, much as they might turn over the china at a new acquaintance's home.

"I suppose it's all right," her father said about something or other.

"The food is good," Mother replied. "For being prepared at twenty-one knots per hour."

To which her father exclaimed, as though this were some sort of scandal: "The food would be good anywhere, my love! Mr. Selvedge told me the chef is quite famous in Paris, and was employed for a time by the great Sarah Bernhardt. The man is an artist."

A part of Vida's brain listened to her parents' small talk. But another part was focused on the other first-class passengers, strolling on deck or lounging nearby; on the sweep of her petal-pink dress spread over the deck chair and onto the polished boards of the deck itself; and the angle of her hat which, while protecting the pale perfection of her skin, still showed just enough of her face that if Fitzhugh were to come passing by he would see her immediately from her best angle.

A couple were ambling toward her in the direction of the bow. Her blood quickened. For a few seconds together her eyes were sure the man was Fitzhugh. The woman on his arm was uncommonly beautiful. Her dress was a shade of blue similar to the wide sky that went on forever and ever behind her. A broad hat decorated with little white flowers topped her head. Ropes of blond hair were twisted around her neck and down her breast, like a maiden in a fairy tale. Her mouth was a small red fruit and her eyes were wide lavender lakes. Vida's heart sank a little with this sight, and even when her eyes adjusted and she realized it was *not* Fitzhugh, but merely a man very like him, she still felt a little helpless over how much she had cared.

"Striking similarity, don't you think?"

Vida had been staring, she realized, and was so focused on the passing couple that she had not noticed Dame Edna arriving on the chair beside her.

"My, you do pop up," Vida said before she could think better of it.

"Get used to it, dear. If you want to move in the best circles, that is. I long ago mastered the art of arriving in silence. One does overhear such things that way."

The columnist, too, wore a hat, an impressively ribboned and bedecked thing of vivid green, and her coat was also of her signature color. As Vida took in the coat, she became aware for the first time that the air had a little freeze to it.

"Recognize him, my dear?"

"Oh!" Vida's heart lightened as she came to understand. "That's the brother, isn't it?" She sat up and watched as the figure of Fitzhugh's older brother, Carlton, ambled along arm in arm with the woman in blue. "And his wife, Camilla."

"Yes. Pretty, isn't she?"

"Very," Vida replied, although it wasn't really Camilla's prettiness that concerned her, but what kinds of leisure activities she enjoyed and how Vida might sort of accidentally come across her, and become friends with her, thus making her conquest of Fitz all the more inevitable. Plus, when they were sisters-in-law, Vida wanted to be sure she was invited to all the best parties. "What's she like?"

"Oh, she's even fancier than he is, if you can imagine it. She's an Astor on her mother's side, and her father's family, the Joneses, own half the copper mines in this country, and have been deciding who is and isn't invited to things for half a century. Their wedding was one of the most anticipated matches of the decade—they were married in Grace Church, and it was a frenzy among New York society to be invited. Many who weren't are still bitter."

"And what sort of secrets do you have on her?"

The couple had disappeared between one of the ship's mighty smokestacks, and Vida's parents were on to discussing the comfort of the beds in the first-class cabin, the relative virtues of the sheets and softness of the pillows.

Dame Edna tilted her head and her mouth flexed in amusement. "I do have a little story, though you may not wish to know it."

Vida hoped her face didn't reveal how much she did in fact wish to know it. "Tell me," she breathed. "I will be ever so much in your debt."

"Well." With an expert gesture Dame Edna had one of her little cigarettes lit, despite the wind, as though her powers were not just over the well-dressed, but also some-how over the elements. "She was with *your* fellow first."

"My—" Vida broke off and her mouth bent in a funny way. She was flooded with such contradictory emotions that she hardly knew whether she should frown or beam with joy. That Dame Edna might so easily refer to Fitzhugh as her "fellow" made her feel as light and free as a balloon floating in the upper atmosphere. But that he had somehow belonged already to that other girl, whose incomparable qualifications Vida could never measure up to—even on the highest crest of her considerable confidence—made her heart black with possessive fury. "My fellow?"

"My dear, you do know I see all you do, don't you? You and everybody else, too. He *is* your fellow, isn't he?"

"But, I mean—" Vida bit her lip. She was utterly sur-prised by this tide of feeling—it was only a game she wanted to win, after all. Why should she be acting like a ninny whenever it was suggested that he had feelings for her? "He's hardly mine."

"Modesty does not suit you, dear. I like you better as yourself. You remind me of me when I was your age. You have the gift of bending the world to your will. He may not be entirely yours now. But he will be yours, if you want him."

"But he was promised to his brother's wife?"

"Oh." Dame Edna batted away the question with her gloved hand. "It was one of many little attachments for both of them a few years back. Nothing close to an engagement. He is seen with another girl at parties and things every season or so, as I'm sure you know."

"Yes, I've heard that about him. I'm not the sort of girl to be troubled by such a reputation."

"I like that about you, and I didn't think you'd be put off by a few dalliances that are entirely historical," the dame said, her eyes narrow and glittery in appraisal of Vida. "I don't think you should be worried about her. I like you very much—you are a young woman of intelligence who knows how to enjoy society, very fun without being silly, with a perfect sense of exactly where the line is between spirited and debauched—and I think you will have quite a celebrated career. I expect we will be friends a good long time, and do each other many little favors."

Vida put on an evasive smile, and decided that she had been quite right to make an ally out of Dame Edna. They would indeed see each other often wherever the adventurous and monied go. Plus, as Vida was beginning to realize, Edna really did believe that Vida could get Fitz—she wanted it for her own reasons, too. "I will look forward to that," she said.

All the while they had been talking the ship continued its steady path, ripping a seam in the endless ocean. They had left the endless blue dome of earlier, and now gray mist enveloped the deck, so that there seemed to be no sky at all, and Vida noticed, as she let the air release from her lungs, that the crowd had thinned out. Only a few strollers remained on the lido deck. And coming back in their direction was the woman Fitzhugh had once romanced—Camilla Farrar, still on the arm of her husband.

Dame Edna stepped in their path. "It's a wonderful ship, Mr. Farrar," she said with cunning directness. "I hope you've been enjoying the space I have devoted to it in my column."

Though Carlton wore the expression of a man who has just bitten hard on gristle, he did shake the hand of Edna, as he might have with a business associate. "Yes, thank you."

Camilla was not so cold. She kissed the dame on either cheek. "We're so glad to have you on board," she said in her soft, breathy voice.

"I've just been talking to the most charming young woman—may I introduce you?"

"Yes, please," said Camilla, and at the same time Carlton grunted, as though to say, *If you must.*

Vida, realizing she was the charming young woman in question, scrambled to her feet.

"Pleased to meet you," she said, offering her hand to Camilla, who took it with an easy smile.

"Mrs. Carlton Farrar," said Dame Edna, "please meet Miss Vida Hazzard."

Camilla's hand went limp in hers, and as quickly as she had offered it she pulled it away. "Oh," she said. And after a long, rather miserable moment, she added, "Well, it was nice to meet you."

The Carlton Farrars strode off, disappeared belowdecks, and Vida turned to Edna to see what she made of the odd exchange. But she didn't seem to have noticed anything awry. In fact she leaned in, quite confidentially, and said, "You'll see if you can use that to your advantage somehow. Now, you must promise me a little something in return, for that is how civilization marches on, by the trading of shiny chits back and forth. . . ."

Before she had a chance to make her request of Vida, the high, fluty voice of Mrs. Hazzard interrupted them:

"It's chilly, Vidalia, we ought to go in." Vida had almost forgotten that Mother was sitting on a nearby deck chair with Father, discussing the dinner rolls, no doubt, and whether they were baked on board or had been brought from the mainland, for all San Franciscans have a belief in their sourdough, and that it cannot be properly made without the special quality of air in their hometown.

"I don't think we've met," her father said, rising to his feet and coming over to offer his hand to Dame Edna.

After a few pleasant nothings were exchanged, Dame Edna said, "I am a great admirer of your daughter. The man who marries her is lucky, for she will take both of them to the stars and back."

"Thank you. We are partial, of course. To us she is the stars themselves."

"Isn't that nice. I was just telling her that the gossip is that an engagement announcement between her and Fitzhugh Farrar is imminent, and I wanted to confirm with her before I print anything."

"Oh, well . . ." Her father seemed unsure about the correct thing to say. "Already?"

But Vida cut him off: "You shall be the first to know, Dame Edna."

"Very good. I am filing my column from Honolulu in four days, and I will have to have a scoop for my readership, who will have been a whole week without good gossip, poor dears. Mr. and Mrs. Hazzard, a true pleasure. I will see you at dinner."

And with that she swished on, her green skirt shifting and then disappearing into the fog.

"Let's get indoors, shall we," said her mother, taking Vida's arm. "I've just realized something terrible—you're in suite seven, and we're in suite six."

"So?" Vida asked, glancing at her father, who rolled his eyes at this superstition of her mother's. Mother had been raised by a nanny from the old country, who had filled her head with any number of old wives' tales, so that the whole family was forever throwing salt over their shoulders.

"How can you say that? Together they make thirteen, and that's bad, very bad. Let's go in. We shouldn't go out tonight."

"Yes, by all means, we must beware portentous numbers," her father agreed lightly as he took Vida's other arm. After a contemplative pause, he mused: "My dears, do we trust that woman?"

"Oh! Vexations everywhere," Mother said. "We can't really trust anyone but each other. And then there's what she said. She said this young man, this Fitzhugh, has had a string of associations. But it's too late, of course. Vida simply *must* marry him. God forbid he doesn't propose. And then what shall become of us all?"

Vida wasn't sure whether she was more annoyed with her mother for calling him "this Fitzhugh," or that she had obviously been listening in on Vida's conversation. "It's hardly his fault," Vida replied hotly. "Women just throw themselves at him."

"Be that as it may," her mother replied, "it is your reputation that will suffer if this engagement rumor comes to nothing."

"Really." Vida sighed in irritation. "We have danced together all of three times; I hardly think anything has occurred that could *tarnish* me." But even as she said this,

Vida's eyes burned a little at the thought that her mother was right, that girls' reputations were ruined all the time over less, and then they were never invited anywhere, and were shut off from the world to grow old alone, and what a terrible waste that was.

"Nevertheless," said Mother.

"It's cold tonight," said Father. "Doesn't a nice broth and a game of cards sound lovely? What say you, Vidalia, can we stay in tonight?"

"Arnold, you can't be serious, she *must* keep it up tonight."

"But my dear, you just said—"

"Never mind that. Think, Arnold, you must think! If she is absent, another girl might swoop in—if this Fitzhugh is so easily distracted, she cannot miss a chance to meet him."

"My dear, have you not heard the phrase about absence and the heart growing fonder?"

"Oh really—do you think that's how I got you?"

"Wasn't it? Do remind me."

"It's not your memory that is the problem, darling. Men know nothing. You can trust me on that."

And so her parents blathered on in their gentle, anxious way, as they descended from the high deck, through stairways and corridors toward their own well-appointed cabins. Vida was only half listening, nodding just enough that she would seem obedient to both of them. Her mother always won these little exchanges, anyway—and even if they had both been opposed, Vida would have found a way to the first-class dining room later on. For once she had set her sights on something, she did not rest until it was hers.

FIVE

"Miss Vidalia Hazzard."

The butler announced her arrival, and then Mr. Selvedge arrived at her side to escort her through the grand first-class salon. Vida felt wonderfully unhurried about her entrance, and also about everything else. She had spent several pleasant hours with Nora getting ready, and she knew herself to be incandescent. The crowd buzzed at the sound of her name. Maybe because of the swirling rumors, or maybe because of her appearance, which was immaculate as usual but possessed that extra brightness that comes with a crush. She was wearing an absolute confection of a gown, tiers and tiers of a pink just slightly redder than white—*suggestive* of matrimony, without being too obviously a wedding dress.

Her dressmaker on Union Square had convinced her to buy the thing some months ago, saying that it was particularly flattering on her. It had been a little *too* much for any event she had yet attended. But now, with the idea firmly planted in Fitzhugh's mind, not to mention everybody else's, the appearance of Vida in a dress that could not but invite a picture of her veiled, at the altar, seemed opportune, and perhaps the perfect stroke to bring her campaign to the brink of success.

The night was perfect, and she felt that she was, too. She accepted Mr. Selvedge's hand and he escorted her through the crowd to meet the Duke of Devonshire, and his wife, Margarita Hollings-Blue, the famous hostess, and then two young Astors, and a man who had invented a new process of petroleum extraction, and whose entire life was now a grand tour.

"Charmed," she said to the young man, Henry Dries Stahl, when she had determined he had nothing more of interest to say. She had a creeping suspicion that he might ask her to dance and wanted to get away from him before he did.

"We must play a game of tennis before we arrive in Honolulu," she said to the Duchess of Devonshire, when she was sure that lady's friendship was a coup she could undertake at another time.

"Isn't it strange?" Lilly Adell, the young widow of a

department store heir, asked her, just as Vida was trying to escape her company. Lilly, she had just noticed, was sort of drifting with Vida from one cluster of people to another.

"What is?" Vida asked, startled by the peculiar question.

Mrs. Lilly Adell had seemed in a light, elegant mood moments before, but her expression had another quality now. Strange, and rather faraway-seeming.

"This carpet." She was gazing fixedly at the pattern of exuberant curlicues of purple and gold beneath their feet. "I mean, it's beautiful, just acres and acres of such beautiful carpet. But it's all just to make it *seem* like we're on land. We're not! We're a thousand miles from anywhere, and the ground floor of our building, if you can call it that, is the surface of the ocean, and beneath the surface of the ocean— it's just a vast unknown, do you see what I mean? It could be mermaids down there, but also monsters."

"Oh, Mrs. Adell," Vida said, trying not to laugh at this morose turn. "Did you have too much to drink at lunch?"

"No. It's just odd, do you see what I mean?"

"That all of a sudden you believe in mermaids? Yes, that is odd."

"I'm sorry. It's such a lovely party, yet such a heavy feeling has come over me. The weather's bad tonight. Don't you think?"

Vida squeezed her hand. "Have these bores done you in? You don't have to stay, you know."

Lilly squared her shoulders in resolve. "Oh, yes I do. I am twenty-five. If I don't meet a man this year who seems likely to marry me, I am done for. They say you're the kind of girl the men flock to, and that if I stay by you, I'll meet some worthy fellows, too."

"Oh." Vida shuddered at Lilly's assessment of her situation. "I hardly think that's the right mindset in which to meet a man."

Lilly glanced at the beautiful people leaning on columns, showing off their fine clothes, their enviable social connections, their jewels, and their spouses. They were enjoying being looked at, and looking at everyone else. Vida had heard the story, how Lilly's husband was trampled in a streetcar accident two years ago, but she had seemed perfectly gay until this moment. "My God, it's freezing," the widow said. "Oh, maybe I should go to bed early."

"Absolutely not." Vida made her expression very serious. She had not realized what a strange person hid within this beautiful and conventional façade, but she liked Lilly very much for revealing her weirdness now. "Upon reflection, I have concluded you should not be alone tonight. You must stay where there are people and have some fun." Vida grabbed Lilly's hands and pulled her toward the fireplace. "Come, let's pretend to be getting warm while we look around and see who might be worth your time."

They whispered together tête-à-tête while covertly

glancing at the gentlemen in the room. Henry Dries Stahl was rich, but had nothing to say. Freddy Flynn, Flora's brother, was handsome, but liable to drink too much and become boorish. Hollis Granger was funny, but he had a peculiar smell. And then there were a lot of men who were all-right-looking, and were capable of holding a conversation with a woman, but were already married. Finally, Vida's eye settled on an Englishman with some title or other, who was tall and wore a pleasant, open expression, and who she had seen at breakfast alone reading a book. Mr. Selvedge was passing then, and Vida wasted no time flagging him.

"There's a favor you must do for me," she said.

"Anything," Selvedge replied with a little dip of the head.

"That British fellow who sits alone at breakfast, what's his name?"

"Oh, that's Lord Morrow."

"Is there a Lady Morrow?"

"His mother, but she retires early and sleeps late."

"Would you mind sitting Mrs. Adell beside him this evening for dinner?"

"Wonderful idea. Let's make the introduction now." Selvedge offered his hand to Lilly, and she took it, and off they went.

Vida watched Lilly walk away. Her head was high and

steady as though the rest of her were pulled on wheels. Her lips swayed with that subtlety exhibited by girls bred from birth for a smart marriage, and her black train trailed over the carpet that had inspired her to say such melancholy things. For a moment Vida felt melancholy, too, thinking of all the years her new friend had labored to mold herself into the perfect bride, only to be left as she was now. But she would be all right, and meanwhile Vida had her own match to pursue. She turned to the grand hearth, pushed her bosom in and up so that it would catch the best light, pivoted to grab a passing glass of champagne. She sipped and took in the room. Mr. Selvedge was coming back her way.

"Any more seating changes you would like me to make?" he asked. His eyes were merry, and she could see he wasn't really annoyed.

"As it happens, my parents won't be coming this evening after all. I'm sorry to tell you so late—you do go to so much trouble. Perhaps you could find another table for me to join?"

"It's no trouble at all. And you weren't seated with your parents this evening in any case."

A sweet wind filled Vida's lungs. "Why not?" she asked with a coy sideways glance.

"Mr. Fitzhugh Farrar asked that you be seated at his

table. I do hope you don't mind. All the sporting fellows always ask to be sat with him, so you may find it a bit of a bore."

Oh, I don't care about that, Vida very nearly said out loud, so thrilled was she to hear that not only would they be seated together, but that Fitzhugh himself had requested it. "I'll manage, somehow" was what she actually said with a little wink.

"It is always a pleasure," Mr. Selvedge replied, winking back, "to be of service to a young lady who enjoys herself. May I escort you to your table, Miss Hazzard?"

A happy gust surged in Vida, and she held her hand aloft for him to take, and then he paraded her past the Blues of Park Avenue, and Mr. and Mrs. Louis Jones, and the rows and rows of footmen and waiters, past the oil paintings and statuary and potted palms and gilded doodads, and into the dining room, where a quartet was playing mildly, and where many of the first-class passengers were already seated, just waiting to see her as she came through the door. Mr. Selvedge commented on who was who, but she scarcely listened. For one thing she knew already, and for another she was concentrating on moving just the way a girl like her was supposed to, with grace but also with a little frisson of flirtation, and on lowering herself into her golden chair with as much elegance as possible, while still keeping her waterfall of a skirt away from her feet. She was as Dame Edna had described her—she knew just how to walk the line. To be decorous enough not to run afoul of good society, yet never falling into conformity.

"Can I get you anything?" he asked as he poured champagne from the large bottle in the silver urn.

"No, thank you, Mr. Selvedge," she replied, letting her fingers rest at the base of her champagne flute. "I have everything I need."

Beyond several plates and sets of silverware and glasses of every shape was a small tent of white cardstock with her name scrawled in dark ink. At the next setting, there was an identical name tag that said simply *Fitz*. As the other members of their dining party leaned in to find their own names, she nodded and smiled a remote, elegant smile, all the while thinking to herself that the real fun would begin when Fitzhugh sat down beside her. Fitzhugh, with his neat and gleaming hair, his tails and tux and white tie, and she, in a shade just slightly pinker than a wedding dress, beside him like they were already a match announced. It had been her parents' idea, of course. But she was making it her own, moment by moment, spinning pleasant fantasies of the adventure her marriage would be. Rosa de Hastings was at a far-off table this evening, looking a little dour, and Vida thought of the sense of triumph she'd feel when it was all settled. Dame Edna's article would proclaim it in the newspapers, and everyone who doubted Vida would have to admit that she had taken a grand prize. She was trying to calculate how many days until then—until they reached shore, and the news could be cabled back to San Francisco—when the chair beside her was pulled back. Her smile flickered on, and she turned, hoping to see the young man whose name she had just been savoring in her thoughts.

"Oh." The word echoed between her ears and escaped her mouth before she could help it. Disappointment dragged down her smile, and her shoulders, too. "It's you."

The nobody wore a face of mild amusement, just as he had when she saw him last. He was dressed as plainly as he had been that day at the map room. It was only one of a dozen things that irritated her about him. But he could have shown a little respect to the women in that room, who had given their afternoons to getting dressed, by putting on a tie. "Not who you were expecting?" he asked. His tone made clear that he knew the answer.

"Why would I be expecting you?" Vida asked. She had not been drinking the champagne that Mr. Selvedge had poured for her—she had wanted to wait so that she could toast Fitzhugh with a full glass—but now she took a big gulp and stared off at the dining room, still full of people dressed their absolute best, but somehow a little less sparkly than in the moment before. "The name tag is quite clear on who is sitting next to me, unless by some strange coincidence your name is Fitzhugh as well."

"A bit of weather, I'm afraid, and the captain required Fitz's expertise at the helm. He sent me to make his excuses. My name is Sal."

"Sal?" She was trying to hide her contempt, but not really very much. "Just Sal?"

"I have a family name, but no family anymore, so I don't bother with it much."

"I suppose you want me to feel sorry for you."

Though his expression was placid his words came back like a whip: "Why would I want something like that?"

"If you think I'll be sweet to you," she replied, fast as he had, "and tell you that I am not disappointed by the fact that the seating arrangements had me next to Mr. Fitzhugh Farrar, of the shipping Farrars, known around the world for his exciting explorations of places unknown, and instead I find myself wasting my breath on a nobody—well then you must believe I am as polite as I look. I assure you, politeness is just a costume I wear sometimes when I find it advantageous."

"I am getting the feeling you don't like me very much."

"I don't have to explain myself to you. But you must know you were quite rude."

"At the map room, you mean. Is that what makes you so sour toward me? I am sorry, my lady, and I do humbly beg your pardon. It's just that girls are always slipping or falling or twisting their ankles wherever Fitz sets up his headquarters."

Was he being ironic? Her cheeks flushed dark with rage. "You can't be implying that I did it *on purpose*."

"No." He shook his head, as though he had never heard of anything quite so ridiculous. He was either utterly in earnest now, or a very good actor. "No, of course not."

The attempt at sincerity was even more infuriating, and she very much considered rising from the table, marching out of the dining room, and finding her parents, so that then she might at least enjoy them, and their card games, and their idle chatter. But then she imagined this Sal laughing at her in his imperturbable way, and that seemed like the worst fate of all. She could not stand the idea of him thinking of her as silly and a liar. But neither could she stand the idea of him thinking other girls silly liars—like poor Lilly Adell, making herself miserable to meet a man. She felt a sudden fury on behalf of all the women who had ever lived, giving so much of their wit and youth and beauty just to be noticed.

"So what," she said hotly.

"What do you mean 'so what'?"

"What if I *did* do it on purpose, what would it matter?"

She could see that he was making an effort not to smile at this, which made her angrier still. "But why would a girl of such obvious pride do a thing like that?"

"Well, why do you think?"

"I haven't a clue what goes on in the mind of a high-class girl like you."

"Oh please." She had no desire to hide her indignation that though he was calling out hypocrisy in others, he too was shading the truth. "I mean, you sail around with a young man of not a little social importance. You see how he lives, do you not?"

"Yes, I've traveled with him since we were children; of course I see how he lives."

"He gets to go on all sorts of adventures, and everyone applauds him for it."

"Yes, he's very brave."

"He is, to be sure. But there are other young men who go in for boating, and sporting, and adventuring, are there not?" She waved her hand at the men who sat at the table, each of them trim, and able, and rich, and used to going where they liked and doing what they pleased for their own amusement and not thinking of the many others who made all their leisure possible. Beside them sat their sisters and wives and cousins, who were a very lovely roving audience for the triumphs of brothers, husbands, and cousins.

Sal leaned his elbow against the table and angled his head in curiosity. "Some."

"And do you know any young women like that?"

"Well—no."

"And why do you think that is?"

"I guess young women just don't like adventure."

Now it was Vida who smiled in amusement at Sal's half-blind way of viewing things. "Have you *asked* any young women if they don't like adventure?" she prodded. "Now, I am not one to make an argument with the world as it is. In fact I quite enjoy the world as it is. But if you have eyes, then you can see that all the things that are expected of girls—that they be pretty, and dress like ladies, and wear skirts and make houses lovely, and all the other fixed ideas of female purity—are perfect ways to deter young women from a life of adventure. Anyway, I like a big gown, and a big party, and to have everyone saying how beautifully I am dressed. So what?"

"Which is it? Do you like the fussy dresses, or do they hold you back?"

"Have you never felt two contradictory things strongly, truly, and at once?"

He considered that, but was too slow in replying, and so she charged on to win the argument.

"The world is full of contradictions, and I am not trying to change it. But I assure you, the desire for the new and novel and to go exciting places is in all of us. Or most of us, anyway. And certainly in plenty of young women. Our adventuring is of a different kind, by necessity—we adventure in ballrooms, and with the dressmaker, in our imaginations, and in our hearts. That leads to real adventure, if we imagine right—adventure on the arms of our husbands. And if we choose well in that category, then we shall see all manner of wonders. That is the hand we ladies are dealt. I for one am quite good at playing this particular game and making a laugh of it."

But Sal frowned at her perfect logic. "I guess I've just never taken up the hand that was played me."

"I wonder."

He held her gaze. "Nobody tells me what to do. I go anywhere I like, and my life is what I make it."

"You seem to think balls and things are very silly, and yet you serve a master who attends them all the time. Your life is what *he* makes it, no? Look me in the eyes and tell me you go where you like, and that your life is exactly as your soul would make it."

But he couldn't quite look her in the eye. She spent a few moments studying him, and concluded that he might be sort of all-right-looking, from the right angle and in the right light. He had dark eyes and lashes, and a nose that curved nicely, and a full mouth, but it was all so funnily put together, as though his face had been left out in the sun, and melted slightly, and would remain forever with its features not precisely aligned.

"I don't usually underestimate people," he said after a while.

"From you that must be a high compliment!"

"Do you care about this dinner?"

Vida glanced at the others sitting at their table. "You mean the rolls and the squabs and the potatoes dauphinois? Not even a little."

"If you are really so keen to see the map room, I could show it to you."

He had already stood up from the table, taken a step back from the opulent dinner that was just then being ferried through the room by a hundred uniformed waiters and deposited plate by plate before the first-class diners. Vida hesitated a moment—for what would the room make of her leaving early? Would her parents hear that she had not stayed put, that she was not acting like a marriageable young girl? Would she end up in worse trouble? But Sal had made clear that Fitzhugh would not be coming. She hated the idea of everyone seeing her waiting around for him. She had another look at her dining companions—the men with nothing to talk about but boating and racing and sports, the women absolutely stuffing their faces with Waldorf salad out of boredom—and decided to do what most excited her curiosity.

"All right," she said, and led the way to the closest exit,

to make sure that as few of the other first-class passengers as possible saw her leave with the nobody. But once they were through the door, and she saw the glitter in his dark eyes and a hint of that amused smile, she thought she had better clarify for him, too: "Only because I have nothing better to do at present."

SIX

"This does not seem the most direct route." Some girls, saying a thing like that, would affect a treacly coyness. Not so Vida. She'd had a look at the layout of the many decks of the *Princess* and she knew where she was going, and that they were taking a very meandering path to the map room. She followed the nobody who called himself Sal down a flight of stairs, and—eager for Sal to know that if he were playing a trick on her, she would see to it that he lost his job—spoke directly. "Did you hear me? I prefer a direct route."

He glanced over his shoulder but didn't quite look at her as he reached the bottom stair, pushed open a door, and led them onto the polished blond deck of the open-air promenade. "You like telling other people what to do, don't you?"

"Well, who doesn't?" A gust of night caused her to shiver. Strangely, though the air seemed very still, it had energy. Not like sea spray close to land—which always had a whiff of rot—but instead a kind of dense, clean-smelling weight. Beyond the railings, she could see almost nothing. That heavy air crept in like a spirit. "I like things done right. And sometimes," she went on, "that means telling other people what to do."

"You said you wanted adventure," he replied simply.

She almost smiled at that. "Did I? Maybe. But I don't remember asking *you* to take me on one."

"Yes, I know. You only wanted to see the map room. But you were very eloquent regarding what ladies of your kind are allowed to do, and what they are not. I thought we'd go the way we are least likely to see the first-class diners coming in late for dinner."

"Oh." She resisted thanking him for thinking of that, but did sort of nod a little in agreement.

"That, and . . . I wanted to feel this weather. Isn't it something?"

Vida gazed out. "I can't see a thing."

"Not much, I'll give you that. But be quiet, and see if you don't get a sense of what's out there."

He closed his eyes, and his face assumed a beatific

expression. Vida narrowed her eyes, and wondered what sort of mystical nonsense this was. Nonsense, surely. And yet before she could successfully dismiss his behavior, she did get a hint of what a vast mystery surrounded them. Felt what a colossus she rode over the watery plain, how they rocked gently on their forward path, giving in to a motion that was much larger than any of them and dwarfed even the mighty *Princess*. Before she could help it, her eyes had closed, too. She did not so much hear as experience in a gentle vibration that originated between her toes and rose up the backs of her legs the enormous engines of the ship, the impact of the wind as it slid around the ship's high walls, and the waves, always shifting, way down below.

When she opened her eyes, Sal was staring at her with his dark, impenetrable gaze, and she remembered that this might all be some kind of trick.

"It's bad weather out there," he said, turning on his heel and leading them on.

She almost laughed. "You must be joking. It's still as the dead."

"Didn't you know that the calmest place is at the heart of the storm?"

"Are you speaking some sort of riddle?"

"No, I am being very literal. You know how, when you are sitting in a room, the hot air rises to the ceiling, and so you tend to feel a draft around your feet?"

"Yes, I suppose that's true."

"Well, the atmosphere is the same—hot air warmed by a patch of sea rises, and cold air rushes under it as wind. But of course we are not in a little room anymore, we are talking about the wide, watery Earth, and as Earth turns, so the atmosphere turns, so that the system of weather begins to spiral. Meanwhile the hot air is cooled on high, its moisture becomes rain, the whole thing takes on tremendous energy, the wind begins to whip around the warm center, so fast it forms a kind of protective wall, a kind of hollow tunnel, and in that tunnel there is no wind, no rain, and things seem to be calm."

For the first time on this voyage her chest tightened— was that feeling fear? She was not often afraid, but guessed that's what the sensation of fear would be like. "Are you saying that we are in the middle of a typhoon?"

"No, no." And his easy, willowy manner assured her that they were in no danger. "There is a big storm out there. But a typhoon—if it is a typhoon—moves very slowly, and a ship—well, a ship of this size can't move fast exactly, but it can certainly get out of the way of a typhoon if the captain sees it in time. That's why there's a watch all day and all night. If they see bad weather, it is almost always possible to avoid it by changing course early."

Vida stared out at that grayness, wishing she could see into it, that she could see all the way to the horizon. Her heart was beating in such a steady, intense way. But for some moments she felt oddly disinclined to move her feet. Ordinarily her evening clothes, once put on, seemed no less a part of her than her hair, her fingernails. And yet as she lingered, the night air seemed to slip in beneath the fabric, separating her from all that silk, lace, boning, ribbon, and she became keenly aware of her skin. It tingled with excitement.

"We should hurry," Sal said. "Once Fitz and the captain have determined the course, he will most likely have dinner in the map room, so if you want to see it before he gets there, we had better hurry."

"Oh—" A funny little moment followed in which she wasn't sure what he meant. She shivered, and it came back to her—he really thought she *was* that curious about a map room. "Yes, of course." The loveliness of weather, of moisture, of the air so suggestive of things to come, renewed her pleasant prospect of Fitz, of knowing more about him, of making him hers. What could it hurt to know what went on in his private lair? Anyway, she enjoyed this sneaking, this little bit of mystery.

"Come on," Sal said, and she followed.

They went quickly now, up and down stairs and into the hall where a few days ago she had schemed, hesitated, and flopped. Sal did not hesitate now. He leaned against the door and pushed it open with his shoulder.

They both jumped a little in surprise when they saw the female figure.

Vida's mind was slow to catch up—there was supposed to be no one here. But there was someone here. A woman was here, with eyes wide in surprise to match Vida's own, framed in the doorway, blocking their path.

The woman's hand was lifted, her arm extended as though she had been about to grab the doorknob, as though she had been about to leave the map room Vida was trying to go into. The woman's beautiful fair hair was spilling over the front of her dress. Her cheeks were ruddy with some feeling that Vida did not like. She made an exclamation, somewhere between an "Oh!" and an "*Ahhh . . . ,*" flat at first and then soaring upward in surprise.

"Who's there?" barked a man's voice, deeper within, at about the same time that Vida's mind put together that this was Camilla, who she had found so beautiful earlier on the deck.

A little hope burst through Vida and died. For a minute she had thought maybe it wasn't Fitzhugh; maybe it was the brother who looked so like him. And then she knew that wasn't the case. It was Fitzhugh. Sal's long body stepped sideways to block her view. She tried to see around him, though she was at the same time contending with a strong urge to turn and run away.

"Fitz?" Sal's voice was pinched with confusion. "I'm sorry," he said, backing away. "I didn't think . . ."

"Sal—" Fitz was saying as he came out of a dark corner into the illuminated part of the room. His hair was as polished as usual, and he was dressed for dinner in white tie and tails, and he was comporting himself with the sureness that made him so winning to newspaper columnists and the ladies who read those columns. "I asked you to see to Miss Hazzard."

"He did as you asked," Vida said, pushing around Sal and not hiding at all her stricken expression. Camilla stepped backward, maneuvered herself behind Fitz. "But maybe you should have been straight with him about what you were doing. Then he might have known not to bring me here."

Now she could see Fitzhugh Farrar's famous map room and felt sad for herself and all female kind that they were made to pretend that this was a fun place to visit. The walls were paneled in dark wood, and the ceiling was carved wood, and on a large wood table many old papers were spread out. It was just like every uncle's study. There was a painted globe, and a lot of leather-bound books, and a nook with a pair of large leather chairs and between them there was a glass tray with a set of crystal glasses and crystal bottle full of amber liquid. In the midst of all that solemn furniture stood the lovely Camilla, the wife of Fitzhugh's brother, and Fitzhugh's former fling. Or maybe not former. Vida was finding it difficult to make sense of the scene.

"We were—" Fitzhugh began.

But Vida couldn't stand to hear an explanation and began to drown out his speech with her own: "I know what you were doing. Please. I am a lady. I really oughtn't hear such things." Why had she said that? It was precisely her unladylike behavior that had gotten her into this mess in the first place. She had acted too free, and now look at her. She'd behaved like all the other girls foolishly chasing after men who were indifferent to their efforts. And hadn't a little part of her been hoping that maybe Fitz would kiss her, in the dark of this map room, just as he had apparently done with Camilla? It felt better to act indignant than to appear hurt, however, so she went on frowning as though this scene really had offended her delicate sensibilities.

"I have no idea what you are suggesting," Camilla Farrar said. "Fitz is my brother."

"Brother-in-law," Vida corrected for some reason.

Camilla's red-painted lips parted slightly in malice. Somehow the cruelty of that smile did nothing to diminish her beauty. "My," she breathed. "Aren't you well-informed?"

Of all the facts that now stabbed at Vida, Camilla's cool dominance cut the deepest. In the years of her social career in San Francisco, Vida had never overplayed her hand so badly as now, had never had to face an adversary of higher social standing and more self-possession in quite so obvious a way. "Isn't he?" was the only reply she could muster, and she knew it was the sort of weak and witless response that would repeat and repeat in her thoughts all night and all tomorrow like a torturous melody.

"We were only talking," Camilla replied as she walked in a cloud of careless irritation past Vida and into the hallway. There she paused, revolved, and the way she gazed at Vida made Vida feel that all of her—her physical self, and also the high spirit she had believed herself to be—had been shrunk down to a pitiful nothing.

A little fire sparked in Vida's belly. In the next moment she was aflame with anger. She let the heat build inside her, let it become a kind of tower. Any moment now, an absolute dagger of a rejoinder would occur to her. She knew it would. She waited for it, smiling at Camilla, facing her down as though they were two soldiers at a duel. Camilla smiled back, and Vida opened her mouth to let this woman know what a dangerous adversary she truly was.

Then Camilla was gone. Before Vida could manage to be astonished, she was struck by the sound—although it took several seconds for her to comprehend that what she was experiencing was a sound. It was so loud, for one thing, and also it was so many sounds at once. Somehow a scraping and a moaning and an echoing, and also the sound of a thousand wailing banshees, and also the wind, and also the complete absence of noise one might hear at the end of the Earth. She felt it deep in her belly and her skull as though she herself were a bell being tolled by whatever *it* was. She became aware that her feet were no longer on the ground, that she herself was almost floating. Then the wall (or the ceiling—she wasn't sure which) smacked her left side, and for a moment her vision was a sparkling blur.

"What was that, what was that?" she heard Camilla shrieking from what sounded like not so far away.

"We've hit something." That was Sal, and his voice was low and steady, which somehow made everything seem more frightening. "The ship hit something big."

"Are you all right?" Fitzhugh asked, and his voice was so close that she knew the arms lifting her up must be his. Though she struggled against him, it was no use. That liar Fitzhugh, who made bright girls stupid, had snared her in his arms when she was too weak to protest.

SEVEN

How calm everything seemed for a while, and then never again.

Just after the world-ending sound and the shock of impact, Vida said she was all right, and would Fitzhugh please put her down, and he did. Camilla got up from wherever she had landed, and Sal approached the doorway, and they all stood there, very quiet, looking from one to the other with a hopeful question in their eyes—was it possible that they imagined it?

Then they heard the pounding of feet above, the shouting, and they knew they hadn't imagined anything, that something had indeed happened. Wordlessly they followed Fitzhugh toward the exit to the promenade.

The oil paintings that had hung in the hall were now flung across the floor, and they could see, even before they arrived, that the door that had once led onto the promenade was gone. On the floor above them the shouting became more frenzied. They heard what sounded like a stampede of horses. They walked, as though compelled to do so, to what had once been the end of the hall. They stared out at what had once been the promenade—that wide, polished walkway that went all around the ship. A section of the promenade had been ripped away. They went to the edge, peered over into the abyss, and saw that it was not just a piece of the promenade that was gone, but a whole section of the ship's outer wall. Below them an unearthly fog unfurled, and far below that was the splashing, churning sea—the sea that was even now pouring in through the gap that had been torn into the side of the ship. The vast red-and-black iron flank of what must have hit the *Princess* slid past them and into the vast darkness of the ocean at night.

Vida's heart was oddly still. Everything seemed not quite real. But she didn't at all like the terrible expressions on everybody's faces. "Say something," she said in what she had meant to be an irreverent way. Instead it came out sort of soft and trembling. Nobody did say anything. Fitzhugh revolved and began walking and then running down the hall, and first Sal, and then Camilla, and then Vida followed.

They ran up and up, through the fine halls of the

first-class quarters, until they reached the top deck. The chaos Vida saw there made her a little less embarrassed about what all that running had done to the arrangement of her hair, the loveliness of her gown. And she forgot, too, the hope of a reprieve from all these long faces. Every face she saw had a sickly pallor, every pair of eyes seemed not quite to see. Bodies charged, yelled, pushed, grabbed at anything to no obvious purpose. Some people had arrived in their nightclothes, others in their topcoats and carrying their suitcases. But what could be *so* wrong, she reasoned. The ship still floated.

The lights were still on, illuminating the wide field that was the open-air part of the ship. The fog hung over them but there seemed to be no wind, no menace in the air, and Vida glanced at Fitzhugh, at Sal, at the awful, terrible, beautiful Camilla, for some sort of agreement that perhaps the worst was over.

She found none.

She knew by the way Fitzhugh was speaking to the captain, who had appeared suddenly in his crisp blue-and-white uniform, that the worst was yet to come. "I saw it," Fitzhugh told him, his voice low, even as his eyes roved constantly, alert to all that was said or done around him.

"A steamer?"

Fitzhugh's head jerked in swift agreement. "Hit us amidships on the port side."

"Must have ripped a damn big hole. There's already flooding in the engine room."

Fitzhugh's steady blue gaze rose up and met the captain's eyes. "This ship is unsinkable."

The captain nodded. "Of course, sir."

"Practically speaking, she is unsinkable."

"It is a Farrar ship, sir," he said dutifully.

"The newest and most modern of our fleet." Fitzhugh averted his eyes. "But as a precaution we should get the women and children into life vests."

"We'll want to keep things calm."

"Yes." Fitzhugh drew breath into his chest, as though trying to inflate his very stature. Incredibly, he did look a little taller. "Someone get me a bullhorn."

Vida watched him climb onto a deck chair and boom his voice across the night, and she felt her skin crawl with the strangeness of it all. Her mind couldn't quite keep up. None of this was real, was it? She couldn't seem to believe that any of this was real. That bizarre and pathetic scene, in which a hundred people milled around, and ceased their clamoring for answers, and listened to a handsome young man who wore a tuxedo with the logo of the Farrar Line embroidered at the lapels. He was telling them there was nothing to fear, it was only that every precaution must be taken after a collision in the open ocean. What nice words he chose, and how good he looked in command, his expression serious, his brows drawn together, his body, compact and strong, gesticulating in such a way that the crowd did quiet. They sighed, relaxed, nodded to each other in agreement that with someone very impressive in charge they could trust in things again, that they were safe.

But the tiny little hairs on Vida's arms, the coolness in her heart, told her otherwise. She had ever been the sort who made her own luck—as a little girl, she had wanted a pony, and so it had been. When she was grown enough to want finer things, she had decided that she would make herself the most talked-about young woman in San Francisco society, and so it had been. And she had wanted to do it her own way, and have more fun than all the debutantes hunting for husbands, and so it had been. She had voyaged out on the *Princess of the Pacific*, in the name of getting Fitzhugh Farrar, who everyone wanted for a husband, and so it should have been. But it wasn't. Because besides everything else, the ship had been hit.

And so while the passengers did as they had been told, and kept calm, and put on their life jackets, and as the crew did their orderly preparations so that the lifeboats could be loaded and lowered if necessary, Vida glanced about as though nothing at all was to be believed but this: the ship had been hit hard. Her own eyes had seen how much iron had been torn away by the passing ship. She *could* sink, and every utterance of the word "unsinkable" was an invitation to the fates and furies to have their destructive way with them. All of it seemed of a piece—that terrible moment of realization in the map room, which made her earlier humiliation at its door seem like a laughable nothing, and the fact that all her bravado was just delusion.

A lot of time must have passed, but time seemed an alien concept in this strange, still place.

Only when the ship began to list did Vida's heart start beating again, a wild beating, though not because she was surprised. Because she knew finally that the worst was coming. She had been waiting for this moment, for the other passengers to understand what she understood: this had all been a mistake. They were land dwellers, and should not be where they now found themselves, far from shore, on a beautifully polished surface that was tilting, slowly but surely, as though to spill them into the infinite watery world below.

All this time, for reasons she did not understand, she had stood close to Fitzhugh and Sal and Camilla, as though their togetherness at the moment the ship was hit could bind them together in misery forever.

The crew began urging women and children into the lifeboats, and Fitzhugh looked at her—really looked at her, for the first time since he had picked her up and she had demanded to be put down—and said that she should go in the first boat. Then he touched Camilla's elbow, and told her that she should go, too, that the two ladies ought to stay together, and they would be back onboard soon enough, once the ballast was corrected. What with everything, Vida should not have cared that he seemed to treat them the same, should not have wanted the pure blue of his gaze fixed upon her and her only. But she did, and she drew back from Camilla.

"Not without my parents," Vida said, and for the first time since everything got turned upside down she thought of her mother and father, and realized they must be in a state of high agitation.

"All passengers will be roused and evacuated." Fitzhugh cast a worried glance at Sal. "We are boarding several boats at once, so they may already be gone."

Camilla's face had a stone fury in it, and she turned away from their little party, and extended her arms to the waiting crewmembers, who gently lifted her over the railing and lowered her into the waiting lifeboat. The tail of her gown trailed over the rail and she was gone.

"Please," Fitzhugh implored Vida.

An orderly line had formed behind them, and Vida stared at these strangers, at their odd complacency in the face of calamity. Her heart refused to go ahead of these poor souls. Not out of altruism. Altruism had never been and was not now Vida's chief characteristic. It was that very little of her wanted to be safe. She wanted only to see her mother and father and know they were all right and face whatever the night held with them.

"I must insist," Fitzhugh said. He did the same trick he'd done before—he took a breath and seemed somehow bigger afterward—and Vida felt sorry for the part of herself that still admired this ability of his.

"Must," she muttered, chewing and spitting the ridiculous word, and charged down the line to see if her parents were among those who had queued up in a vain pretense of normalcy. She did glance back, but Fitzhugh had already given up insisting. He was holding a lady's hand as she went over the rail into the lifeboat, and only Sal, who held the lady's other hand, glanced back at her with that dark and impenetrable gaze.

Vida stalked the deck, shouting her mother's and father's names. The crowd was so dense by then, and she knew she was upsetting the others with her frantic searching. They did not want her to disturb their sense that this was all very normal, that this was all just fine. Their numbers dwindled, and the ship slowly, slowly angled to the port side. Soon empty lifeboats were brought up, along with the happy news that the ship that had hit them was nearby. The other ship—called the *Artemis*—was a bit bashed in at the stern, but she had taken on no water, and so passengers from the *Princess* were being brought on deck.

A cheer went up when that news arrived, and people

began joking that they should make a quick run back to the dining room for a bottle of champagne to lighten the mood on the way over. But the news did nothing to soothe Vida's agitation. When she had been back and forth across the deck a thousand times she tried to force her way belowdecks, to search the cabin where her mother and father had intended to spend a peaceful evening. A sailor was blocking the door that led below.

"You can't go that way, miss," he said.

"Well, why not?" she fumed. "I bought my ticket just like anybody, and it's my life to risk if I so choose."

"There's nobody down there," the sailor insisted. He had pink cheeks and fair stubble and Vida wondered if he were even younger than she was.

"How do you know?" she demanded, confident she could bend him to her will.

"We have knocked on all doors, miss. Now, please. I must insist you get to safety."

"Oh *must* you?" Vida shot back with bitter irony. "Captain's orders, is it?"

"No—his," replied the young man, and she saw Fitzhugh striding in her direction.

"Don't you dare!" she shouted as he charged forward to pick her up.

She resisted, her legs bicycled wildly, but it was no use. He was much stronger than she was. All her delicate walking, all her careful eating, all that whittling of her already petite person made her the perfect target to be lifted from around the waist, hauled across the deck. A crew-member who stood at the edge of the deck picked up her feet and together they lifted her over the rail and deposited her in the lifeboat fastened to the *Princess*'s side. Then Fitz signaled, and other crewmen began to slacken the ropes to lower the lifeboat down.

"Wait!" Vida screamed, and stood up as though she might actually grab the *Princess* by the railing and haul herself back on deck.

One of the other women in the vessel gasped, and Vida realized that she had risen so suddenly, and with such fury, that she had no control of her own body's trajectory. She might have thrown herself clear out of the boat. Fear spread its icy fingers over her breastbone. Yes, she might have fallen a long distance to the ocean below, where she could see other boats being rowed away into the dense fog. Some-one had reached out and grabbed her by the wrist, though. He was holding her steady. She had a final view of the deck of the *Princess* cleared of all passengers. Only the crew, in their neat navy-and-brass uniforms, remained. Fitzhugh saluted them, gave a final order, then leapt over the edge and landed beside Vida in the lifeboat.

"You bastard," she said through tight teeth.

She thought he would respond with equal fury, but he enraged her further by smiling amiably, like the hero of newspaper columns. He smoothed the surface of his hair. "Maybe—but one who keeps you safe, my lady."

Only then did she glance at the person who held her wrist, and saw Sal. She jerked back her hand, and he did not try to hold on. The little boat lowered along the wall of the ship. As they descended she had glimpses into a dining room where all the plates had spilled off the table, into abandoned cabins, into the white-painted halls. The great ship went on tilting, so that at last it loomed over them. She could hardly breathe staring back up its monstrous, looming side, which went on winking at them from its many illuminated portholes.

Meanwhile the water lapped gently and when at last they touched the surface of the ocean she allowed herself a little guilty burst of relief. She hadn't wanted Fitzhugh's help, or his empty assurances, but as they rowed away from the *Princess* she understood again what a massive, wounded beast the ship was. Soon enough the crew began to lower themselves in the last of the lifeboats, and Vida watched, numb and refusing blankets or reassuring words from the twenty or so others who huddled on the wooden benches around her.

A lifeboat! She shuddered as the real meaning of the phrase occurred to her.

What had they left, then?

Well, the answer was painfully simple. It was a death ship now.

Up above, the lights of the *Princess* had begun to blink on and off. The crew was shouting that the final boat must be lowered. The others who surrounded Vida with their anxious, breathless waiting fixed their attention on that last boat of crewmembers, and when its tethers were released from the big ship, a great collective sigh escaped from the other passengers on Vida's boat.

That last lifeboat rowed toward them, and then both boats began to row in the direction they believed the *Artemis* to lie. Though no one spoke, it was not quiet. The air crackled with their fears. They were so small under that tower of ominously winking windows. And yet they were smaller still when, quite suddenly, the lights went out and the darkness surged over them.

"The electricity's gone!" cried one of the crewmembers in the other boat.

"That means the water is in all the boiler rooms," Sal called back. "She'll be sunk soon."

"Is Carlton with you?" cried the crewmember in the other boat.

"He went to the *Artemis* some time ago," Fitzhugh shouted.

Once again Vida thought that time was a very odd concept that explained nothing. It seemed to her the ship had only just been hit, but also that she had lived a whole life since then.

The water had begun to bear them up and down more forcefully, and the crewmembers in the other boat seemed not to have heard.

"What did you say about Carlton?" Fitzhugh shouted. "Why would he be there?"

The man was shouting, and though the name "Carlton" came clear over the din of the water and the wind, little else did.

"Why would Carlton have been with us?" Fitzhugh asked Sal, and Sal said he did not know. "He must have been back on the ship somehow. If he's back on the ship, I can't leave him."

Vida glanced around at the other people crowded onto the benches of the lifeboat. Their faces were immobile, and their eyes averted from Fitzhugh as though they did not want to know what he was suggesting. There must have been about twenty of them—a few crewmembers, men she recognized from the first-class dining room, several ladies in their nightdresses, and two women with hair that had never been arranged for a party, faces that had never been painted for an evening's entertainment, holding tight to four small, frightened children. Vida swallowed to see those little bodies hiding in their mothers' humble shawls. Vida knew what he was suggesting, and it infuriated her.

She opened her mouth to tell him so, but no sound came. And suddenly she realized how terrified she herself was.

Fitzhugh ordered the men to row. The other lifeboats had rowed hard away from the dark, listing ship, but the Farrar crewmembers obeyed Fitzhugh; they piloted their lifeboat back.

Sal's voice was even, but Vida thought he betrayed some anger, too. "It's too late, Fitz. The bow is starting to lift."

"Oh God," said Fitz, and the tone in his voice was enough to make the other men stop rowing.

In the darkness Vida could see the massive form of the *Princess*, but no other detail, as half of the ship lifted up out of the water. She rose slowly, awesomely—she seemed almost alive. A mammoth sea creature showing its true size just before it dove deep to see what was below.

"Hold on!" Fitzhugh shouted. "Stay low!"

And Vida, and the others, gripped the rails of their boat. They bent low, they held tight. *Stay low, stay low,* Vida repeated in her mind. It was the last thing she was able to think clearly before the *Princess* stood on her head and began to slide out of view. In a matter of minutes the ocean swallowed the great ship whole. Her fingers ached from clinging to the wooden rails. A massive swell rose beneath their own tiny vessel, twirling them around and around and around. They were powerless—the sea had them—and they were flung into the darkness and the unknown.

PART
TWO

EIGHT

Vida had not known how alien the dawn was until she saw it from a lifeboat on the high seas. She was cold, numb, hopeless, and nothing she could see seemed real.

Of course she had seen the sunrise before, usually after a long night of dancing and a little dazed on champagne, from the stone terrace of a fine house on Telegraph Hill, through the frame of the surrounding elegant buildings. She and Bill, or Whiting, or whoever it was, would have had a whimsical notion to say good morrow to the sun, and they would do so laughing, letting their fingers graze each other's arms, and then they would go back inside to drink the bouillon being passed by waiters in livery.

Tonight had been a very different kind of long night.

Her mouth was a desert and her lips were dried leather and her dress had been soaked through with the water that had washed over them in those terrifying minutes (or hours? It was very hard to know anything for sure anymore), so that the fabric had tightened around her body (except where it was still damp in the corners), and her mind had been absolutely rinsed empty by the tears she couldn't cry. The children—two boys and two girls, none of them older than ten years—had not cried in the rage of the storm, and so she knew it would look wrong for her to do so. But oh, oh, oh, how her insides beat with despair and horror whenever she made the mistake of wondering what had become of Nora and Mother and Father. All through the deepest darkness of night, and then the lightening of the sky, she had tried her best to be stoic and not think about any of that.

And now across the unending plateau of the horizon the sun surged, first staining the sky and then the sea with such a multifariousness of unreal colors that it frightened Vida more than the hours of darkness. She saw Fitz and Sal, their presence taunting her with the vanities and petty ambitions of worldly existence. And there was Flora Flynn, who she had described to Nora as an ungifted conversationalist for no good reason at all. And a few members of the *Princess*'s crew, who were trained to survive the ocean in all sorts of ways Vida had never even bothered to think about.

After the ship went down, the ocean had surged beneath

them and their little bark had been carried away from the field of wreckage left by the *Princess*. The atmosphere had seemed so still and calm while the great ship took on water and tilted in the night, but afterward they caught the edge of the hurricane they had been trying to avoid. The wind and spray whipped their faces and Fitzhugh and Sal and the others strained and labored to keep the boat free of water, to steer out of the worst of it. Vida huddled with the two mothers, shielding the children from the gusts of seawater and trying to prevent their small bodies from bouncing into the swell. For stretches it seemed they were alone, the only people in all the world, with no moon, and no stars. Then they would see another ship being carried back and forth by the storm. They'd hear cries, and even once or twice glimpse a face, but these were not the kind of faces one recognized. They were faces hollowed by terror, so wide were their frightened eyes, their fearful mouths, and thus unrecognizable as anyone Vida could have met in her old life.

While the sea had battered them, Vida had been senseless with fear. The only idea her mind managed to form was that this would all be over soon, and perhaps she would meet Nora amongst the beautiful underwater coral castles, where they could hold hands and float along as the pretty corpses of fashionable dead girls, or otherwise be entertained by the legions of strapping mermen who had saved them.

In the relentless brightness of morning, it was almost impossible to hold a pleasant fantasy for even a passing moment. The sun was all. It hovered over them. It sparkled the crests of the little waves and sucked up what was left of the ocean within their boat. It made them thirsty, and warm, and then hot, all while reminding them, with the steady path it blazed above, that it would soon abandon them to the cold and dark of night. In the previous days, she had been consumed with different ways of holding the interest of Fitzhugh, and now here he was. He was trapped with her in a small boat. Yet she had nothing she wanted to say to him, or to anybody. No one else seemed to want to talk either. If they began talking they would have to admit what a terrible situation they were in.

Late in the day they saw a dark form against the sherbet sky. A distant ship. The others stood, screamed, made crazy motions with their arms. Vida just went on holding on to the rail. They would not be saved. There was no goodness. Everything Vida had counted on her whole life seemed reversed now.

That the sky was blue, for instance. That water could quench thirst. Now she knew that everything was much more complicated. The riot of color that the sky displayed throughout the course of the day sickened her. She was surrounded by water yet her thirst desiccated not only her skin, her mouth, but also her brain, her bones. In a long-ago time

aboard the *Princess*, Sal had insisted the ocean was a wonder. He didn't now. He watched the sky, the waves, what
mysterious forms swam below them, as though reading an
ancient text, and said almost nothing.

Fitzhugh said things. He said them in his sure and jocular
way, as though this too was another adventure in a string of
adventures. *We'll catch up to that ship,* he said. *Another will be
along soon.* But Vida did not listen much. She did not believe
in him anymore. Like the twenty-odd others, crowded
onto the benches of the boat, she huddled and stared downward, but really at nothing, not entertaining much hope,
just waiting for a fate she did not dare imagine. They were
only bodies now, and had lost their standing in the world
of men along with their luggage and their futures. The big
ship in the distance was absorbed by the falling night, and
they were alone again.

Now that the storm had passed, the dark curtain of the
sky was pierced with a million stars. It might have been
beautiful, Vida thought, although she no longer put much
stock in beauty. Sleep seemed like one of many luxuries
Vida had taken for granted in her old life and would never
know again. But she must have slept, because she woke
up with an ache in her neck and her chin slumped on her
shoulder, and saw that it was light again, the very beginning of morning, and heard the anxious murmuring of all
the others. A little life came into Vida's limbs, but she tried

to be reasonable, and not to allow anything as ridiculous as hope to enter her thoughts. The others were craning, gripping the rails. At the rear of the boat Fitzhugh and Sal were using the remaining two oars to row as hard as they could.

"What is it?" she asked one of the mothers.

"Mr. Farrar's man saw a gull," she replied.

"So?"

Her son, who had not said a thing during their trial, flexed his brow as though wondering if Vida were serious. "You only see birds near shore."

"Right, of course."

The mother resisted returning Vida's gaze, and Vida thought she understood why—if their eyes met they would surely shine with excitement, and if they allowed themselves to become excited over nothing, the disappointment would break their spirits permanently.

NINE

The endless horizon was endless no more. At first it seemed a kind of mirage, but slowly and steadily it became more real, even as Vida blinked, shook her head to get the stars from her eyes, even as she forgot to breathe. The others had gone silent. There was only the heave of the oars, the splash and ripple of the sea, the labored sighs of the two men at the stern. As they pulled, as the floor of the boat went up and down with the water, Vida felt her blood move again, felt the wind on her face, and she was surprised by the conviction that they *must* reach that bit of land growing ever larger before their eyes.

There, contrary to the direness of her heart, was an island. An island! An island with a rocky promontory, crowned with palms, toward which flew the birds that promised other forms of life. Beyond the beach rose green peaks. She gazed and gazed at it. She was afraid to look away, afraid it might disappear.

So—she did still want to live after all.

The waves bore them into the land, and no one said anything or looked at each other until they could see the sandy bottom only a few feet beneath the surface. Then Fitz jumped from the boat and began to pull them in.

But not until she felt the beach under her own feet did Vida believe they would be saved.

Then she felt solid land beneath her and all the sorrow and pity about what had happened surged up and over-whelmed her mind.

She felt, too, the ocean's rocking. The movement of the water beneath the boat over their long night lost at sea fol-lowed her onto land. All that still moved within her body. She was dizzy and fell to her knees. For a moment it was all too much, and she gasped to hold back the tears. A few sprang to her eyes, but in moments she had mastered herself. The ocean still swayed within her, but she forced herself to stand and go to where the others had gathered.

"This way, that's right!" Fitzhugh was saying. He went on saying such things, somewhat indiscriminately, as the men dragged palm fronds, sticks, and whatever they could find at the edge of the jungle that spread from the beach back into the interior of the island. Sal and others were erecting a few shelters with what they could find. "Ah, Vida!" Fitzhugh said when she approached. He grinned, flashed his strong teeth. He was still wearing his formal pants but his jacket was removed and his formerly white dress shirt was rolled to the elbows. "Feeling all right?"

She nodded. "What can I do?" she asked.

"Just stay in the shade. We can't have you burned by the sun."

She nodded obediently, and walked toward the shady spot where the other women and the children were huddled. But the way he'd sent her away rankled, and seemed somehow all of a piece with everything that had been between them. The flirtations that had obscured the cruel dismissals. She didn't want to join the frightened huddle. She kept walking, along the place where the white sand met the dense vegetation, irritated with this young man she had pursued so energetically, and knowing full well that irritation was among the least appropriate feelings to have at a moment like this.

To her left stretched a wide, flat beach; to her right the unknown island, the dense greenery that was the way into the interior.

At sea there had been only two questions: survive or perish.

Now here she was, still alive, and she couldn't seem to shut her mind to bothersome little thoughts.

For instance: If Fitzhugh was concerned about her getting sunburned, did that mean he had a romantic inclination for her after everything? And if so, should she allow herself to care?

For instance: Did Sal judge her for not helping with the building of the shelter?

For instance: Why had she worn this pastel dress? It had been the faintest of petal pinks, but now it was yellowed, stained by the sea water, muddied at the hem by the dark, wet sand she'd trod through to reach the safety of land. The strange lacy bell sleeves would snag the moment she headed into the jungle, which they would have to, sooner or later, for water and food. Why had she chosen a dress with so many laces, so many little details—how would she ever get it on and off properly without Nora? And meanwhile her hair had frizzed, had gone absolutely mad with the salt air, with the humid wind gusts—how would she manage to tame it, here, so far from any apothecary with a decent hair tonic for sale? And then she almost laughed. Here she was, on an improbable outcropping of land, safe—or safer than she had been—and she was concerned with her wardrobe.

But, just as soon as she had convinced herself not to dwell on such petty matters, she reached the top of the rocks at the edge of the beach, looked down into a little sheltered cove, and saw that there *was* a better color to have worn for a shipwreck.

Camilla Farrar was wearing it.

The color was aubergine (oh, *eggplant*, Vida said to herself, what does it matter now, just call it *eggplant*). The gown itself was as glamorous and somehow as fresh-looking as when Vida had seen her framed in the doorway of the map room with that lovely face, rosy and bright with the spirit of feminine combat. Even here, in a desperate and remote corner of the Earth, her beautiful hair hung half-loose down her back, as though she had arranged it that way on purpose. Jealousy struck Vida like snake venom, and she almost turned away. Then she heard the sound—a moan like an animal dying. When she looked again she saw the scene below for what it really was.

Fitzhugh's lovely sister-in-law, the girl he had been romantically attached to at some time in the not-so-distant past, was bent in a beautiful aubergine curve, her waving golden hair lifted by a gentle breeze, her head hung low, as she tried to protect the body splayed out on the beach. A dead body. Even at a distance Vida knew that body possessed no life. A body that wore a formal black tuxedo, and that belonged—or anyway, *had* belonged—to Fitzhugh's brother. Again Camilla made that horrible sound, and Vida felt it, low in her stomach, and before she could help it a sense of sadness for this widow on the beach had invaded her heart.

Very slowly Camilla lifted her head. The wind pulled

her hair back from her face, and Vida saw that the woman's beauty had been undone by loss. Anguish had drawn its paw across her features. Her mouth and gaze were ripped open. Nobody had told Camilla to stay out of the sun—her face looked charred by the elements.

"Hello!" Vida tried, with the same verve she might have used on the top deck of the *Princess*. She lifted her arm and smiled wide, and then immediately thought better of it. She wrenched her arm back to her side. Camilla's eyes were bloodred from crying—in those eyes was the whole story of their ordeal. A man was dead. Her man. The life they had lived together was an ocean and a country away and they could never go back there. The glittering world in which Vida had first encountered the grand Mrs. Carlton Farrar was gone—the ocean had swallowed their way of life whole.

TEN

The funeral was held at dusk on the high rocks that separated the cove from the wide, flat beach. The survivors of the wreck of the *Princess* gathered around and bent their heads as Fitzhugh Farrar spoke some words about his elder brother. Though Vida felt numb inside, she had no trouble looking sad. She wasn't sure her face would ever be capable of anything but a sad expression again.

"Carlton Farrar taught me everything I know," said Fitzhugh, hands clasped behind his back and head hung low.

Vida's eyes darted between the two distinct rows of mourners. On one side were the fine people, of which she was one, mostly in tattered evening wear. On the other were the crew and other third-class passengers, whose appearance was slightly less ridiculous than the first-class passengers', on account of being mostly dressed in dark fabric and adorned with a minimum of frippery. Not that *she* was going to be the one to call attention to a torn silk skirt's ridiculousness. They were a morose group, and Fitzhugh's solemn tone seemed to admonish her for thinking such things.

"He was a man who embodied righteousness, a man of rigorous intellect. He was a husband, a son, a steward of a great enterprise. He was the keeper of the family's values, and a man of indubitable practicality. . . ."

Vida was stern with herself not to roll her eyes. This last bit was, as almost every member of the assembled now knew, untrue. The story of Carlton's demise had spread rapidly throughout the long afternoon. How he had been among the first of the passengers of the *Princess* to evacuate, but upon realizing that the crew was abandoning ship, had insisted on returning to see that all was being done to preserve his family investment. And his wife, who had already been drinking tea in the captain's quarters of the *Artemis*, had heard of his rash behavior, and insisted on going after him with two other members of the *Princess*'s crew. He had been ascending the side of the doomed ship when she began to sink, and he was feared lost in the following chaos. But Camilla commanded them in her husband's name to remain close to the scene of the wreck, so they had managed to recover his body before they, too, were swept up in the storm. All night she had keened over him, and into the morning as he became rigid. And when they crashed into the rocks in the darkness she had insisted that the two young seamen carry his body ashore, where he had remained for several hours before Vida thought to climb up on the rocks and see what was on the other side.

Nobody spoke of his reckless behavior now, of course. They lowered their eyes, polite even at the extreme edge of existence. Their heads bobbed along with Fitzhugh's words as though they were the gospel truth.

In her old life—in a life where her hair was straightened and arranged, where she changed her clothes three to six times a day, where she kept a luminous and very full schedule of events, most of which involved the serving of many small golden plates topped with rare and elegant bites—Vida had been a master of such displays of etiquette, such upholding of customs amongst moneyed and prominent peoples. But that had all been a mask she wore so that she might do what she pleased. She certainly felt no compunction to wear such a mask now. While the others kept their gaze piously averted, she lifted her chin and took in the scene. For one thing, she could not stand to be looked *at*—not with her appearance so frightful. If anyone was going to look at her, she wanted to be ready with a warning expression. But also she felt so entirely impious about everything, and could not tolerate if, along with everything else, she had to pretend that the great Carlton Farrar had perished in some noble pursuit, when everyone well knew he had died on a fool's errand.

There were thirty-nine survivors. Four children who with their mothers were traveling to meet their fathers (laborers on a sugar plantation in Hawaii), five members of the crew, six ladies—some of whom had been dressed for dinner, and some for a quiet night in—eight gentlemen, nine men and women who had been employed as servants to the first-class passengers, Fitzhugh, Camilla, Sal, Vida, and the celebrated gossip columnist, Dame Edna Sackville. Although she was tight-lipped about what had transpired during the sinking of the *Princess*, it was said that she had been among the last to evacuate because she had wanted to report the story of the event in all its gruesome detail.

("A shipwreck on the first page is guaranteed to sell out," Miss Flora Flynn claimed to have overheard her say, and she said it to her lady's maid, Eleanor, who repeated it to Vida.)

The gentler amongst them had been warned that there might be more bodies. All afternoon, as the men had worked to build shelter, materials had been ferried in by the tide. Pieces of lifeboats, doors, trunks, and other debris. So it was possible that the people who had clung to these items in the final moments of the *Princess* would come, too. But the band of survivors tried to put this out of mind as they sought water, food, shelter from the sun—and from whatever came at night.

Through the afternoon, nobody had spoken of what might hunt them in the night.

Whether this strange island had residents who might prey upon their humble beach encampment. How the winds might roar, or the sea surge over their lean-tos.

When a search party led by Sal returned with fresh water, they all cheered, and said they had been saved.

When they had managed to turn over a damaged life-boat, and prop it on boards to create a kind of gazebo, they said they had been saved.

And when the oldest of the children—Peter, a boy who had comported himself throughout the ordeal with a heartbreaking seriousness—managed to make a cross of two sticks, bound together with the dried centers of palm fronds, the whole band cheered that they had indeed been saved by God.

They had labored through the day to be ready for night. Now night was falling. But they did not speak of the uncertainties. No—they spoke of Carlton Farrar, who ruled the shipping concern to whom they had all entrusted their safety. The cross that Peter had made was used to mark Carlton Farrar's final resting place, in the soft earth between the high rocks and a great gnarled tree, with roots that spread like an octopus from jungle to beach.

The sky blazed pink and purple as the sun mellowed to a great gold disc hazing into the watery horizon.

The breeze picked up, whipping the already messy hair of the assembled.

It was plain from looking at them who had worked during the day, and who had not, by the relative paleness of their skin. They wore the clothes that had marked their places in the hierarchy of the *Princess*—elaborate dresses, or simple ones; formal jackets, or uniform ones—although not in the smart manner of before. Now everything was tattered, dirtied, either loosened or shrunk by the assaults of the ocean and the sun. To a one they were a disheveled parody of their former selves. But none so much as Camilla. The sunburn on her face had mellowed in the course of the day, but the extreme contrast of her light eyes against the reddened skin gave her the appearance of some strange creature from the depths of the ocean. Or maybe from the clouds. She walked a little bent over all the time, as though she had just been hit hard in the stomach.

"But to me," Fitzhugh said, bringing the eulogy to a close, "he will always be my brave and strapping older brother. He is with God now. May his soul be at rest."

With this, Camilla threw back her head. A croaking

sound came out of her mouth, followed by a wail. Sobs wracked her body. The first-class passengers of the *Princess* stared at her, not sure what to do. They were a staid sort of people, disinclined to displays of emotion. They appeared horrified by her unlovely grief. Vida wondered if someone would do something. Then she noticed that someone already had. Fitzhugh had reached for her, he had taken her hand. As he squeezed her hand, her sobs slowed and became less frequent until she made no sound at all. There was only the rise and fall of her lovely breast.

She had, with his touch, become lovely again.

Vida disliked herself for caring. But she had believed that Camilla was no longer the possessor of uncommon beauty, and she was disappointed to find that it had been there all along, lying in wait until she had the attention of this young man again.

They looked like the perfect pair—rumpled by the elements, yet somehow still handsome, with their light eyes against sun-darkened faces. And Vida, who would not have thought she could be moved by anything so trivial ever again, was shocked by the sharp pain that spread from the left side of her chest.

Fitzhugh had seemed as good as hers, but he belonged to another. The absurdity of the entire situation did nothing to assuage her unbearable loneliness.

She could not let these people see her cry, so she turned

away, made her way carefully back down the rocks, to the wide beach where they had arrived that morning.

Could it really only have been that morning?

It seemed as long ago as the beginning of time.

At the water's edge she sank down and gazed out. The little ripples went on forever, through crests of magenta, midnight blue, turquoise, bronze, to the mellowing sun. What a fool she had been to chase such a man. A man she thought she knew, but who she didn't really understand at all. And where were the people she had blithely put at risk to chase a chimera? Nora, and her mother and father—where were they? Had they slept through the last hours of the *Princess*? Did they only realize at the final moments that the great ship was going down, when the cabins were flooded with the ocean and they could no longer escape? Vida wished them safe, but she couldn't make herself believe they were safe. A happy ending seemed such a naïve and childish notion, now.

Sobs rocked her shoulders. Before she knew it, the water had crept up, had soaked the hem of her dress, of her petticoat. She glanced up at the rising tide, wiping the snot and tears from her face, trying to get control of herself, to put a stop to those heaving sobs before someone saw her.

Too late she noticed her skin prickle, that telltale sign that someone already had seen her.

A little way down the beach, back toward the rocks,

stood a tall figure. At that hour he was just a silhouette. But she knew it was Sal—she recognized the leanness of him, the way his hair grew long around the ears. She couldn't make out his face, but his body was turned toward her, and she could feel his gaze. So—Fitzhugh had sent his servant to see what she was doing.

For another moment Sal watched her, and she watched back, daring him to interfere.

After a little while he bent his head in understanding, saluted her, and returned to the others. Vida was alone. She did not want to be alone, but nor did she want to be with any of the people she'd washed up with. She had no choice but to stand apart and contemplate the vast unknown that spread out before her, on and on to the very limits of her vision.

ELEVEN

Vida blinked into the white sun of high noon, trying to think what day it was. She was relatively certain this was her third day of residence on the island. Which would have meant it was a Thursday. But it might have been the second—things did all run together.

And she wasn't even all that sure that they had sunk on a Tuesday.

What was a Tuesday, anyway?

She was very hungry, and this further confused things. And then there was the monotony. She had been braiding together the dried ribs of palm fronds, which was what Fitz had asked all the ladies to do, and it was the sort of task that dulled the mind to nothing.

In San Francisco, she had been the celebrated habitué of what in retrospect were only a handful of well-appointed rooms. Yet, when taken together, those rooms—elaborately decorated and filled with the sort of person who practiced the art of charm and loved to talk and talk—had seemed vast. On this island she could see, from first light to last, that the world was much bigger than she had known.

It was rather horrible how it went on and on.

For Vida was afraid of what lay beyond those first clusters of trees at the top of the beach, how the jungle thickened and cried out with its mysterious, indescribable sounds. She could only say that the sounds the island made at night chilled her, although the atmosphere itself was mostly warm. She was afraid of the ocean that crept up and down the wide crescent of the beach twice a day. So the overall effect was that her life had shrunk down like a puddle in the sun.

There were only these other survivors, and they were as scared as she was. They huddled together under the makeshift shelters, these little huts made of fallen palm leaves, the debris of the wreck, tablecloths, and other items that had washed up in the wake of the storm. They did not speak much, because when they spoke they would often accidentally talk of what had happened, and the memory of what had befallen them and those who had perished in the disaster worsened their misery. Vida especially did not like to think of the time before this, which led her to thoughts of her parents, and how they fretted over her. How they had gone on this fool's errand to protect her reputation, neglecting the fact that she had probably already ruined it. Maybe she had been born ruined.

"A word to the wise." A voice interrupted her thoughts.

"Yes?" She glanced up wearily at that odd phrase, which had made perfect sense in her old life, but sounded curious and all wrong here.

"My dear, don't take this the wrong way," Dame Edna said as she sank down out of the sun and became visible to Vida. She was wearing what had once been an emerald-colored evening gown and a bonnet that she must have constructed for herself out of a bent palm leaf wrapped with a piece of green silk that (Vida presumed) had been repurposed from some part of her undergarments. "You're beginning to smell."

"Oh." Vida instinctively lengthened her neck and did a trick she had learned in ballrooms, which was to keep her expression very placid and relax the focus of her eyes so that she could take in who was close by and within earshot.

"Don't worry, I'm not trying to humiliate you, dear child. Nobody can hear."

It was true—they all sat far apart, as though to discourage small talk. But *still*. The blood surged to Vida's face. She felt it was of the utmost importance to defend herself. She parried with: "What does such vanity matter now?"

The gentle smile with which Dame Edna returned this comment was even worse than a true rebuttal.

Of *course* Vida still cared how she was perceived. It was only that she thought she had been keeping up appearances. She had plaited her hair and wound it at the back of her head, and she had gone with the other women to the cove to bathe in the ocean yesterday, and then Miss Flynn's maid had helped her put her dress back on in as proper a fashion as they could manage. It pained her not to be able to check her appearance. Not knowing *precisely* the depth of her hideousness felt like torture, though she knew it was a blessing. Hadn't that always been her trick anyway? To believe herself the most beautiful girl in the room with enough verve that everyone else believed it, too?

Well, here was Dame Edna, to tell her that she had become a stinky, slovenly mess.

At night, crammed together in the makeshift ladies' shelter, she had smelled such human odors as she had not known existed, but she had assured herself that these were not the emissions of her own body. Now her ears clanged with shame and she tried to think quickly back to whether or not Fitzhugh and she had been in close proximity recently.

"There's a lovely pool, not far beyond the trees. Fresh water that comes down in a little waterfall from the high peak of the island," said the dame. "The trick is to bathe in fresh water, and take off all your things, give them a good rinse, and let them dry on the rocks while you do."

This was against everything Vida had been taught. How long did it take for an evening dress to dry in the sun? She had never seen to such a task herself, but she guessed it would take some time, and that in that time she would be uncovered in public. And as she contemplated this prospect another blush crept up the skin of her neck. Despite some notable rebellious behavior, she had been taught since birth that revealing the skin of her elbow could diminish her standing in the world. Apparently some of that sense of decorum had stuck. "How do you . . . ?"

"I was born in the British East Indies, dear, and began my career sending dispatches from the First Boer War. There are certain situations in which you must try very hard to forget everything you know about propriety."

"But I would have to be . . ."

"Naked. Out of doors, yes."

The word "naked" sent a sudden heat to Vida's cheeks. She would have thought she was beyond that kind of humiliation, but no—she had blushed at a mere word.

The dame noticed her embarrassment.

"Perhaps I have overestimated you." Dame Edna's face was like that of a faded fox. It was apparent now—without makeup, in the stark light of the island—that she was a woman with many decades behind her. But whatever lines marked her face, whatever frost had settled permanently in her hair, her eyes had the fire of eternal youth.

Vida gazed back and wondered if the dame *had* esteemed her too highly. She was feeling very sorry for herself, and wished that she had stayed in San Francisco and been satisfied with making a good match and living out the life her parents expected of her. But some deep determination forced Vida to square her shoulders and say, "No, you haven't. And thank you for telling me. I shall look forward to a nice bath—and showing you that I am still myself."

Edna nodded. Just then Fitzhugh bolted from the trees, dashing past them and down the sand, where he leapt and dove headlong into the next gathering wave. He emerged seconds later, pushing his hair back from his forehead, his muscles gleaming as the sunlight glimmered on his wet skin. He had rolled his dark trousers above the ankle, and went about retucking his undershirt under his waistband as he strode back up the beach.

The ladies who sat in the shade, braiding the long, dried stalks they had spent the morning collecting, stopped what they were doing and stared openly. As he approached his mouth broke open into a hearty grin. *Oh what a stupid animal is the female heart,* thought Vida. Her own heart had fluttered alive at the sight of him.

"Isn't it a beautiful day?" he called.

"He's very impressive, isn't he?" Dame Edna said at a volume only Vida could hear.

"Don't you mean delusional?"

"Oh, he's worried. I've seen a few men in extreme circumstances, and I can tell you delusion is a frightening thing that any sane person recognizes immediately and shrinks from. No, he knows what a bad spot we're in. But he's a leader, and he knows that we are in greater danger if we lose our will. Don't you think?"

"It was his unsinkable ship that sunk and got us here," Vida said as she picked up her handmade rope again. "So you'll forgive me if I withhold my judgment."

"My men and I spent all day climbing these trees," Fitzhugh boomed so that all the survivors could hear him. "And we have brought you lunch!"

As if on cue, the men who had been crewmembers of the *Princess* emerged from the trees carrying a ripped piece of tarp heaped with the coconuts that Vida had, until then, only seen high on the palms, or broken and emptied on the ground. Upon waking that morning, she had sucked the water from an empty husk that she had placed on the roof of the ladies' hut to collect dew. It had a faint taste of something savory and sweet, but she had not yet tasted the meat of a coconut. The other ladies lay down their handiwork and began to buzz. They stood and moved toward the men, who used their knives to cut holes in the furry brown hides of the fruit, and showed the women how to drink. When the milk was gone, they split the coconuts on rocks and shaved off pieces of the white innards.

"Aren't you hungry?" asked Dame Edna.

Oh yes—seeing the others eat made Vida's stomach tighten and howl. But she did not want to be one of those desperate women clamoring for any little scrap. She had fasted at least this long on several occasions in preparation to wear an especially fitted gown. She had her pride, still. "Not hungry enough to participate in that spectacle," she said.

A little smile flickered on the older woman's face. "So— you *are* the girl I thought you were."

"I don't know if the girl I was could survive a place like this."

"Well, if she does, it might be the beginning of the greatest love story I have ever written," the dame said with a little nod toward the man who had separated from the crowd.

Fitzhugh was coming her way. Vida was flushed with renewed mortification. Dame Edna was right. There was a ripe, human smell coming off her person, and she had no idea how far away this smell could be detected.

"Miss Hazzard," he called, revealing his strong white teeth. "How are you this morning?"

"All right," she replied in as disinviting a tone as she could manage.

"That's good." He nodded, as though this were an ordinary answer on an ordinary day. "That's good. Aren't you hungry?"

"I'll let the others have their fill first," she answered coolly.

"Nonsense." Fitzhugh's brow flexed, and his smile softened without losing its ironic curl. "If you wait, there will be none left."

He was coming toward her all this time and she was willing him to stop but he didn't. She stood as quickly as she could and stepped backward and away.

"Don't be ridiculous!" he said.

Oh, how it curdled her heart to be called ridiculous. Ridiculous was, to Vida, even worse than being ugly, worse than being unwanted. She would rather be a girl with a great mess of a face who no one ever asked to dance (*that* she could work with, or else enjoy the solitude) than a girl who showed up in a laughable dress expecting everyone to admire her. But before she could think of a biting reply, Fitzhugh flung himself at the nearest tree and began to haul himself up. He had a time of it—she could hear his labored breathing as he ascended the tall trunk—and she willed him to fail. He didn't, though. He knocked a coconut from its high, sprouting nest, and it fell at her feet. Then he slid down, jumped, and was, to her horror, within range of her underarms.

"My lady," he said, stooping to fetch the coconut and kneeling as he punctured its side with a blade.

Vida retreated with a hasty "No, thank you."

"Vida," he implored as he followed her.

"I beg your pardon," she replied with haughty formality. "Are we friends?"

"Miss Hazzard," he corrected himself, and slowed his pace.

Without thinking she had marched farther into the jungle than she had yet traveled. The smell of the earth, of trees just sprouting new growth, not to mention the dense perfume of some sort of flower she had yet to see, overwhelmed her nostrils, and she was relieved that she had at least this dignity—that the forest's bursting life would mask her own sweaty scent.

"You don't know me at all," she said.

"I know you a little," he replied, catching up. "The night we met I kept thinking to myself it was easier to talk to you than any girl I'd ever known. It was like we'd met a hundred times before. And then, on the *Princess*, I felt I wanted to know you more and more."

"Yes, for some reason you wanted me to believe that,"

she snapped. "I can't think why you'd still want to convince me of such falsehoods now."

"How can you say—"

"Oh *do* let's be honest with one another. I know about you and Camilla."

The sun here was filtered by the high green canopy. His face was all dappled. His expression shifted, became serious. "Yes? What about me and Camilla?"

"I saw you together! On the ship—and yesterday, holding hands. Or the day before. Whenever it was. And I know what was between you in the past."

"No, that's not . . ."

The air was denser here, so full of tiny floating specks of life. Vida felt pink all over. The dress constricted her arms, her waist. Her underclothes chafed at her thighs. She was feeling so many things, certainly too many at once. Mostly she wanted him not to come any closer. She wished that she had never wanted him; that he had never been. That she was Mrs. Whiting de Young just now, or even Mrs. William Halliday, and that she was reading the *Chronicle* in the garden court of the Palace Hotel while she drank her tea and petted a little lapdog. And that she and Rosa de Hastings could go on pretending that they were lovely young ladies forever, who had only lovely things to say about all their friends and all their enemies and of each other.

Instead she was here—hideous, tired, harassed by tiny insects.

"That's not *true?*" she prompted. "Do you mean to tell me there was never anything between you and Camilla Farrar?"

For a long time he said nothing, and Vida knew what hope was again. She had hoped—still! After everything!—that it had not been true, that she had misinterpreted things in the map room, that Fitz and Camilla's intimate history was just rumor. But his silence confirmed things, and Vida learned there was still sufficient sensation in her trampled mess of a heart for it to sting with fresh humiliation.

TWELVE

"Don't you dare come after me," she said. With a brisk little turn she marched on.

A few moments later she glanced back and saw that he had heaped yet more insult upon her by doing as she asked and not pursuing her.

On she marched—yet her abjectness marched on with her. Soon snotty tears were running down her face, and she gasped and sobbed and lost any sense of where she was, or who. She had *believed* herself somehow better than other girls—a girl especially adept in the fine art of being wanted. *Now look at yourself,* she thought. A sunburned wreck who sobbed in the ugliest fashion, and who, apparently, smelled like a back alley on top of everything else.

All she knew was the misery inside herself, and for a while she had no sense of her surroundings. Then a shock of pain spread in her toe—a rock had stopped her forward motion. She lost her balance entirely, and before she could grab hold of something she was facedown on the ground. The soft earth filled her palms.

"Oh," she wailed pitifully.

Too late, she considered the tattered remnants of her once-civilized appearance. The tiers of pale pink lace, the belled sleeves she had lifted in her ship cabin to dab her wrists with tuberose perfume, were already stained by water and yellowed by sun, like some old doily left too long in the window of an unloved house. Now her garb was stained also by the wet soil of the jungle floor. In how many ways could she become more ugly? The idiocy of it all hit her at once—that her own vanity had further marred her appearance. She began to laugh and cry at once.

As she sat up she went on laughing and crying. It was distinctly possible that she was going mad. But laughing and crying at once felt good, so she went on laughing and crying until she heard the shriek.

The shrieking split her ears, zoomed past her and upward.

She gasped in terror and scrambled to her feet. Her blood coursed, and fear seized her throat—she couldn't make a peep, much less call for help.

A burst of exquisite orangey red was disappearing up into the ropes of greenery overhead. *A bird,* she reassured herself, *just a bird,* and her breath came back to her, and she saw where she was.

A little clearing, lit by a small skylight that opened in the high foliage, at the base of a rocky hill that was grown over with vines, with small trees, with flowering bushes. Her heart still pounded, but it was slowing back down to normal again.

The bird still squawked, and another bird squawked back, and then she heard the symphony of the place, the chatter of birds and rustle of leaves and the rush of water down the side of the hill where it filled a rocky basin. This must be the bathing spot Dame Edna had told her about. Vida was still frightened, but she fixed the fear in her sights and told it to come along with her, if it absolutely must.

Holding back her skirt so as to protect it from the mud, but mostly to prevent herself from tripping again, she advanced to the pool. The surface rippled outward from the spray of the falls and it sparkled in the sun. At the edge, she removed the satin slippers she'd worn to dance in on a long-ago night, and carefully lowered herself into the still water. She knew, then, how warm the air was. The coolness of the pool stole her breath and her chest rose in shock. She knew the water became deep quickly by how cold it was on her bare feet. The water soaked her skirt, made it heavy, so she hurriedly undid the buttons at the small of her back. She slipped out of the thing and heaved it onto the sunniest piece of rock.

She reviewed sweet memories—perfumed baths Nora had prepared for her, the taste of strawberries dipped in chocolate as served in the de Young's dining room, the sensation of Bill Halliday's fingertips on her cheek when he was trying to lure her to a private corner. But her memory could summon nothing that felt quite as wonderful as this fresh water against her skin. Dame Edna had said naked—she didn't go that far. She left on her bloomers and her corset (which would have been difficult for her to undo herself). The water seeped against her skin nonetheless. The trials of wind, sand, sun—all of it seemed undone by this sweet coolness that she submerged herself in again and again until her hair was unbound and she felt washed clean.

As she lay on the rock beside her dress, letting the heat absorb the beads of wetness from her skin and underclothes, the dampness from her dress, she listened more closely to the whispering of the wood. It seemed to be telling her a secret. The secret was a sound like the ocean as heard from the coil of a shell, telling her that which she had seemed to know but hadn't really:

I am alive.

Well, of course I am, was the practiced and civilized rebuttal from the voice that went on unceasingly in the space between her ears.

But the secret persisted in its resonant tone—I am alive, I am alive, I am still alive—so that the knowledge of her aliveness seemed to echo throughout creation and also into the deepest, darkest corners of her person. And she knew it to be true in a way she hadn't in the fog of her misery and the awful slog of survival.

Coldness seeped into her skin, making gooseflesh of her clean limbs.

The jungle was abundant with sound. So it was strange that she could hear one in particular. It was a sound that did not belong. She sat up suddenly and jerked her still damp dress over her partial nakedness.

"Who's there?" she demanded.

Light burst against her field of vision. There was so much darkness and so much blazing color.

Her imagination conjured a great sleek cat and a three-headed beast. A thick snake hung from a low branch.

Then she saw that the snake was just a vine, and afterward she understood that the great cat was just a man. A young man. The young man was Sal, and he was bending in such a peculiar way. Bending as though he wanted to assure her with his eyes that he was not a danger—and at the same time to not look at her directly.

"What are you doing?" she demanded. "I am not dressed."

"I'm sorry." He shielded his eyes and turned away. "You're such a lady," he went on. Not in the judgmental way he might have onboard the ship, but in a curious tone she could not place. It sounded almost like a lamentation. He was wearing those same clothes that had looked all wrong in the dining room of the *Princess*, but had fared well through their ordeal. They were that same color as before, neither white nor brown, and no more or less rumpled. "So I would not have thought you would—" He paused, struggled for the word. "Disrobe."

Laughter burbled up and escaped her mouth. To hear that euphemism, spoken by a boy who had proclaimed himself free of such hypocrisies! "Dis*robe*? Is this a newspaper serial for church ladies?"

"You know what I mean," he said.

"Yes. I suppose I do. Stay that way, I'll just be a minute." She was amazed by how quickly the dress, even with so many layers of lace and tulle, had dried. This was not the city she grew up in, where a thing, once damp, stayed damp a long time. "Don't look," she warned, but when she glanced up from the task of bringing her enormous skirt over her cotton knickers, and the bodice over her boned corset, she saw that he was already fastidious in looking away. "I'll need your help with this last bit."

With an awkward little jump, she came off the rock and toward him, holding the back of her dress closed.

"It's just a few buttons. I know you're a rough sort of person, but I think you can manage," she assured him.

He made no sound of acquiescence, but he did as she asked.

Or tried, anyway. He had done half the buttons when he began to undo them again. His breath became short, and she realized he must have missed some.

Now he was slower, more careful, and it seemed a long time his fingertips moved up along her spine.

When he was done she turned to him, her expression pert. "Thank you. You can enjoy your bath now."

As he considered his reply, she realized that she had misinterpreted his presence here.

"Oh," she said. Her anger flared. "He sent you after me."

Sal's dark eyes were still reluctant to meet hers. "He said you seemed upset."

"*Did* he." She strode past him, back toward the beach.

"Vida."

"Just like your master," she called over her shoulder, trying very hard not to trip on any hidden rocks or roots. "You seem to think you know me well enough to call me by my given name."

"Miss Hazzard."

"Oh, *what*," she replied tiredly as she continued through the dense hanging vines.

"That's the wrong way."

She stopped. Her mind rebelled. But he was right—this was not the way at all.

"And he's not my master."

"What would you prefer?" She half turned, but he was too obscured by the shade of the jungle to see his expression. "Don't tell me you want me to call him your *friend*."

"Your maid, who you boarded the *Princess* with . . ."

She squeezed her eyes closed, thinking of Nora, of what might have befallen her.

"Was she not your friend?"

"Of course she was my friend!" Vida replied with sudden fury. "She *is* my friend," she corrected. "She is," she repeated, and her anger was doused by the soggy mess of tears she could not help. "She is, oh God, please, let her still be."

"I'm sorry," he whispered. "I'm sorry. I'm sure she's all right. So many passengers were transferred to the other ship."

She wavered like a kite in a high wind and her hands covered her face. "But what if she wasn't? What if she was asleep, and didn't know the ship was going down? What if they didn't let her on a lifeboat? What if some first-class type insisted she go back after their luggage? What if . . ."

"Stop."

Vida sucked in a breath. Her fears had tumbled out, and all along the sunlight found its way through the high leaves, the buzz of insects and birds continued, the jungle busy and indifferent to her existence. When he began to walk, in what she presumed was the correct direction, she followed along. "How can I stop? How can I not wonder?"

"It doesn't do anything, worrying."

"You don't understand. She was my responsibility. She took that journey on my account. My parents, too. And now what? Now what? I must forget her, just because I am stuck here, at the ends of the Earth and can do nothing about it? No, I will not pretend it was not all my fault."

"You?"

Ah. *There* was that smirk. She had rather missed his smirk. Being smirked at made things seem normal, and she knew again who she was supposed to be. She was the formidable Vida Hazzard, wild, vain, and selfish. If one squinted, they might be two civilized people strolling in a particularly ill-kept corner of the Golden Gate Park.

"Yes, me."

"Miss Hazzard, you are very grand, but you could not sink a ship like the *Princess of the Pacific* all by yourself. Only nature could do that."

"I think I like it better when you laugh at me."

"Well, there's plenty of reason to do that."

"Oh really?"

"No. Not really. Actually there are very few reasons to laugh at you."

"Because I'm so awful, you mean? Having risked the lives of my dearest ones for a big lie like the love of Fitzhugh Farrar." Sal was silent a moment. She hated the silence, and blathered on: "Oh, don't be like that. We both knew that's what I was up to."

They had come through the thickest bit of jungle by then and could see the beach through the thinning trees. Beyond that: the endless marriage of sea and sky.

"Don't worry. It doesn't help. I can't promise you that everything is all right. But Fitzhugh and I have been all over the world, down rivers and canyons where no man had ever been, with fewer resources than we have now, thirsty, hungry, doomed. We always find a way."

"Oh? What are you going to do? Build a boat that will take you to California?"

"No. We only need to get as far as Hawaii."

She wasn't sure why, but there was something about hearing this plan from Fitzhugh's inscrutable servant that made it more believable than if Fitz had said it in his own confident and beautifully articulated way.

"Meanwhile," he went on, "we will build better shelter, and get better food. This island has resources to sustain us forever if need be."

Forever. Her mouth went dry. She had not thought of that. She had never thought she'd do any one thing for very long at all.

They passed out of the shelter of the palms. The people on the beach glanced at them. Flora Flynn was sitting on the beach, arms wrapped around her legs and her head rested on her knees. A little down the way Jack, who had been a deckhand aboard the *Princess* and whose face was fuzzed with the beard he could not grow, and Henry Dries Stahl, who had been introduced to Vida as an inventor, were trying—not very successfully—to build a shack at the edge of the trees. It kept slanting, threatening to fall down. The notion of forever with these people made Vida's stomach drop in despair. She gave Sal a formal little nod and said, "I do wish you luck in all your endeavors."

He bowed in return. Although she saw the laughter in his eyes, his reply was as formal as her own had been. "Thank you, Miss Hazzard."

They were about to part. But quickly, before it could seem they had been talking too long, she bent her head and asked, "Sal. Tell me the truth. Do I . . . smell?"

His dark eyes met hers in surprise. "You will never get the sea out of *that* dress."

"Oh, damn it all." She sighed and stepped away from him.

"But I don't mind it," he murmured. Or that's what she thought he said. As she made her way toward the huddle of ladies braiding their palm ropes, she glanced back once and saw that his dark eyes were still upon her.

THIRTEEN

In the days that followed Vida's visit to the little pool, the girl she had been in the first days after the wreck shrank and disappeared from view. Sal's reassurances that they would be all right here began to seem less empty. Had she really bawled in public, and run off through the jungle like a madwoman because she was afraid the famous Fitzhugh Farrar might smell her? It was true that until now her fortitude had been adapted to a very different milieu. But she found that she had fortitude still, that she was capable of surviving not only the wilds of a ballroom but also of an island far, far away.

What Sal had said was true. They had plenty right here. In a matter of days their circumstances were transformed.

Vida acknowledged, though only begrudgingly, that this was largely Fitzhugh's leadership. He kept the survivors busy from first light till last with a multitude of tasks, and though Vida initially dismissed the smallness of their various assignments (she had privately believed he was keeping them occupied so they wouldn't go mad), she marveled at what their steady output created in a matter of days. The children had managed to collect several large empty turtle shells which were set up to collect rainwater, as well as many useful bits of detritus that had washed up in the days since the wreck.

Doors, planks, nets, pieces of textile, glass jars, and one fine metal platter.

The women had managed to make so many braids of dried palm fronds that they could braid the braids together. In this way they created mats to be used as flooring in their shelters. Instead of the two small, propped-together shelters—one for females, and one for males—they had managed to construct six houses with thatched roofs in that lightly wooded area separating the jungle and the openness of the beach. These were open on the sides to the breezes, but situated far apart enough that they offered a kind of privacy. The especially delicate ladies had taken to hanging the outermost layers of their skirts from the roofs to serve as walls while they slept. When the wind ruffled those skirts, they filled like beautiful sails.

Each day, a group of men ventured farther into the jungle and returned with the fruits of the trees. Not just coconuts, but wonderful sweet-tasting bulbous things with bright skins and gleaming seeds. There were rumors of game in the hills. But they were not ready yet for that, said Fitzhugh. He and several of the other former crewmembers had escaped the ship with blades on their persons. But they did not have weapons sufficient to protect themselves from—much less hunt—a wild beast.

That was how Fitzhugh phrased it. He said "wild beast" and the little group of people, which he had begun assembling in the morning, gasped at the phrase.

Having regained some of her personal dignity, Vida found herself once again in possession of her incredulity. After Fitzhugh's morning speech, she followed him to ask what he'd meant.

"Wild beasts?" she demanded.

Fitzhugh looked up from the piece of bone he was whittling. "Don't worry, Miss Hazzard, you will have something better to eat than tree fruits, soon."

"That's not at all what I meant, Mr. Farrar. But I do think it's cruel to scare everybody."

"Are you scared?" he asked, rising to his feet, showing her the breadth of his shoulders and the sweet puncture of his dimple and grinning at her in a way that she still found (against her will) sort of pleasing. Only on an aesthetic level, of course. "Don't worry, we are taking every precaution, and the shelters are well situated in case of attack. . . ."

"That's not . . . !" Vida protested. But she only knew her desire to protest, and not precisely what it was she was protesting. She ran out of words before she succeeded in making any kind of point.

"Don't tell anybody. I want it to be a surprise. But we'll have a celebration tonight. Can you and one other lady with discretion see what you can collect in the way of kindling?"

"For a fire, you mean?"

He only smiled at her.

"Are you trying to call the attention of passing ships?"

Still that evasive and annoyingly handsome smile.

"Have you seen a ship?" she pressed on, her heart lightening and her lips curling into a smile even though she wanted to maintain her antagonism, wanted him to know how much she objected to his exaggerations, his secrecy. But she hadn't permitted herself such a fantasy—a passing ship, a sudden salvation, a warm bath and glass of lemonade—and now she had. Her mind wrapped around this hopeful vision as surely as a suitor's grip might grab hold of her delicate wrist. "Have you seen a ship passing close enough to see us?"

"Even better," he said, and strode off down the beach.

As she watched him half run, half walk toward the water she felt the heat of the sun, which grew hotter with every passing moment. A strong, gentle breeze ruffled her skirts. The day was noisy with the whisper of human hands weaving fibers together and the smacking of planks that had once been part of the *Princess* as the men separated them into two piles. One for wood that might be used to build structures, and one for pieces too shattered and broken by the rocks and the coral that hemmed in the island.

There was also the mélange of island sounds: the high rhythmic chirps of birds, the smash of a coconut falling from its lofty place, and always, always, the low sizzle of the ocean waves washing up and falling back from the beach.

There was the turquoise water spreading forever beyond the long white beach, the cornflower blue of the sky, the big gray rocks.

And there was herself, Vida—the same girl whose name had once appeared in society notes in newspapers—encased in that pale pink dinner dress, which had been dirtied and magically cleaned again, almost bleached white, by its trial in the elements. That lace and cotton fitted tight to her body. Her small body, which she'd walked in all her life. For long, unthinking stretches of existence that body was all she really knew. Now her physical form seemed a tiny, insignificant doll thrown against the infinite variety of sights and sounds, harsh and sweet, which themselves were nothing when compared to the incomprehensible vastness that rolled out from the beach.

How deadly, Vida thought with a shiver. *I am being awfully profound.*

She turned away from the scene, and looked around for an accomplice in kindling-gathering. Ideally Eleanor, Miss Flynn's maid, who was the most level-headed of the female survivors—the least mute with despair, and the most able when it came to almost any task. But when Vida's eyes settled on Eleanor, she saw that Eleanor was busy drying seaweed on the rocks (unfortunately, this had become a staple of their diet). Miss Flynn would have been her second choice, for though she was not as clever as Eleanor, and tended to tire easily, her desire to be considered helpful was deep and abiding. But she caught a glimpse of Miss Flynn— who had been fated to live out her time here in a flowered nightdress—hurrying away from the group in the direction of the private grove where the ladies went when they were called by an activity that they found too shameful to name.

The children, because of their enthusiasm, were always off collecting something or other.

And the men, for reasons everyone found too obvious to discuss, were always engaged in building a structure or a better, more elaborate water-gathering system, or something else that Fitzhugh deemed too important to be known by the group at large.

The only idle body anywhere was that of Camilla, who

sat by herself halfway down the beach, her arms wrapped around her knees and her head bent.

So Camilla, who had not bothered to be faithful to her husband while alive, was so devastated by his death that she could now do nothing to contribute to her own quite tenuous survival, while all around her others worked?

In her old life, Vida might have well enjoyed an hour in uncharitable analysis of Camilla's state (though Nora, who was ever Vida's ally, had an inner sweetness and could not abide that sort of chatter). And now, in this place, having subsisted on rainwater and kelp and the occasional coconut shard, Vida would have liked to savor the spice of another's contemptible self-pity and hypocrisy.

She did try.

But before she could sink her teeth into that thought a different thought had her attention, which was that the pale skin of the back of Camilla's neck was exposed to the sun. It would burn, and blister, if Camilla just sat there in silent mourning.

Vida walked briskly over. She cleared her throat. "Mrs. Farrar."

Camilla sat motionless and the ocean waves continued to lap at the shore. "You must really hate me," Camilla said eventually, speaking into her knees.

"Why would you say something so stupid? Of course I don't hate you."

"Oh?" Camilla raised her face and Vida saw how washed-out her eyes were and how puffy the skin around them had become. After all these days it was hardly news, but it still amazed her how different a lady appeared without the preparations of makeup, of comb and lash crimper, minus the enhancement of sparkling ornaments. "Then why would you use that name?"

"I'm sorry," Vida replied impatiently. "What would you prefer?"

"What does it matter?"

"Well, if you want to be like that. I mean, why does anything matter?"

Camilla thought about that a while. "What do you want?"

"Could you help me?" Vida tried to sound as entreating as possible although she wasn't sure she really wanted Camilla's help at all. "Fitz asked me to do something, and said I ought to find a discreet accomplice."

"Oh."

"And if you stay where you are, your neck will burn."

"All right."

"All right you want to burn?"

"All right, what do you want my help with?" Camilla extended her hand, and though Vida felt a blush of outrage at Camilla's expecting to be assisted in this way—when of course they were all weak and fatigued, when they all needed a hand to help them—she let herself be a steady support as Camilla rose to her feet. "Discretion," Camilla muttered as she brushed the sand from her silk skirt. "As though I want to talk to anyone anyway."

"Well," said Vida brightly, "you certainly don't have to talk to me."

If Camilla was insulted by this, she didn't show it. She just nodded and followed Vida past the first trees in search of fallen bark, leaves, twigs, and other combustible items. They didn't talk any more than they had to, but kept always close enough to the beach that they could hear the others. Every now and then Vida would glance up to assure herself that she could catch a glimpse of the endless ocean through the trunks and hanging vines.

They foraged a long time in silence.

Then the sky was purple, and then pink. As they returned to the camp carrying a tattered tablecloth piled high with small, dry scraps of the forest, they saw the others gathered around a new structure. It was the bashed-up shards of the ship, propped together like a teepee. Fitzhugh beamed when he saw Camilla and Vida appear, and clapped his hands.

"Thank you, ladies, you have brought the final ingredient," he said. And as they stood holding the tablecloth, he and the other men began taking the kindling they'd gathered and shoving it inside the structure. When it was all gone—all their work, jammed under the old boards—Fitzhugh whipped a tinderbox from his pocket. An old-fashioned tinderbox like the ones Vida had seen in antique shops when she was slumming with Bill Halliday back in San Francisco. Fitz worked it and for a moment Vida was afraid for him, afraid the promise of the big pyre would fall flat because he couldn't get this pathetic little antiquity to work. Then she saw the spark and her heart started. The spark initiated a small flame. His palm sheltered it as he kneeled. The flame touched a dried leaf, caught a dried branch. No one spoke. They just watched until the fire spread, became a big pyramid of fire.

It was not that they had been very cold. They had been wet, and at night chilled occasionally. But mostly the dense air held the sun's heat even after dark. They hadn't been warmed like this, though. The heat off the flames warming the skin of their hands and faces. They smiled and laughed—that variety of amazed laughter which is mostly relief.

Vida turned from them, gazed at the horizon. As the others talked, marveled at the fire, she watched that eerie strip of green, a reddish line, and above that a deepest blue. She strained to make out the silhouette of a mighty ship. But time passed, and she saw nothing. She was brought back from her disappointment by the excited exclamations of the others, and she turned to see how Sal and Fitzhugh used long sticks to carefully remove what had been hidden on the stones under the pyre. A package, wrapped in banana leaves. Before she could hope for anything specific, she saw Fitzhugh open the package. Inside was a large, blistered fish.

Everyone lined up and each was given a steaming cut of white flesh, placed on a ripped piece of green leaf. Some went to sit on the sand, while others were too impatient and stood devouring their portion. Their first helping was gone almost before anyone noticed and then they came for seconds. Everyone buzzed happily, but Vida, overwhelmed by an emotion she had no name for, walked away from the crowd and sank down on the sand. The stars were emerging against the great, dark dome of the sky.

"Here," said Fitzhugh. He had sat down beside her before she could tell him not to.

She stared at his outstretched hands offering her a piece of fish on a square of leaf. She resisted, not so much because she wanted to spite him (she did, though oddly not with the same verve as before). Mostly it just seemed bizarre to have something so like a meal offered her here.

"Try some."

Before she knew what she had done, her fingertips had dug into the white flesh, the flakes had melted on her tongue, and she knew that taste of salt, of fat in her mouth, and the wonderful satisfaction of food absorbed by her belly. She had almost forgotten what it was to eat and feel satisfied.

"It's good, isn't it?"

She glanced sidelong at him. But her irritation at his having seen her eat with such abandon, at his knowing smile, was short-lived. "Yes," she said. "Aren't you going to have some?"

He showed her his own banana leaf plate, which she had not noticed in her frenzy. Her old anger at him was like internal fireworks—it soared, exploded with light, fizzled into nothing at all. She was left with only a glowing trace. Meanwhile he took bits of fish in his fingers, chewed thoughtfully, then wiped his fingers on the banana leaf, and tossed it off. He sighed and leaned back, his elbows propping him above the sand.

"What do you think they're eating now in the Palace Hotel?" he asked.

She didn't have to think about the answer. "Oysters," she said reflexively.

"And after that?"

"Lobster bisque."

"And after that?"

"Duck confit, followed by a walnut and celery salad, followed by squabs and madeira, followed by berries and cream, followed by baba au rhum."

"And then?"

"And then everyone will moan about how uncomfortably full they are. And then they will all have to retire to their little salons—the men for cigars, the women to loosen their corset strings—and then when everyone is refreshed, they will return to dance."

"Do you think they're dancing now?"

"Oh no. Not yet. It feels late because it's dark. But in San Francisco it's early, they are only just beginning their evening." She held his gaze, her lips parted, and she knew they were both thinking of that moment when they first saw each other across such a room, and forgot to talk to anybody else for the rest of the evening. "And in New York?"

"In New York perhaps the dancing is just beginning. They are all catching their second wind, and saying a little tipsily that the night is full of possibility."

"And here we are."

"Yes." He sighed again, not in the satisfied way of before. Now he sounded weary. "Here we are. It is good to hear your voice, Miss Hazzard, thank you. I always liked listening to your voice, to you saying anything. It makes me think we might be all right."

"I am surprised to hear you talk this way. You never seem to think that everything won't be all right."

"Good. That's how I should seem. But you must know how precarious our situation was, especially in those first days. Is. Everything is still precarious. We should enjoy these moments. These precious moments."

Her lips parted. She wanted to look at him, but was afraid her eyes would betray some yearning. She wanted to ask him exactly what he meant. But she only nodded and whispered that she understood. "We'll be all right," she added, not knowing quite where this conviction came from.

The women were sitting together and talking by the fire that was sparking off into the night. The children were laughing and racing back and forth, everyone happy and relaxed. She didn't see Camilla anywhere, but there was Dame Edna a little apart from the rest, outside the bright reach of the fire's light. It was difficult to see in the dimness, but Vida thought the dame was scribbling on a piece of bark with that little pen that dangled from her wrist.

Suddenly aware that they were even more observable here than in a grand room, Vida said, "We should go back."

"Vida?"

She was so startled by the seriousness with which he held her gaze that she almost laughed. It took some effort, but she managed not to by pressing her lips together. "Yes?"

"I want to tell you something about myself. The person I am in newspapers and things—I made all that up."

"What do you mean?"

"I mean . . . I wasn't born the dashing adventurer type." He met her gaze again, and gave a little roll of his eyes, and she couldn't help it, she liked him for this show of self-deprecation. "I was actually quite a sickly child. Had to wear leg braces until I was ten, and the doctors said they didn't think I'd live to adulthood. I wasn't supposed to know about that, but I did. You can learn almost anything when you spend most of your day in bed. It was awful, mostly, but I was educated by private tutors. At fourteen, I'd read more than most can read in a lifetime. Only my best friends know that about me. It is very important to my family that my . . . my weakness not become public. But I am grateful for that time, in a way. It was during the years of my infirmity that I became absolutely fixated on getting to see the world, on making myself strong and able, so that I could go anywhere, everywhere—to all the places I was told I'd never see."

The fire was throwing off sparks, and so too was her heart. In the hothouse of the social swirl, Fitzhugh had seemed a shining object, desired by all the marriageable girls. Yet unbeknownst to her he had been just like her—a rather imperfect person who by the force of their own imagination and ambition had created a new and more magnificent self.

Just like her, he was determined to go where he pleased, and see all of life.

Fitzhugh gazed out in the direction of the ocean. "Anyway," he said, "you're right, we should go back," and with a gesture of weariness and regret he was on his feet. He offered her a hand so that she, too, could come to standing. "I'm glad we're friends again."

"We can't be enemies," she said. "Not here."

"Yes, that's true," he said.

As they walked back in the direction of the others he let his fingers linger for a moment at the small of her back, brush down her skirt, and fall away.

FOURTEEN

The morning after the bonfire, Vida once again fetched Camilla to be her partner in kindling collection. She wasn't sure why exactly. She didn't particularly want to talk to the widow, and Fitzhugh's silly subterfuge didn't matter now. But the other woman was sitting in the sand staring off at nothing in particular, and Vida felt stabbed with pity. Her sense of charity insisted it would be a good deed to nudge Camilla into some sort of action. Well, that, and—Vida had to admit, to herself, if to no one else—it was satisfying to feel sorry for her rival rather than the other way around.

After the second day of searching the jungle floor for little flammable scraps, it seemed established that they would do this every day, together but in silence, acknowledging each other only when necessary.

Vida had learned to be absorbed in tasks. She had learned to braid her hair with the same intensity that she once used to parse a seating plan. To sift leaves, bark, twigs, for what was truly desiccated and would catch fire easily, with the same attention she'd once scrutinized fabrics for the colors that would most flatter her complexion.

This fixation, however, was not a perfect defense against certain thoughts.

Thoughts were often upon her before she could dodge them.

The worst thoughts concerned Nora and Mother and Father. What might have befallen them on the stormy sea. She also imagined her own grisly death, shuddering to think what might have become of her. Her mind wandered to what her friends were doing in San Francisco. Bill and Whiting, his sister Ellen and cousin Louisa.

She speculated on her appearance. This category of thought was as bothersome as a hungry street dog that would not be dismissed, yelping for attention with:

The wreck of your hair.

The ruin of your face!

The complete ignominy of your dress—is it even worth it to be saved, when the saviors will never forget how hideous you really are?

Whenever Camilla appeared in the running chatter of

her mind it was always as "my rival." But why, thought Vida, should Camilla be her rival, when they had nothing whatsoever to compete for? Yet the word stuck.

Meanwhile, she and Camilla wandered into a part of the forest where the trees were overgrown by a vine that sprouted magnificent pink flowers. Their petals were big, with a texture like crepe paper.

As Vida marveled at these lovely petals, Camilla picked up a conversation that they had had the day before yesterday. Her voice was sharp against the dense and fragrant air. "I know perfectly well why you don't like me."

"Who has the energy to like and dislike anything?" Vida crouched to examine a pile of leaves. "The girl I used to be had the privilege of preferences," she went on snappishly. "Now I am grateful to eat whatever will not poison me, and sleep anywhere I won't be rained on."

Camilla made a high, sharp noise through her nose. It was like a laugh, but wasn't quite. "They were right," she said. "You are clever."

Vida glanced up. *They?* Although Camilla's face was not as marred by weeping and sunburn as before, she was nonetheless unrecognizable as the beauty Vida had encountered on the top deck of the *Princess*. Without makeup her features had a childlike sweetness. Her complexion was reddened by the sun, hardly that alabaster tone that she, like all the women of their tribe, protected with broad hats and delicate parasols. "Who is *they*?" she demanded.

"So you think you are the only one who talks to gossip columnists?"

How pitiful that Vida should be surprised by this, that she should still care. Vida had not thought that Dame Edna was her friend, precisely, but she had believed that their alliance was an exclusive one. She went on tossing aside the wet leaves, but with the extra zeal of this fresh embarrassment.

"Everyone knew you were after Fitz."

"What do you think you're accusing me of? I didn't make it a secret."

"No, I guess you didn't."

"I must have looked foolish to you. But I didn't *know* he was yours," Vida said, fast as she could. She was glad to have it outside of herself and in the air.

Camilla snorted. "He was hardly mine."

"No?" Vida sucked in breath and narrowed her eyes. She was overcome by two strong and simultaneous desires: that Camilla explain that statement immediately and in elaborate detail; and that she herself seem supremely above caring at all. "I thought you were what the columnists call 'an item.' Before you were married."

"Yes, once upon a time the famous Fitzhugh Farrar

and I were known to be romantically entangled. We went around New York together and had all kinds of fun. But he gets bored easily, haven't you noticed that? And he only likes the ones who know well how to play a game of hard to have."

"Hard to have?"

"Oh yes, we played all sorts of games. He would make a promise and I would demur, and he'd go to lengths for my attention, and I'd think he was mine at last. And I would say all manner of desperately sincere and adoring things. And then *he* would disappear on some sort of trek down the Amazon!"

"Sounds romantic." Vida had meant to sound sarcastic, but there was another part of her—not a part she was especially proud of—that *did* think what Camilla described sounded exciting.

"Oh, it was."

"Why did you marry his brother, then?"

"Me and Carlton—that started as one game of many. I thought if Fitz read in the papers that his brother and his girl were known to be dancing with each other he might come home. But he didn't. And then he still didn't. And then the game with Carlton had gone too far—I found myself engaged, and walking down an aisle, and promising to be his in this life and the next."

Vida took in a big breath of the fragrant jungle air. "Oh."

"But marriage is different than you think it is." Camilla straightened up and glanced away and hung her head and put her face in her hands. She made a funny sound that began as a sigh and ended as a laugh.

"Oh?"

"Yes," Camilla said, and the word was so heavy she seemed pushed down by it, her body sinking to the ground. "As a young girl you run around trying to get a husband, thinking that getting a good husband is the only goal of life. Then you have him. Well, it's not romantic, your heart doesn't beat like mad, and you don't fill pages and pages of keepsake books with the precise way in which his eyes lingered on your bare neck. It's something else than that. Suddenly, it's really all you have."

She looked very small there against the massive, knotty roots and big green leaves of the hanging vines. "I'm sorry you lost him," Vida said.

Camilla cocked her head, unsure of Vida's sincerity. "Thank you," she said at last. With a sigh she wiped the wetness from her eyes. She seemed fatigued by having talked so much. "Now let's be good Yankees and never speak of it again, please."

"Lady's honor, we shall never speak of it again."

And like that, the idea that Camilla was any kind of rival disappeared.

And, for the better part of the afternoon, Vida was as good as her word.

The sun traveled across the sky and clouds came and threatened rain, but passed with only a few little drips, and sweat beaded on their foreheads, fell salty against their tongues. They did not speak very much and yet they communicated more than they had before as they moved into the jungle, helping each other to reach old, dry leaves stuffed into the crevasse of a big tree, holding hands as they struggled over a slippery knot of roots. How frightening the jungle had seemed to Vida at first, how lush and lovely now. When they had collected enough leaves, Camilla plucked two flowers and carefully placed one behind Vida's ear, weaving it into her hair.

"Here," said Vida, and did the same for Camilla, tucking a bright pink burst of petals into her tumble of golden hair. Then Camilla smiled. Vida realized she'd never seen Camilla smile, not really. It was a wonderful, surprising smile, and before she could remember to be standoffish and difficult to please, Vida smiled back. It was only as they approached the encampment that Vida considered breaking her word to Camilla. She began a vociferous internal debate within herself over what could be assumed by the phrase "lady's honor."

In the course of the afternoon she had come to think of Camilla as her friend. And her friend Camilla had said very clearly that she did not want to talk about what had been between her and Fitzhugh anymore. Yet Vida very badly needed to know what exactly she had seen in the map room.

And just as Vida was trying to decide whether or not she could ask about that, she already had. "If Fitzhugh wasn't yours, what were you doing with him?"

"When?"

"That night."

"Oh." After a moment Camilla said, "You mean what were we doing when you interrupted us?"

Vida's pulse quickened as she remembered all that had happened since that moment. Those unreal hours when she and Fitzhugh and Sal remained close together as though that could undo the disaster. The sea, and everything after. "Yes."

Camilla shrugged and squinted through the trees, in the direction of the bright beach. "He said he wanted to see me, and I was quite thrilled. We never really stopped, you know, even after I was married. But it would be only now and then that he'd pay me special attention. I lived for those times. Carlton was good to me. But he wasn't loving, he wasn't an exciting conversationalist, he didn't . . . well, a lady doesn't talk of that. So, when Fitzhugh did remember that I existed, it always thrilled me, and I couldn't wait till we were together."

"And so you were together that night? Again, like you used to be."

"No. . . ." Camilla shook her head. "No. I thought we would be. But when I reached for him in the old way, he said it was over. That it was really over this time, and I must not hope for it to be revived." Her face was drained of color—the memory seemed to age her in an instant.

Some small and demanding part of Vida whispered, "Did he tell you why?"

Camilla's lips trembled. Her eyes took on a faraway quality. "I can only guess. I didn't want to hear that, and I left—or tried to leave—before he could explain."

Vida's thoughts raced. She needed to hear the end of this story. Yet she sensed she must somehow learn patience. Camilla would tell the story in her own time. They kept walking and Vida had to hurry to keep their piece of fabric piled with kindling aloft. In the encampment, they wordlessly lowered their haul to the sand. Camilla stood, stretched her arms up to the sun hovering over the placid expanse of ocean.

"There was something different about him that night," Camilla said. "I could tell it was not the same old game. I don't know what had changed him," she went on with a shrug. "Maybe he finally felt too guilty about Carlton. Or maybe it was you." She lifted her arms to undo the knot of her hair, so that her golden mane spilled down her back.

They stood together in a silence thick with significance.

Down at one end of the beach, the Misses Van Huysen had climbed the high rocks. They too were looking out. Miss Flynn and Eleanor and Dame Edna and the two women whose husbands were employed by the sugar companies in Hawaii—Ingeborg and Sonja—were sitting in a huddle watching the children. The children were using a piece of driftwood to whack a small drained coconut that served quite nicely as a ball. One of them shrieked—an actual shriek of pleasure—and then another one of them laughed, and it was a real laugh, the kind a person can't help, or fake. That true and joyous sound filled Vida with such a feeling—it was either all the feelings, or one that was new to her.

A smile overcame Camilla's face and she began walking toward the water.

"I feel like putting my toes in!" she called over her shoulder. Soon she was running down the sloping beach.

Vida wondered over what the widow had said. That phrase—*maybe it was you*—coursed through her body, was her very pulse. Meanwhile Camilla had reached the water's edge. She laughed with abandon and did a twirl; her dark skirt flew up and revealed her lovely legs.

FIFTEEN

For a while Vida remained motionless, her gaze fixed, her mind drifting, soaking in the happy mood of the camp. The children playing, their mothers at ease. Camilla a beautiful silhouette against the glaze on the surface of the water. And there, down the beach, was Fitz, striding in his confident manner from the dazzle of the sea. With him were the men who had once been sailors. They rested their makeshift fishing poles over their shoulders and hauled in the fish they had caught. Fitz's pants were rolled, his voice buoyant with salty air.

He was looking around for someone.

For Vida.

When he saw her, he smiled and raised his hand.

She raised her hand in reply. What Camilla had suggested recurred to Vida with a little drumroll of triumph, a blush of fear, a bright spike of hope, a warm wanting. Maybe she *was* the one who could tame the famous Fitzhugh Farrar after all. But in the brilliance of that lovely moment she felt no great need for anything to be different. To possess more than she had right now. She knew that in her old life she would have rushed to secure Fitz's affections. Instead she turned, leaving the kindling she and Camilla had collected, and moved back into the shelter of the palms, wondering if she even was the same girl she'd been before, the kind who was always campaigning, strategizing for what she wanted. Or if she should be—if she already was—a different sort of girl.

She had no idea, so she walked on, in a new direction, and eventually into a little grove surrounded by strange and mighty trees. Those trees were gnarled and vast; their branches reached out to form a great halo of leaves. Their roots were massive, spreading across and deep into the earth. Little birds with bright yellow plumes darted between the high limbs. Yet at the same time there was a profound and living stillness in that grove, as though the place was animated by a spirit of the divine.

The spirit was laughing. For a moment it really seemed like that, like there was a wood nymph and it was laughing at her. Then it occurred to Vida that the laughter was rather masculine, and her eyes adjusted, and she saw Sal sitting on the edge of the lifeboat that they had spent so many hours in. The boat had been transformed, however. Additions had been made, including a contraption that attached what looked like floating planks to the sides, and a mast where she supposed a sail should go.

"What are you laughing at?"

"I was just thinking about the first time I saw you. All dressed up. How impossible it would have been for me then to imagine you as you are now."

Vida blushed at this reminder of how far she had fallen, appearance-wise. "I didn't know you imbued our first meeting with such extraordinary meaning." She had meant this as a riposte. But his eyes went reflective and she knew too late that he did view it with some meaning. "Oh."

"It was dramatic, you must admit." He had a laughing way again.

She hadn't really seen him that night, she realized. There was something about Sal that was easy to look through. His long, lean body posed with a sure confidence, his longish dark hair pulled away from his face. But his dark gaze was shy to make contact.

"It was," she admitted. "You used to make me so angry. On the ship, that is. In my mind, I called you 'nobody' so that I wouldn't be cut by your judgments."

He smiled. "That's fitting. I am nobody."

"Oh, come," she said. "Don't be metaphysical. Of course you are *some*body."

"Your kind of people are always trying so hard to prove you are somebody," he said with a shrug. "Not me. I go with the current," he added with such finality that, though she wasn't sure precisely what he meant, she had no desire to question him.

"Anyway." She averted her gaze and dried her palms against her skirt. "What's this?"

"It's our ship."

"Ship?" she echoed with mirthless irony. This strange, patched-together raft was nothing like the colossus of the *Princess*, which, despite the spectacular way it had failed them, still seemed magnificent and stylish, a triumph of oceangoing vessels, in her memory.

"You don't think much of it," he replied, still smiling. "Like you don't think much of me."

"I never said—"

"That's all right. I know, it is not impressive like the ships you're accustomed to. But you know, the people who populated the Hawaiian islands, they came by ships not much larger than this, carved from a single tree, across a greater distance than we sailed on the *Princess*. All the way from the antipodes—without engines, or a crew of hundreds, on seas that were surely rougher than what we experienced. They knew the currents, and their ships, and the weather, and they survived the crossing."

"But there's no one here now," Vida said in a small voice.

"No, I don't think so. Though what's on the other side of the island, beyond the ridge, we don't know. If this place had inhabitants they'd have made themselves known to us by now, for better or worse. But I've seen signs that plants were cultivated here by humans—there are trees that grow giant yams. Those must have been transplanted. They aren't native to this part of the world. Someone brought those here from far away. Not white men."

"How do you know?"

"White men usually leave more signs of themselves, for one thing. And, particularly in the wild, they live by the gun."

She shivered at the thought of such distances, of people who would trust their lives to the sea. "Where are they now?" she asked. "The people who brought the yams here."

"Who knows. Maybe they continued to the larger islands we now call the territory of Hawaii to join their kin. Maybe they were lost, like us, and just stayed here a time to regain their strength."

She nodded. She wanted him to tell her how a person came to know such things, but did not want to betray her ignorance.

"Come on, we had better go back—Fitzhugh will be wondering where you are."

For a moment she thought Sal was going to offer her his arm, but there was none of that. He just passed close enough to her that she felt invited to walk alongside him as they made their way back to camp.

Through the evening—during the lighting of the fire and the cooking of dinner and the appearance of the moon over the waves—Fitzhugh was busy and Vida watched him. Her earlier tranquility was gone. She had become a little obsessed with how to strike up a conversation with him, how to test what Camilla had said. Then he was there at her side, with an attentive heat that reminded her why his company was sought by so many.

"Miss Hazzard," he began very formally. "Would you do me the honor of going on a walk together?"

He offered her his hand, as though this were the salon of a grand house and he was about to take her for a turn around the formal gardens. Vida—wary of seeming eager—tilted her head, ignored his hand, and said, "If you wish it, Mr. Farrar."

"I do wish it."

"All right."

She walked in the way she had practiced as a younger girl—shoulders square, head high, little steps that made her skirt sway in a feminine way. She did not look at him, yet she felt his presence, how he fixated on the ocean and chewed on what he wanted to say.

"Yes," she said at last. "What is it?"

"I wanted to thank you."

"For what?"

"For being so kind to Camilla. She needs a friend now."

"We all do," Vida said.

"Yes," Fitzhugh said. "Yes, that's true."

"Anyway, I wasn't being kind. I needed her help. That and—I like her."

Until that moment, Vida had maintained the cool command that was her customary manner on courtly rambles through the Golden Gate Park; but the knife of envy twisted in her side at this reminder of Camilla's special importance to Fitz.

"I admire you, you know. How strong you are."

They had moved far enough from the fire that the sound of its crackling was overwhelmed by the gentle waves washing against the sand. The moon was bright as silver; it was almost as bright as the sun. He didn't say anything for a long time, and Vida's curiosity got the better of her. She glanced his way. His mouth was bent, and his eyes reflected the glitter of the moon.

"Are you laughing at me?" she demanded, more surprised than angry.

"Not because I think what you're saying is funny. It's very serious, of course. It's just that you aren't afraid to tell the truth. I'm not sure I've ever met a girl as determined as you are. I admired that before, too, you know."

A moment before, her body had been cool, but now her heart was wild. "You and Camilla—"

"We have been entangled a long time."

"Oh."

"We were entangled. Before she was married, but after, too." Fitz watched her, waiting to see how Vida would react. Though this was only confirmation of what Camilla had told her, still it stung. "I kept telling myself it had to end. And then it kept beginning again. But that was the end of it, in the map room, when you came through the door."

"That was the end of it," Vida said, needing for him to be very clear on this topic.

Fitzhugh was staring out at the ocean again and she couldn't catch his eye. "That's why we were there. I had just told her it was over when you came in."

"Why?"

"Well," Fitzhugh's blue eyes met hers and his smile cut a dimple in his cheek, "because I met you."

Vida felt woozy and the best response she could manage was a limp "Oh."

"Do you understand?" She saw the fire of sincerity in his gaze.

"Yes," she said. She was concentrating on breathing normally. She knew what it would be like when his strong hands held her face and brought her mouth to his.

"Yes." He tilted his head in agreement. A rueful laugh escaped his mouth. "Things didn't go the way I thought they would after that. I thought I would begin to court you, on the *Princess*, as I would have in New York."

"Oh." Why couldn't she think of another word, of something witty to say? She hoped he would go on talking, even though she sounded so simple and foolish.

"I would still like to take you out, as I would have in any of those places."

"What—here?" Vida threw back her head and laughed.

"I like hearing you laugh."

"Oh, well, keep promising the impossible, I will laugh and laugh."

Another man might have cowered at this, but not Fitzhugh. "Good, that's what I'll do, then. I plan to take you on a date, like I would in New York. In New York, I'd pick you up at six for a light meal followed by a ride through the park and a show at the opera, followed by a supper and dancing."

"Wouldn't that be charming?" she said, and began the walk back up the beach. The fire was blazing, and the other survivors surrounded its brightness. Although she sensed they were watched, Vida couldn't make out one figure from another. The only figure she could identify was Sal, on account of his height, and because he stood slightly apart from the rest.

She offered Fitz the back of her hand to be kissed and then stepped away in the direction of the ladies' huts. "You can pick me up tomorrow at six, then."

SIXTEEN

A celebratory mood arrived like a gust of good island weather and, in the heat of the next afternoon, Vida, along with a small band of ladies, set off for the wooded pool to bathe in anticipation of her date with Fitz.

The promise of romance enlivened the rest of the survivors of the *Princess*, too, during this, the second week of their residence on a desolate rock in a vast ocean, and the work they had become accustomed to was forgotten in the name of new tasks. The children shrieked and jabbered, the women shushed them and glanced at each other with excited eyes. Dame Edna, too, was alert to the general buzz of anticipation. Vida knew that the gossip columnist's attention to all the minor proceedings signified the true importance of what was now transpiring.

Inside, Vida was all aflutter.

But, she resolved, she must be formidable.

She must not come across too girlish or silly or swoony.

And she must look her best.

Thus she waded into the pool with Eleanor and Miss Flynn, Camilla and the Misses Van Huysen. They pressed cold water to their faces and washed their clothing and let it dry on the rocks. In San Francisco—in any city in the country of her birth—servants would have on such occasions brought her and her female companions painted trays of refreshments, would have perfumed the rooms, would have laid out their jewelry on velvet. Here she gathered with the other young women under the protection of trees, took in the perfume of bark and pollen, and drank from the spray of the little waterfall with cupped hands.

Everyone wanted to hear a happy story, and Vida very much wanted to tell them one.

Perhaps this was the reason that she lost her usual firm hold on her emotions and nearly burst into tears when she felt how Eleanor struggled with her hair.

Vida had braided it in those first hours on the island, and had occasionally retightened the plait, but had not dared to take it all apart for fear of what knots had formed and become permanent. Fitzhugh was "picking her up" at six, however. The whole group of ladies was effervescent with expectation. She wanted to look her best, but some things could not be helped.

"Oh, say something."

"Shhhh," Eleanor admonished. "Don't speak now."

"It's awful, isn't it?"

"It's not . . . not awful."

Vida glanced toward her lap and saw how her hands whitened into fists, and she felt all achy in her throat. The ache of a little girl in whom sobbing is imminent. But no: she couldn't disappoint the others by losing control. She flinched back tears. She breathed in the humid air. "I'll have to cut it, won't I?"

"Oh no," said Miss Flynn, rousing herself from the rock. "No, you can't do that."

"But the tangles are too bad, aren't they?"

Camilla came and rested a hand on Vida's shoulder. "We'll pull it back and wrap it in a sort of bunlike thing. It's only hair. It's your eyes he'll be looking at."

"But it's hopeless, isn't it? I'll have to cut it."

"Tomorrow," Camilla said.

"Tomorrow—tomorrow I will cut the damn braid off."

"But tonight it looks fine, and tomorrow it will grow back."

Then Vida braced herself and let Eleanor do her best with strong fingers to make the horsetail of her hair into a big circle above the nape of her neck.

When she had pinched her cheeks for color and curled the little wisps at her earlobes around her pinkie; when she had asked Camilla one too many times if she really looked all right, if she was sure the sight of Vida wouldn't turn a man like Fitz to stone; and when she knew that she could not ask again, they walked together as a small flock back to their shelters, situated themselves on the slope of sand by the area that corresponded roughly with the front door of a house back in the city, and waited in that state of feigned inactivity they had often assumed in drawing rooms, posing in anticipation of gentleman callers over cold tea.

The arrival of Fitzhugh was foretold by a gentle hum of feminine excitement.

Vida kept her face turned away, her gaze focused on something not quite there.

"Miss Hazzard," he declared with the formal baritone a man employs in a ballroom when he is about to ask a girl to dance.

"Oh, hello, Mr. Farrar," she replied, and her mouth did the thing it used to do in those same ballrooms, when she was upholding the pretense that this meeting was all very chancy, and that nobody had any idea what was about to transpire. Even though all parties knew precisely what was about to transpire, and there wasn't the least smidgen of surprise to any of it.

He was only a few feet away.

She paused a few more seconds and met his gaze.

He grinned. "You look well."

Vida let her eyelids sink in demurral, the better to keep any rogue smiles at bay. "Don't let's exaggerate."

He offered her his hand, and she thought that—if they were not performing the ritual of fine young men and women meeting with all eyes upon them—she might have said how lovely he looked, too. He did—it pleased her eyes to look at him, all trim and sunbrowned. His black trousers were rolled as they had been, but he had donned the black jacket that she had not seen since their arrival here. His hair was polished with some sleek stuff—in the dining room of the *Princess* she might not have noticed this change at all, but here it had a dramatic effect.

It made the whole ruse seem real.

"Would you walk with me?" he asked, and pulled her to her feet.

Together they began to stroll past the little huts, past the watchful crowd, his elbow raised to support her arm, her pace matching his.

"Did you have a good day?" he asked, and she answered. They conversed like this on and on, with the surface gentleness that had been the tone of all their social gatherings in their former lives. They didn't say much, for that wasn't the point of such conversations. Their tone was polite, gentle. When they reached the rocks that separated the long peaceful beach from the little cove, he bent, heaved her up into his arms, and carried her over the rise.

"I thought we would have dinner," he said, and gestured at the place down on the beach where a table had been constructed out of two small boulders and a board. A cloth (a cloth that had once been white) was spread over this arrangement, and a metal platter, which she remembered from that early tide of refuse, held it down. The wind billowed the edges, giving it the appearance of the last table at the very end of the Earth. Fitz smiled when he saw how she smiled at this humble attempt. He gestured toward the sky, where the sun was making its downward trajectory. "And after dinner," he said, "a show."

"How lovely." When he didn't immediately put her down, she clarified: "I think I can walk from here."

They went down into the protected cove, to the smaller beach, where Fitzhugh pulled back a stump for Vida to sit upon. Then he assumed the position opposite her. The eldest of the children appeared with a large banana leaf heaped with cut coconut. He placed the food between Fitz and Vida, did a flourish and a little bow, and swiftly departed.

Here, as everywhere, this sort of engagement between a

male and female of the species followed a well-established formula with predictable timing.

At first the conversation was light, with almost no meaning. Then began a subtle flirtation, imperceptible to anyone who might have been watching, yet marked by both parties in their altered breath and posture. Vida waited for Fitz to initiate this change—which he did by paying her a compliment that might have been perfectly proper if bestowed upon a grandmother. ("You have a healthy color in your cheeks" was what he said.) She furthered the flirtation by glancing up and allowing him to hold her gaze just slightly longer than before.

"I've been looking forward to this," he said.

"Oh," she pronounced in a significant tone. She glanced away, forced herself to blush.

"We're being watched," he observed.

He pointed toward the high rocks that formed a barrier between the little beach and the big one, and she saw that not only the children—who presumably would continue to bring them food as though this were a fancy meal with dozens of courses—but also several of the ladies, and even some members of the crew, were peering at them.

"That's all right," Vida replied. "I am quite used to being watched."

"Yes, that is one of the things I first noticed about you."

"Oh? I didn't think you were noticing anything about me at all."

"On the contrary."

"What else did you notice?"

"That you had a kind of force. That you were determined. That you could arrive in a room full of fancy people, and chart a course through them the way I might chart a course into an unknown territory."

She raised her chin—the better to catch the beautifully blazing light of that hour, and in order to show him her face at its very best angle. "Oh, really? Seems you've thought quite a lot about me."

"Yes" was his answer, and its simplicity had a weight that a lot of words never would have. It sounded more true than any of the theatrics that had come before.

"I suppose there's no reason not to admit that I've thought a lot about you, too."

"And what did you think about in particular?"

"What you told me the other night. About what your childhood was like."

"Oh, what about it?"

"A person who is just strong and able without trying is rather boring, don't you think? A person who has made himself that way by dint of his own will is much more interesting. That's the kind of person they put in books and songs and things. I'm that way, you know—what nature failed to give me, I decided to make up with my own ingenuity."

He nodded. "I didn't know that," he said. "You seem immaculately yourself at all times. But maybe that is what I noticed about you—the ways in which we are more similar than I could have guessed."

Vida's blush was more earnest now—though the lowering sun was pinking everything. "But it's not for vanity's sake. It's because I didn't want to be told I couldn't go anywhere. I wanted to make myself into the sort of person who *could* go anywhere."

"I understand exactly what you mean."

She had almost forgotten the others when the eldest boy reappeared, this time with a board upon which was piled fish cooked in blackened banana leaves.

Their familiarity held at about that level through the eating of the fish, the serving of a third course—empty coconut shells filled with a sweet yam mash—and the to-ing and fro-ing of the children, who were gay in their performance of butler and waiter.

"Time for the show," Fitzhugh said when the empty coconut bowls were removed, and Vida smiled, and glanced at the hammered gold of the sunset on the water. This was indeed magnificent, and she thought that was the entirety of the show he meant. But then she heard the harmonizing voices of the children, and Fitzhugh offered his hand.

She felt the thickening of emotion in her throat at the sound of the music. She had almost forgotten what music was. How it played in the body and lifted the spirit. Music moved them, as it was apt to do, moved her and Fitzhugh into each other's arms, so that they began to dance, not exactly as they had on the *Princess*, but close enough to make Vida's heart skip. The skin of her face was warm, she felt a giddy rush; she was so close to getting that which she had sought.

"This is nice," she said.

"I'm enjoying myself immensely." He smiled at her, but his brow knit together. "Are you sad?"

Her chin quivered in puzzlement. She *was* rather ecstatic—for Fitzhugh had done what a man always did when he became serious about courting. He had arranged everything, and then kept his gaze steady upon her. And yet. And yet her lungs were so peculiarly light and heavy at once.

"What is it?" Fitzhugh asked.

"I'm not sad exactly. . . ." She let him see how difficult it was for her to smile, and was gratified to feel how his grip drew her in at this show of emotion. "It's not because this isn't lovely. It is! That's not even the word, really—it's so much more than lovely, it's beautiful, it hurts my eyes to see something so beautiful. And yet at the same time . . ."

"At the same time?"

"Is this life?" she whispered. Of course she knew that she ought to have expressed her fears for those loved ones she'd been separated from when the ship sank. But this was not precisely the source of her melancholy. "When I boarded that ship, it was with the goal of getting close to you. My parents said I had better, because of the spectacle I'd made with you that night in San Francisco. But I didn't picture getting to know you *here*. And now we *are* here, and it *is* beautiful. I just thought—I thought somebody would have come for us by now. And if no one has come for us—does that mean no one will?"

"I understand you perfectly." He knelt, and she had that strange flash of panic that she'd had when previous beaux sank down on a knee in proposal. But the panic passed quickly. He was gathering his strength to pick her up at the waist and twirl her around. "How wonderful you are!" he said with sudden energy, and she heard how the crowd of watchers exclaimed over his proclamation. "Come," he said, placing her back on the sand and taking up her hand. "I want to show you something."

When they reached the height of the rocks the others parted for them, their expressions happy and knowing. As Fitzhugh led Vida up the beach the others followed at a respectful distance, and all the while his hold on her hand was loose but firm.

"'Is this life?'" he repeated. "How well you said that. It is life, of course. But you must know it is not all of life, not *our* life."

How handsome he was! Vida gazed at his face and thought that if this life was theirs together, then that face was hers to look at forever. She had to turn away so he wouldn't see how she beamed. The press of his hand, the light of his eyes, were all so delightful that she stopped paying attention as they walked on.

"Don't you want to be alone?" he asked.

"Yes," she whispered.

He pulled her by the hand, and they darted away from their audience, through the trees, into the jungle. In a few moments she found herself back in the grove she'd seen yesterday. That open space in the thick of the vegetation that vibrated with awe.

The boat that she had seen—yesterday, when she came across Sal by chance—had been transformed. It was no longer a patched-together affair. The thing had a gleam of sturdiness, and she knew just looking at it how it would sit high over the water.

"I'm going to get you home, Miss Hazzard."

"On that?"

His laughter surprised her. She wasn't at all certain why he was laughing. "Of course not," he said, when he realized that she had been serious. "Me, and Sal, and a few members of the *Princess*'s crew have been building this bark. We are going to get help, and bring you home in style."

"And then?"

He laughed again, but it sounded different to her this time, softer, so that she felt she was in on the joke. "I should've known it would take more than that to impress you. To impress the famous Vida Hazzard." But she would not look away from him, and he didn't dare end their exchange with a joke. "*And then* I would like very much to take you to New York."

"But," she said, "that certainly won't do for a sail."

Fitzhugh glanced at the mast, at the old tablecloth that was wrapped around the mast.

"It's already ripped, for one thing," she said. "And for another it's heavy damask. What you need is a modern fabric, strong yet light."

She let him puzzle over this a moment. Let a little drama build in the air between them. Then she bent, turned away for modesty's sake, and unhooked the petticoat underneath her skirt. The balloon of the underskirt came out from under the ornamented top skirt, and it was obvious what a good sail it would make—even in the still atmosphere, it looked ready to fill with wind. She saw how Fitzhugh watched her and gave him a subtle little dart of a smile. A strong energy grew in him, lit up his face.

His hand found the narrow of her waist. A pretty glaze blurred her vision.

They stared at each other a moment and she dropped the skirt and her lips parted.

His face moved toward hers, his chin tilted—in a moment she would close her eyes to accept his kiss. His hands spread over her waist, and she felt the press of his mouth against hers, and the warmth of his breath, and the pump of his heart.

"I've been wanting to do that a long time," he said.

She might have replied in kind, but she instead draped her arms around his neck and leaned closer so that he would know he could kiss her again. He gripped a fistful of her skirt. But he hesitated a moment, and then she heard a rustling from the tree above. Somebody was up there. That somebody jumped down from a high branch, and dashed past them toward the beach. Fitzhugh's brow creased in concern.

"I'm sorry," cried the somebody, and Vida recognized Sal's voice.

"Damn it," said Fitzhugh, drawing Vida protectively toward him. He watched Sal go with fire in his eyes. She'd never heard Fitz sound angry before. She felt cold and hot at once. Was she angry, too? She remembered how irritated she had always been in the presence of Fitzhugh's manservant back on the deck of the *Princess*. He had always been getting in the way of her finding Fitz.

"I didn't know you were coming here!" Sal called as he retreated into the trees. "I'm sorry!"

Vida's anger burst so hot and sudden that it was almost a kind of pleasure, and she stared after Sal hoping he'd look back and she could show him with her eyes what she thought of his meddling. Or, if he wasn't meddling, the impertinence of being where he wasn't supposed to be at all. Or—but then she wasn't sure what she wanted to show him, and he had disappeared into the night, and it didn't matter anymore. Fitzhugh's mouth had found hers again.

When Fitz led Vida back to the beach they saw against the darkness the hanging lamp of a magnificent moon. It whitened everything, even the stars, which had previously been too multitudinous for it to be possible to make out any pattern in the sky. Around the silent white disk, like some celestial spirit, radiated a series of pale halos.

"How beautiful," Vida whispered.

Fitz put her fingers to his lips. "I ordered that moon especially for you."

"It reminds me of winter." She laughed at the absurdity of this thought. "Do you remember winter? Isn't it funny to think about winter here, where it's always hot even when it rains?"

"Yes. You'll remember this heat when we are in New York and the snow drifts are higher than a man's head and we can't get out the door."

"Oh!—snowed in—what*ever* shall we do?"

"We'll make a fire in the fireplace."

"Yes, do go on."

"And we'll take out the blankets, and we'll play bridge, and we'll have cocoa and whiskey and we'll dance—and if it's only us, we will dance a little wildly, and nobody will ever know."

"It will be our secret." She faced him, the air between them absolutely buzzing with meaning, and let him hold both her hands, and kiss each—his lips lingering at her knuckles as though to make the most of this chaste gesture. "Thank you for a lovely evening, Mr. Farrar."

"Yes, thank you, Miss Vida."

Then she sank her eyelids, let go his hands, and slipped along the shelters to the hut she shared with Eleanor and Flora Flynn, moving in that rocking gait that was the custom of such moments. In such moments, it was understood that a man would stand still and watch, and that a lady would let her form and carriage be appreciated as long as possible. And though Vida's heart was furious to look back, to meet his eye, to exchange the knowledge of what had grown between them, of their secret kiss and the way he had touched her, she was firm. She maintained control. She focused on what was before her and let him watch.

SEVENTEEN

The air rustled with the dreams of others. Vida's eyes opened wide. The moon was shining brightly through the thatched roof of the hut. How would it happen, she wondered—how would she and Fitz be pulled apart and come together again?

All great love stories have a series of thrilling and agonizing setbacks. Dame Edna had said this love story might be the greatest she had ever written. Vida wanted the story of her and Fitz to be grander than them all, to be legendary— but the specifics of those setbacks were hard to imagine.

If this was not precisely how she phrased things in her own churning thoughts, it was nonetheless the spirit of the uncertainty that troubled her sleep like a bad tooth. She lay in her slip on the bed of her dress and knew she would not be able to fall back asleep.

Then she heard the whistle. Soft, but distinct.

Flora and Eleanor were still sleeping, their bodies curled against each other in a feminine heap of salt- and mud-stained skirts.

Again she heard the whistle, so she rose from her place of slumber and went to see who it was.

To the west over the water the sky was still a deep, mysterious purple. Vida took one of the empty coconut shells that had been rigged to catch the dew and drank away her thirst. She pinched the skin of her cheeks with her fingertips to bring life to her face—an old instinct to try to look her best whenever she might encounter a member of the opposite sex. Her body was just about to complain that it was tired after all, when she heard the whistle a third time.

He was sitting a ways down the beach, gazing out at the sky. As she approached his head turned in her direction. There was something in the movement that told her he had been expecting her.

"I hope I didn't wake you," Sal said.

"No," she said. "I couldn't sleep."

"Me neither."

In a few moments, the girl she was supposed to be caught up to her, reminded her that she should be annoyed that a servant had disturbed her sleep, that he was speaking to her in such a familiar manner. And that Sal in particular was difficult, and that she should be stern with him. But the world was still dreamlike. Nothing was quite real. The darkness seemed to her delicious and alive.

"Were you *trying* to wake me?" she asked. Her voice sounded playful in the early-morning air. Had she meant to be playful? She was an expert at subtle flirtation, and didn't usually flirt by accident.

He stood, brushed the sand from the back of his legs. If he'd heard her question, he did not acknowledge it. "Would you like to know the place to best watch the sunrise?"

"Do you mean to tell me that you've been withholding this information?" She was glad about the moonlight. It was bright enough for her to see how he grinned at that.

"Come on," he said. "I'll show you."

They walked together toward the far end of the beach, where it narrowed. No one ever went that way, for reasons Vida had never questioned.

She knew walking this way with Sal would not have been considered socially acceptable by the old standards of drawing rooms and first-class dining rooms—especially after a young lady was attached, as she now considered herself to be. The whole band of survivors had seen Fitzhugh courting her. Now that he'd kissed her, and implied that they would someday be alone together by a fire in a snowstorm, they were promised to each other. In a sense. All that signified a new level of attachment, surely. Vida knew the rules better than anybody.

But it was early. The world was dark. And Vida thrilled to the idea that she was about to get away with doing something. That bit of mischief that she carried in her heart, and that was always getting her in trouble, drove her now. They crossed the border that Fitzhugh had deemed safe for the general population to inhabit. She followed Sal up the steep and rocky incline at the far end of the beach.

As they walked she understood why no one ever went this way. The little pathway between the trees was narrow and shifting, and stones were scattered underfoot. Then it stopped being much of a path at all. On one side was a steep fall toward crashing waves. On the other side the trees were dense, impassable—their mighty, slippery roots reached beyond the cliff's edge, dangled like loose yarn in the open air. Several times she had to crouch to steady herself, and she was surprised when she realized how high they had gotten so quickly. Cool fear touched her temples, and she knew that a slip would leave her body bloodied and broken down where whitecaps were eating away the land.

"Don't worry," Sal said, as though he had overheard her nervous thoughts. "I won't let you fall."

She was about to demand he tell her how he was going to do that, but she was concentrating very hard on the way ahead to keep herself from slipping. All the while Sal went along beside her, at the very limit of the cliff. It was as though he were walking a tightrope at the edge of the world. They did not speak again until they reached the heights.

Then the idea of talking seemed a little stupid.

The new sun was illuminating the world. She forgot to be afraid.

Sal's eyes were diamantine with wonderment. He sat, his legs dangling over the precipice. Vida stood behind him and watched how the sun broke against the sky, shading everything in an unreal orange and fuchsia. A person only sees light that dramatic if they are awake early. She understood for the first time that a sunrise was different if you saw it by staying up all night. Here it was, a fresh day, so magnificent that you knew your life would never be the same. She and the world were new.

"We won't go today after all," Sal said after a while.

"Go where?" Vida had forgotten that there was anywhere but this place. Her eyes followed where Sal pointed and she saw, to the east, the streaked red-and-black clouds where the sun was coming up.

"That's a storm heading our way."

"The ocean is like a lake."

"It's calm now, but that color down at the horizon, you only see that when the light is coming through dense weather far off. Rough, wet weather. It'll be here sooner or later."

"Are you being very mystical? I thought that was an old wives' tale, that rhyme about sailors taking warning if there was a red sky in the morning."

"Why would people repeat lies about the weather for a thousand years?"

"You have a point, I suppose."

"We should go back."

Vida offered her hand to Sal to help him up. She didn't want to go back, but she knew that demanding to know why would be quite brazen. She knew the reason why. "Thank you for showing me the best place to see the sunrise," she said, very formally, instead.

"It is my duty," he said, but ironically, so that she knew he wouldn't have done it if it didn't please him.

The camp was still quiet as they made their way down from the height and she experienced that familiar feeling of satisfaction, of having gotten away with something, as when she snuck back into her parents' well-appointed home after a long night and knew from the housekeeper's averted gaze that she had survived her own wildness again. Anyway, it seemed unlikely that a little predawn walkabout could unsettle the swiftly-moving love story of Vida Hazzard and Fitzhugh Farrar.

The match was as good as decided.

But once she remembered Fitz, she remembered something else.

"Sal?"

"Yes?"

She didn't look back at him, she just kept walking—haughtily, like a girl who expected to be told the truth. "Where did you say you were going? When we started off talking about the weather."

"It doesn't matter now."

"It does to me."

"To get help. In the boat."

"You were going to—leave us? *Today?*" Fitzhugh had showed her the boat—but it had seemed that that was a ways in the future.

"Fitzhugh thought it best to go now. There may still be Farrar boats out looking for us."

"Oh . . ." A darkness welled inside her. Of course she knew that it was perfectly logical—if she was going to spend the winter by a fireplace in Manhattan with Fitzhugh, then someone was going to have to go for help soon. It was so frightening, the idea of Fitz or anybody going back out to sea. But really Fitz, who she had only just begun to know. She glanced up at the sky helplessly. It was then that she lost her footing. One foot skidded, the other twisted miserably. She fell, rolled, found herself half hanging from the cliff.

"Oh!" she exclaimed, as she clung to the rocky edge with stinging hands.

"I have you," Sal said, grabbing her by the arms. "I have you."

He said so, and only then did she believe him. The rest of her was dangling over the rocks, the water below, but he had her arms firmly. Weirdly, he was smiling.

"Why are you smiling?" she demanded.

"Your face—it's different when you're afraid."

"I almost fell to my death!" she exclaimed. Her heart skipped. "I still could," she whispered, sensing the open air beneath her feet.

"No. We're almost to the beach now. It's only a ten-foot drop. At worst you'd break your ankle."

"I'd rather not," she said, and with a strong pull he brought her up. She kicked at the edge, pushed with her feet, and felt the solid earth beneath her. Beside Sal again, she thought to tell him he should not be so cavalier about her ankles. She had almost found the words. Then she noticed how her fall had knocked the earth way—it was loose, precarious, dirt and rocks scattering beneath them, beginning to give way. She scrambled back without thinking. Meanwhile Sal went on crouching above that unreliable earth. Before she could say anything, it began to crumble and give way. His face was perfectly calm, not even really surprised, as he fell.

One moment he was right next to her, the next he was going down.

It was true what he had said—it was only a ten-foot drop. But when he hit the rock below he cried out in shock and pain.

"Are you all right?" she called to him.

"Yes." But he didn't sound all right.

"I'm coming down to help you," she called.

"No." He shook his head and met her eye. "Fitzhugh wouldn't like it. Go back, before they know we're out here together."

She was afraid that the cliff would give under her as well. Sal's dark eyes met hers, and she saw he was serious. He hadn't seemed to care about propriety before, and she was struck by the oddness of him caring now. He was in pain—she'd heard it in his voice—but his face suggested he was afraid of something else.

In any case, he was right. With a strange reluctance in her heart she made her way back to the camp, where the others were just now waking up.

EIGHTEEN

Without learning of the kiss in any explicit way, the people of Farrar Island (as the men were calling it), knew something had occurred between Vida and Fitz. They knew that despite their tragic circumstances they were witness to what was sure to become one of the great love stories of their time. And because they, like all people, are fed love stories from their earliest consciousness, they understood that matters could not proceed smoothly from this moment. They, like Vida, wondered what the setback would be, how the lovers might be separated so that all could work out happily in the end.

The morning after Fitzhugh romanced Vida in front of everybody, all the survivors wondered how those setbacks, that happy ending, would be accomplished. But by afternoon they had an answer.

The rigged-up boat had been moved from the forest to the beach. It rested on the shore, gleaming, magical. The green mystery of the island as backdrop, and the shifting, glittering blue chop waiting to welcome it back to sea. The boat was like all of them, now: half-built in the manner of the world of civilized men (factory smooth, painted, adorned with the names of ports and shipping concerns); and half-built from scraps (tied together with who knows what, and rather beautiful in its wildness). Vida was like that, too, with her corset and her bun, her tangled wisps of hair, the freckled skin of her face so unpainted it was hard for her to imagine it.

In this curious fashion she was not alone. Those thirty or so bodies wore the clothing that had defined them in their old lives, but it was torn, held together with rope. They were barefoot, their appearance roughed, hardened, embellished by the elements. Fitzhugh summoned them and they gathered, in their ripped, sun-bleached, mud-stained finery. They listened as he spoke of his mission. And she understood, by his grave tone and their intent listening, that the happy hours when she knew he had chosen her, just last night, were almost over.

The signs his love was real were numerous:

He had appeared at her hut that morning to inquire

about her rest and to present her with a bouquet of pink flowers.

His eyes had sought hers throughout those first hours, a silent language of yearning and communion that she had spoken fluently in her old life.

He had told her about their boat, their mission, before anyone else.

And when he gathered them around the boat, he held her gaze as though waiting for her approval, and it was not until she gave him a dip of the chin that he began to speak.

"My friends," he began. "You have all been very brave. I and my family are responsible for your safety and we have failed you. But I hope that we may be redeemed in your eyes. I have traveled the Amazon and trekked the Himalayas. I have never begun such journeys without trepidation, and today is no different. But I have never undertaken a more important mission than the one I shall set out on today. I can think of no more solemn duty than my duty to bring you home, back to your lives, to your loved ones. Luckily," and here, Vida noticed, he left off his serious voice, and employed the dimple and the eye twinkle that she couldn't help but find charming, "I have some experience navigating what others have proclaimed impossible."

Vida's eyes shone. Her heart smiled to see him like this, to see his ability to rouse and reassure a crowd. For the first time she thought it was a little lucky after all that their story should have brought them here. For otherwise how could she have known how right she had been, what a worthy specimen he was?

"The wind is good today," he proclaimed. "It will carry us quickly away from the reefs that surround this island, and will, we hope, bring us swiftly into the path of a ship, if not all the way to the islands that were our original destination."

"What will you eat?" asked Peter, the eldest of the children.

"We have packed coconut meat, dried seaweed, dried fruits. We have stored water in coconut husks, and we hope to be able to fish in the open ocean. But we will be hungry, we will be thirsty—this we know. It won't be an easy passage."

"Can I come with you?" asked Peter.

Fitzhugh knelt, so the boy stood above him, and put his hand on the boy's shoulder. "You're very brave, aren't you?"

"I want to see my father."

"Yes, I want you to see your father, too. But you must look after your mother and your sister, do you understand? And then, when we return in a bigger, sturdier ship, I will personally deliver your father the message of how brave you were here."

The boy straightened and saluted Fitzhugh.

"That's a good sailor," Fitzhugh said, rising to his feet.

"In my absence, my man Sal will be first in command, and young Peter shall be his lieutenant."

The laugh of derision surprised them all, and they glanced at Sal, sitting on the sand, elbows on knees, a bit apart from the rest. "I should be with you," Sal declared, not breaking his gaze from the ocean. He threw a pebble in the direction of the water. She had avoided him since their trek to see the sunrise. She had not noticed he was not preparing the boat with the others, that he was gloomy.

"You're injured," Fitzhugh said. "It could jeopardize us all if we meet weather."

"I told you," Sal said, "there is sure to be weather. Anyway, you don't know how to read the stars."

"Sal, I have been navigating the world by maps all my life; if anyone can find his way in the unknown, it is me."

Sal glanced up, shielded his eyes from the blazing sun. "There is no map for the ocean."

"I can read the stars a little," Fitzhugh added, almost as an afterthought.

Vida's eyes darted from Fitz to his man. She was mystified by this quarrel, and more so by the contradictory feelings it aroused in her. For all that morning her heart had sung a plaintive song of wanting this new association between her and the Farrar scion to continue for all to see, with the romantic gestures and escalating intimacies that were the familiar signposts on the road to an engagement.

But at the same time there was that (strangely satisfying) sting of irritation. The way she'd felt watching the sun come up, and when Sal had pulled her to safety when she fell.

"The wind is good today," Fitz called to Sal.

The tone of his voice said that it had all been decided. The two most senior members of the *Princess* crew, George and Seamus, lifted the boat up and carried it down to the water. Poor Jack had not been chosen for the crew (though he wore a brave face). It was Henry Dries Stahl who went in Sal's place, trailing rather uselessly as they labored to bring the hull beyond risk of rocks. The whole band of survivors went with them into the waves, up to their waists in it. The tide was strong, pulling the bark out into the unknown. The wind pressed their shirts to their backs, pulled their hair to the west.

"Wish us luck!" Fitzhugh cried.

The waves crashed in, but the human sounds were louder.

"Good luck!"

"*Bon voyage!*"

"Viva Farrar!"

Fitzhugh was the last of the men to jump aboard. He stood before Vida, the water dense and swaying between them. She felt what he wanted to do. He wanted to take her by the waist and kiss her once before he went. He couldn't, though. Not in front of anyone. It would be a scandal, and possibly a bad omen.

"I'll be back for you," he said. His gaze had that strange opaqueness that was sincerity mixed with desire. Then his serious façade cracked, she saw his most charming smile, and he said: "You and I have unfinished business."

He shoved the boat once more, and swung his legs over its rail. For a moment he had the appearance of a sailor in a heroic painting, the light hitting him just so as he cut a dashing figure against a magnificent seascape. Then the wind filled the sail and the boat flew into the open ocean and he became a miniature. In a few minutes she could make out no detail of him at all, just the silhouette of the little bark against the endless horizon.

The tide gripped her skirt, which was still heavy despite the layer she had given up last night in the grove. When she turned and tried to make her way back she felt how the ocean tugged at her body. As she dragged herself and the once-fine skirt from the water and onto the beach she heard a growl that seemed to come from above. Over the high green hills of the interior the sky was a dense gray. She saw a brief, pale yellow iridescence. The breeze cooled the tip of her nose, her earlobes. Then all was tranquil, warm, lapping waves again. Sal was staring at her, and she stared back to show him. She knew she looked afraid, but she tried to square her shoulders, prove it was not *him* she was afraid of.

He and Fitz had had their little skirmish and Fitz had triumphed. *She* had triumphed. She had sent her man out to bring back the glorious finale of their love story. But Sal did not look away, and Vida realized this pettiness was a poor match for a day of such consequence in the great scheme of her life.

She revolved to have a final look at Fitzhugh. But she could make out nothing but the endless Pacific.

He was gone.

NINETEEN

The afternoon brought a spectacular sky streaked with peach and robin's-egg blue. It was a perfect match to Vida's inner landscape. She was full of pleasant fantasies. As she gathered firewood, as she ripped the leaves from the spines of palm fronds and wove them into new mats, her mind turned again and again to the man she was sure to be betrothed to by New Year's. She imagined Fitzhugh and his two sailors masterfully steering their boat over big, gentle waves.

Perhaps right now, at just this moment, he was swimming in the open ocean, catching a fish with his strong, bare hands. Perhaps he had just sighted a big boat, and his men were ferociously rowing toward it. Perhaps they were being lifted up to the high deck of a sugar company's cargo ship. Perhaps he had already wired Mother and Father to tell them that Vida was alive and well with the others, and that she would be coming home soon. (For everything was going so well—surely her worst fears were false, surely her parents had survived the wreck.)

Perhaps he couldn't wait. Perhaps he went right ahead and asked Vida's father for her hand in marriage.

But that was stupid, wasn't it? Father and Mother would be in Honolulu, waiting for her safe return. In which case, how would he ever guess where to wire them? Or would they have returned home? And if they had returned home, why would they have done that?

Vida knew the answer to that one.

If they had returned home, it would be to bury Vida. To have a funeral without a body for the girl they had raised to be a lady, but who couldn't control herself, who wanted too much and made a spectacle of herself trying to get it, and had thus put them all in danger.

Vida laid down the mat she was weaving and frowned at her theoretical death.

That it was the imaginary conclusion to an imaginary saga comforted her none at all.

The fantasy of her demise sobered her as though it were real. She glanced up at her surroundings, wanting some reassurance that she was still here, that she was still alive. That was when she noticed how the waves moved in a crazy pattern—now to the left, now to the right. They were all white on top like snowy peaks. She became aware, too, of her physical self, which she had quite forgotten in her daydreaming.

How hot her face was, how the sweat sprang from the delicate skin above her lip, under her chin, at the back of her neck. How her hair frizzed where it had gotten loose from the knot at the nape of her neck.

The air seemed as overheated and significant as in a ballroom when everyone has been dancing, and glancing over their shoulders to see who else is dancing; when everyone is looking their very best, and it is difficult to choose one person it would be most pleasurable to sit next to. The atmosphere was heavy, and she was restless. She stood and went to the place on the beach where Sal still sat gazing out.

"Fine weather, isn't it?" she asked.

He nodded in a way that did not signify agreement. "'Fine' is a funny word, don't you think?"

"How do you mean?"

"People like you use it carelessly to describe anything that you admire. What you mean is that it is refined, or that it is like finery. But how can you say weather is fine? Weather is so much larger than whatever you perceive of it from a picture window in your overbuilt cities. Weather is a beast. Perhaps it is magnificent. Perhaps it has an awesome sort of beauty. It is almost never *fine*."

"Thank you for the lecture. I didn't know you were such a scholar."

"I am not a scholar, but I have listened to nonsense from people like you all my life."

Vida had to smile at that. "It gladdens me to hear you talk this way. When you talk this way I know you are telling the truth. I know where I stand. But when I say fine weather, I am talking about a clear blue sky and a sweet breeze. I am talking about the kind of weather that is perfect for a stroll. Or a sail."

Now he raised his dark gaze to her. "Then this is definitely not fine weather," he replied. Her back straightened when she heard his tone. "It's no day for a sail."

An odd thought occurred to her, which was that Sal—who had in the span of a few weeks caused her such a wild range of irritations—had once been a child. This tall, lean young man, with his skewed features and his long lashes, with his absolute inability to adhere to the rules of decorum and polite behavior, had a history all his own. With Fitzhugh, this was rather obvious. One could not meet him without knowing he'd once worn little suits of velvet, and posed for photographers against elaborately painted backdrops. The story of his life, from his charmed birth to his brave exploits and his rakish adventures of the heart, was whispered about and written of and depicted in newspaper illustrations. But Sal she knew nothing about.

"What could you possibly be thinking with an expression like that?" he asked.

She had the strange impulse to tell him. But before she could, a fat raindrop splatted against her forehead.

Sal saw it, too, and was on his feet. A bolt of pain flashed across his face.

"What happened?" she asked.

"That's rain," he replied. "It's about to pour."

"I meant your ankle." She hadn't noticed how bad his injury was, the terribly bluish stain under the skin, how different in size one ankle was from the other.

"I know, it's gotten worse since this morning," he answered. "I was worried about you, and I fell wrong, and it keeps swelling in the heat."

This morning seemed so long ago. "Oh," she said witlessly.

"Come on," he urged her, but when he put his weight on the bulbous foot again, his face crumpled with pain and he made a sound she'd never heard him make before.

"You can't walk on that," she gasped. "How have you been getting around?"

"Hopping." He laughed, but laughing seemed to hurt him, too.

"Here." Before she could think how it would look, she'd wrapped his arm around her shoulder, put her arm around his waist.

Thus entangled they made their way up the beach.

At first the raindrops were like the first one—large and heavy, but occasional. By the time they had reached the shelters, it was impossible to identify one drop from another. The light had changed. In a few minutes the world had gone dark. She could hear the shouting of the others over the wind, saw them flocking toward the huts at the top of the beach, the rain blown sideways by the wind. The drops accumulated, became a torrent that soaked through their clothes and blinded Vida as she and Sal hobbled under the first thatched roof they reached.

They were breathing hard. Under the roof, they began to laugh. The rain was so sudden and so wild—the change in the landscape so extreme. They could hear shouting in the other huts, everyone calling to each other. Mostly they heard the rain, how it pelted the roof and assailed the beach. The world as she had come to know it—this new world—was soon unrecognizable. It seemed all water.

For a while they were trapped like that. They called to the neighboring huts, asking who was there—and who was in the next hut over—until Sal was satisfied that everyone was accounted for. The joke that Fitzhugh had made yesterday—about the sunset being a kind of show that he had arranged for her delight—had seemed just that, a mere joke. But now she understood it in a different way. Sitting beside Sal—her clothes drenched, her face damp, her chest heaving as her breath steadied—the scene before them was as exciting as any play she'd ever seen. It changed by the second, the leaves blown across the sand, the sea now silver now black, the ocean spray leaping like dancers from the sharp rocks into froth white as snowfall.

Then, quite suddenly, the rain stopped.

The seascape before them was every kind of gray, from the dark, dense, light-absorbing variety to a metallic and reflective hue. In the distance Vida saw the movement of storm clouds, but the sky above her ceased its dramatics. Out over the ocean a column of sunlight fell, a rich marigold beam of warmth against an otherwise silvery field. Sal released an anxious breath, and Vida began to laugh again.

"Peter!" Sal called.

They heard the boy's bright reply from some huts over: "Here, sir!"

"And your sister—still there? All right?"

"Yes!"

"Eleanor!"

"Here, with Miss Flynn, Sal; yes, we're all right!"

"Good!" called Sal. "There may be more weather, stay put!"

For a while, they called to each other, learning how

everyone had weathered the deluge. A few roofs had been damaged by the onslaught, but everyone was in one piece. It was only then that Vida noticed the pattern on the water far in the distance.

"Do you see that?" she asked.

Sal narrowed his eyes at the distant ripple on the surface of the sea. It was unlike any shape Vida had ever seen anywhere.

"Oh," he said miserably.

"What is it?"

"A wave."

"Just a wave?"

"A wave like that can travel halfway around the world if nothing breaks it," he whispered to himself in a tone of such awe that she too felt a shudder rocking across her shoulders. Then he bolted to his feet. Now he seemed insensible to pain. He didn't have to tell her. She could see it in his face: a wave like that had the power to sweep them all away. "Move!" he shouted. "Move, now! Get as high as you can!"

The others heard his urgency, and they ran in the direction Vida and Sal had gone that morning, clutching what they could. Fear wiped all expression from their faces.

Sal ran along the huts, shouting, making sure everyone had heard him. Then he grabbed Vida's hand.

"Did you count them?"

"Yes."

"Was that everybody?"

"I think so."

"You think so?"

"Yes! Yes," she cried, uncertain, but hoping it was true, and hating herself for not having counted more carefully.

Sal's gaze swung back and forth frantically. "All right," he said at last. "All right, come on, let's go."

The survivors of the *Princess* made their panicked, careful way up the rim of the cliff, up and up, clutching at the slick roots, keeping low to the ground so as to maintain balance, with Vida almost at the rear, and Sal behind her, urging them to keep their footing and to make haste. "There's a cave at the top!" he shouted.

"What?" Vida fell, but managed to catch herself with her hands.

"It will be dangerous at the top if they crowd there, tell them to get into the cave!"

"There's a cave!" she shouted at those farther up along the ridge. "Get in the cave at the top."

The message made its way up the line.

At last Vida and then Sal reached the peak, where earlier he'd sat staring out. She saw the opening in the rock behind them—she had not noticed it before. The others had gathered there. Sal walked on his foot as though it didn't hurt him, but his mouth was in a hard line and she guessed he must be in great pain. The wind was thick with salt and droplets and a dangerous energy, blown in from far away.

That mountain of a wave she had seen far out reared like some massive beast of myth. It loomed, crashed down. It smothered the length of the beach, smashing through their huts, flooding even the forest. Where the beach had been there was now a seething sea. Then, slowly, the ocean reeled itself back, taking with it the boards and leaves, the mats and trunks, that had been their safety and their home.

Vida felt she had to hold on to something and grabbed what was nearest, which was Sal's shirt. A sound she'd never made before—like a groan, but far more savage— escaped her throat. Before she could take in the scope of the destruction, she heard Sal urging her in his steady way that they ought to get inside the cave lest the rain wash them away, too.

TWENTY

The night they spent in the cave was the longest Vida had ever known.

During those hours of huddling and shaking and silence she had prayed for the night to end. But the next morning's stark sun terrified her, and as she made her way down the cliff's edge to the beach, her heart beat slowly, thudding with dread. The infinite flat sea went on and on, terrible in its stillness. For the stillness was deceptive. Vida knew now what wild destruction that unending water was capable of. As they made the final descent her chest tightened. The ruins of their makeshift homes lay in pieces on the sand.

If she hadn't known better she would have thought it was another beach. It had been rearranged. Some rocks appeared bashed apart, and new ones had accumulated, and the belt of sand between the water and the trees had narrowed. The trees bent in the direction they had been pulled by the sea, and their roots were naked and exposed.

The sky was blue, but a weak blue, as though diluted. There was no rain. The wind had a bite to it, seemed to whip them with sand and particles of things broken in the night. Vida brushed her hair back from her forehead, tried not to be afraid of the gathering emptiness inside her. The ocean had given them no new treasures—only the same old boards and planks as before, more eroded now.

Then her eye caught sight of something in a bright and happy hue. A pale pink—almost like a wedding dress color, but not quite white enough.

Her throat closed. She rushed toward that burst of color, one hand pulling her skirt back from her feet, the other arm swinging crazily. When she reached the bright petticoat she sank onto her knees. The sand was damp; it soaked her skirt. She lifted the petticoat, and buried her face in it.

She told herself not to cry. She was Vida Hazzard—she was not some flimsy thing. If she lost this last principle of her old self, she feared she would be nothing, nothing at all.

But she could not hold back. The weather inside her was beyond her control. She choked, gasped; her sobs had a life of their own. They came like breakers across her chest. The ugly sound of her heaving, the way her body shook, her waist convulsing within the corseted dress she'd worn when all was fizzy and fine—she was helpless to stop any of that.

The typhoon that had come in the night had left them nothing. So how could a boat made of wood, piloted by a few men, be otherwise but buried in the depths of the ocean?

She knew what had become of them. She knew, and her heart closed around what she had lost.

Fitzhugh, who had been at first a pleasant fantasy, and then a very compelling one. And also a handsome face and an excellent story. A story of a sickly boy who had made himself strong and able. He, that grand self-invention, was surely nothing now. He had seemed a bright star, the lone man who might suit her own impressive self, but he was no more. She had to put both hands against the sand for balance. Otherwise the convulsions of her sobs might be too much; she might break apart, too.

Somehow the weather inside her—like the weather that had come over the island—passed. When she looked up, Sal was the only person she saw. He was a few yards ahead of her, shoeless, ragged, staring out at the horizon. He seemed a person who would like to cry but can't, who is too stunned to have the slightest idea what they feel. Vida knew she was being ridiculous. Fitz had been wonderful. But he had not really been hers—it was just a fantasy she had had, a possibility that had passed through her mind. Sal, as far as she knew, had been following Fitzhugh around the world all his life, and could follow him no more.

Fitz had been their leader. Sal was supposed to lead in his place, but he was in shock. Vida waited for one of the other men to speak up, take charge. To step forward with some brave proclamation, some inspiring plan. But several minutes passed, and no one did anything like that. Vida sighed, rose to her feet, smoothed her skirt as best she was able. She touched Sal's shoulder. "We'll be all right," she told him.

His head moved around but it wasn't exactly a nod of agreement. "It's all over," he said.

His eyes were dark with despair. She wanted to look away from that despair. She would have liked to throw the petticoat out to sea, but she couldn't do that. They might need it yet. She wouldn't give up, or abandon Sal or any of the others. She held his gaze. "I know, but we can't let them think that. Come," she said.

The others were scattered across the beach in various poses of shock—some sitting, some howling, some quite frighteningly still in the face of loss. Camilla was one of these. It seemed strange that once upon a time her very presence had seemed to diminish Vida's own. Now her lips were paler than her sun-reddened face, and her light blue eyes made her seem otherworldly. Vida wanted Camilla to look up, to give her a reassuring glance, but she was absorbed in misery. The Misses Van Huysen held each other and wept. Young Peter sat apart from the rest, scowling out to sea. Vida offered Sal her arm and he took it, leaning on her as he hobbled along toward the others.

"I am sorry," she called to them, in as loud and firm a voice as she could manage. "I hate what you have had to endure. I know you are frightened, hungry, tired. But we cannot think the worst. We must assume that Fitz and the others are safe onboard a ship and that they will be coming back for us soon. Now we must get to work, now we must collect what is useful. We must be ready for darkness." She wasn't sure about anything, but she could see the relief on their faces when they had someone to tell them what to do and how to think. So she did her old trick and summoned all her inner spirit so that her presence loomed impressive—larger than her actual self. She made her voice loud, crystalline: "We will survive the night if we work hard and take care of each other. If we take care of each other, we will be all right."

Inside, she seethed. But she remembered Fitz. She thought about what he would have done, and made herself brave.

PART
THREE

TWENTY-ONE

By noon everyone was red in the face, tired, and hungry, and Vida used what desiccated palm spines she could find to rope the petticoat through the eyelet perforations along the hem and hang it between two trees, and in this way created a small area of pinkish shade. Miss Flynn glanced pitifully at the modest shelter, and Vida gestured to her.

"It's all right," Vida said, when Miss Flynn weakly sank under the protection of the petticoat. "I'm not tired." This was a lie, but Vida saw the relief in Miss Flynn's face, and that made it a little more true. "Rest, the children will be back soon."

All that morning, the children had run back and forth to the waterfall, returning with half coconut shells brimming with fresh water for the others to drink. Everyone else was busy hauling and sorting the detritus on the beach—the planks and branches, the cloths and doors—so that they could plan what to build first. The day they arrived here, Vida had been dismissed from these labors. But Fitz had taken two of the ablest men with him on his ill-fated voyage, leaving only three former members of the crew of the *Princess*, and Sal, who had led the effort on that first day, couldn't do much now. He did try, to Vida's vexation. "Looking at that swollen ankle is giving me a headache," she said, truthfully. He sat awhile after that.

A little later she returned to the top of the beach, hauling a piece of deck chair, and saw that the shade she had created was now crowded. Mr. and Mrs. Charles Brinkley, née Lucy Lawrence, who had been friends of Whiting's in San Francisco, lay on their backs underneath the petticoat, and beside them sat Charlotte Coburg, whose father was in railroads and whose husband was from an old aristocratic family in Europe. Vida's irritation flared, but she knew how these people had lived. They were not any more suited to this place than she was. They hadn't the slightest idea how to do anything for themselves, and they had received one too many shocks. They were afraid of everything— who could blame them? Once she'd deposited the salvaged bit of wood in a pile of similar flotsam, she went behind the trunk of a palm and bent over to undo the complicated ties at the back of her skirt. She was wearing enough fabric to make shade for at least three more bodies.

The corset, as ever, squeezed her insides. Stars appeared in her vision and she exclaimed in frustration at the difficulty of removing the skirt. She was hot, her fingers ached. She was thirsty and weak. Otherwise, she rationalized, it would be easier to undo the ties. But rational thought was no match for the utter fury she felt when at last she freed herself from the heavy, embellished skirt. How had she spent so many years at the mercy of her own clothing? She could not have gotten through a morning, much less an entire day, without the assistance of a person whose entire job was to help her with such trivialities. And there was nothing to do with that fury, except contort herself until she had freed herself from the corset, too.

Removing the finery of her last night on the *Princess* had required almost more effort than hauling a deck chair across the length of beach. Her white bloomers and undershirt were stuck to her skin with sweat.

This shedding of old clothes had been a mad impulse, but now that she saw them lying at her feet, she could not imagine how she would ever get them back on. For modesty's sake, for fear she would lose them, she had never fully removed her clothes since her arrival on the island. Mostly she had washed them when she washed the rest of her. The corset had been on so long it had left indentations in her skin. Without them she felt nervous and naked, but it seemed like a lot of work to dress herself again, and there was other work she knew she must do. She shooed away the thought, took a breath, and was surprised by how much air her lungs could take in when they were not constricted.

"Well," said Dame Edna, returning from the waterfall, a new makeshift sunshade in place, the green of her skirt swaying. "You've given up."

Vida blushed. "I couldn't stand it anymore."

"I thought we were doomed. But seeing you like that makes me a little hopeful. Maybe we will be all right. For one more day, anyway," the older woman remarked. "But prepare yourself for judgment."

Vida followed Dame Edna back toward the beach, where her words proved prophetic. First Camilla, and then the Misses Van Huysen, glanced at Vida, now wearing nothing but her undershirt and bloomers, and glanced away. Mrs. Brinkley stared, and so did Flora Flynn, and even Eleanor looked incredulous. Though their faces had expressed nothing but the purest fear since yesterday afternoon, now they managed to widen their eyes and part their lips in that subtle expression of horror usually reserved for some fashion faux pas of a particularly egregious nouveau riche.

Only once or twice in her social career had Vida made a mistake that warranted such censure-by-arched-brow, and she had forgotten how it scalded. She was surprised to find that even here, where no logic could possibly justify their opprobrium, it was uncomfortable to be held under the light of a gaze like that.

Well, *yes*—her first impulse was to run away and find a high cliff to dive off.

But she couldn't do that. She was in the middle of a task, and would have to see it through before she indulged in any drastic measures. The task came first. Once strung up, her skirt and petticoat together made almost a small room's worth of shade, and Vida summoned Eleanor, and told her to rest under it, before she lost her chance and was elbowed out by the kind of people who had never risen from a dinner table with their own dirty dish.

"There," Vida said with satisfaction. "Don't forget to drink water. And see the children have some rest in the shade when they next come back from the waterfall."

"Look at that," said a high, genteel voice that almost disguised its mean edge as Vida turned away. "She's a libertine again."

Vida flushed with anger and embarrassment. Without glancing back to identify the speaker, she went to Sal, who was leaning against a palm trunk.

"You did good work," he said, when she reached him. "You've reassured everybody."

"What does it matter?" She wasn't sure who she was angry at anymore, but the anger was still hot in her throat, and he was the closest person to her. "Just say it, you think I'm awful, and that this is all my fault."

Sal let out a great laugh, sank down into the sand, flung back his arms like a child about to make a snow angel. His laughter was like the swoon of a string quartet in the afternoon.

"What?" she demanded. "What?"

"Miss Vida Hazzard, I can see you think everyone should be impressed by you. But I think you are ridiculous. You keep taking credit for events far beyond your control. How could this be any one person's fault?"

"Oh. Well." Now Vida found herself in the curious position of not wanting to let go of her anger. In vulnerable times, anger could be a kind of fortress. And yet she couldn't get a grip on that anger, and it was gone before she could help it, and then she was laughing, too. "You think I'm ridiculous?"

"A little. But you've taken off clothing that could only serve you in a fancy ballroom, so I must admit that you are slightly less ridiculous now."

"I hope I have not become *too* serious," she said. Then she turned to the cluster of ladies who she knew were still staring at her and waved theatrically.

"No." Sal grinned, from where he lay on the sand. "Not too serious, either."

And Vida flung herself down beside him, folded her

arms up behind her head, and allowed herself to laugh. He began laughing, too. The ocean was back to its old way—peacefully lapping at the sand—and the sun was in their eyes. After a while, the laughter died out. She brushed the sand from her bloomers, picked up a tall, forked stick, and wrapped her corset around it to form a cushion where Sal could rest his weight. She offered Sal her hand, pulled them both to their feet so he could try the makeshift crutch.

"It's good," he said after a few steps.

Vida, afraid he was just saying this to make her feel better, changed the subject. "We'll never get shelter built by sunset."

"No."

"What will we do?"

"Before the light goes, we'll have Jack lead the others back to the cave. They'll sleep there again tonight. You and I will build a fire and we'll take stock of what we have and make a plan. We'll keep the fire going all night in case there is a ship passing in the night, and we'll take turns sleeping. In the morning, we'll start making new huts, on higher ground this time."

Those top-drawer people—once capable of talking animatedly for hours on such riveting topics as cherry galettes and fancy dress balls; now the most horrendous gluttons for shade—would surely disapprove of this arrangement. But Vida could not bring herself to see anything wrong in what he proposed. The only right thing that mattered was how to survive another day. She was embarrassed to find that her greatest wish at that particular moment was for Sal to say again that he no longer found her ridiculous. To tell her how brave she had been. But she could see the irony in this desire—she was ridiculous to want him to reassure her she wasn't ridiculous—so she went off in a hurry to see what else could be scavenged.

"Miss Hazzard," he called after her.

"Yes?" She shielded her eyes from the glare of the sun.

Though she couldn't really make him out through the overwhelming brightness, she sensed the way his lips curled up at the corners. "You aren't who I thought you were at all."

TWENTY-TWO

In the days that followed, Vida discovered that she was not precisely who she'd always thought she was, either. Her heart ached for Fitz, and when she closed her eyes she felt his brilliant blue gaze on her, and remembered the promise of their first, wild meeting.

But she refused to give in to despair, and worked day by day to keep herself and the others safe and hopeful.

Without trying she had become an early riser, a fact that would have shocked her old friends. Every morning she was up before the others, and would walk along the rocky peninsula near their new encampment—the one that separated the small cove and the long beach—to the highest point out at the end, where she'd climb up and have a look down into the clear turquoise waters below. She would leap, dive. How her blood charged when she sailed in the air! Her body cutting through the surface like a knife, her skin shocked by the cool water, arcing through the deep until she couldn't stand it anymore, and would emerge into the upper air breathless and glad.

For another thing, she had become quite freckled and brown. It had been one thing to be flushed pink all the time—that was still a version of the alabaster complexion she had protected under broad sun hats and pretty tasseled parasols on the manicured lawns of San Francisco—but now her forearms were brown as California hills in a drought year.

And, for a third, she had become quite obsessed with finding stones that had broken open in such a way that they could be used to whittle the ends of sticks to a lethal point. She—Vidalia Marin Hazzard, who had once felt it necessary to have a hundred different pairs of shoes—searched, rabid as an American shopping for a season's worth of clothes in Paris, for stones with a clean, hard break.

As she swam back around the rocks toward the beach she would dive down and peek into the underwater grottoes seeking any useful thing—razor-edge shells, fish bones to make hooks out of, the places where fish were likely to be in frenzy. Although Sal had let her use his pocketknife, the blade had been worn dull by their time on the island.

It was the sharp edge of a recently halved white stone that proved crucial in the making of her own spear.

Around the hour the girl she used to be would have been welcoming Nora into her bedroom with a tray of strong tea and fresh pastries, and gossiping about the various intrigues of last night's party, Vida put down this stone and tested the tip of the stick she had carved into a spear against her index finger.

"Oh!" she exclaimed, and frowned at the drop of blood beading on her skin. Then an expression of pure joy suffused her face. She scrambled to her feet and went to find Sal.

When they had first crashed onto these shores, she had been told she couldn't help, and then she had been assigned to search for kindling all day. Now it was Flora Flynn and Mrs. Charles Brinkley who collected firewood, and Vida put her mind to matters of life and death. Thus it had been since the night after the storm.

That night Vida and Sal had sat by the fire until dawn, keeping the flames high enough that a raft in the dark would see them and know where to paddle toward. They had discussed many things—how much "lumber" had been lost, and what sort of shelters they could build with what was left. They agreed that this time their shelters should be by the rocks over the cove—the land was higher there and it would make a better lookout and was more likely to survive another storm. They discussed, too, the best ways to collect coconuts, and who should have the benefit of their milk first. And they wondered what there was of the island, beyond that first band of forest, beyond the waterfall, over the ridge. Whether the wild yams could be cultivated for a greater yield. What else they didn't know about their home, for good or bad, which might now be their home for a long time yet.

But mostly they had talked about Fitzhugh.

Neither dwelled on the likelihood of his survival. Vida was afraid that if she acknowledged how impossible it would have been to live through weather like that on the open ocean, she might actually do him some harm—that whatever remote chance of his having lived through it might be dashed by careless speech. But they weren't hopeful, either. Vida kept waiting for Sal to say something like "The great Fitzhugh Farrar would never succumb to a watery grave."

But he didn't.

Instead he spoke of how Fitzhugh had been when they first met—that frightened, eager, sickly child. Sal's father had been a bosun with the Farrar Line, and had been killed in an accident involving the engine of one of Farrar's Atlantic steamers. Sal's mother had died on the day of his birth, and so it was that at nine years old he was all alone in the world, and old Winthrop Farrar decided that he owed it to the boy's father to give him a livelihood. At first this just meant keeping the nervous, easily fatigued Fitz company, but when Sal told tales of all the far corners of the world he'd traveled with his father, and all he had learned of navigating by the stars, or steering around a storm, Fitz became less melancholy, and it was decided that Sal would be in charge of teaching the young heir to be brave. Once Sal had taught him all he knew—as they were just becoming men, then—he was given a budget to hire every sort of trapper, sailor, cartographer, wrangler, so that they could learn how to live by their wits and survive outside the safe, walled cities of man. How to live close to the land. Fitzhugh became a different person with Sal's companionship. He had invented a whole new self to inhabit.

As the night passed, as they fed the fire twigs, Vida and Sal kept Fitz alive by talking about him. In the morning, there had been no sign of the raft that had sailed into stormy seas. But, having learned of all the transformations that Fitzhugh was capable of, Vida knew that she, too, could change.

And she *had* changed. It shocked her how much and how quickly. Even Dame Edna had remarked on it—said she wouldn't have minded having Vida along with her when she followed armies to report on battles.

Vida still looked out at the horizon as though Fitz might be there, but she had begun to accept that he probably never would be.

Three days had passed. She was hopelessly freckled. She had become accustomed to walking on bare feet. She had begun to wear her own fate like a light summer slip.

Her fate, as it turned out, seemed to involve quite a deep interest in sticks and stones.

And here she was now, rushing to Sal to show him how perfectly she'd whittled a stick into a spear.

"Let me see." Sal grinned as he examined the fine point in the light. He was crouching by the fire, where they kept a few embers going through the day, and weaving a fish trap out of dried vines.

Vida had not known how badly she wanted his approval until the long pause that followed. He examined her spear and said nothing. "Well?" she demanded.

"It's good." His dark eyes met hers as he handed it back. "What will you do with it?"

"Me?" She stared at it in puzzlement. Somehow she had thought she was making it for him, or for Jack, who had once been an ordinary seaman on the *Princess,* to do something manly with. What exactly that might be she couldn't say. She went on staring at it, but the spear refused to proclaim its fate.

"You've made it," he said. "Surely you know?"

She was on the verge of making something up—lest she look a *complete* fool—but then she noticed Camilla passing by the camp, her face a little wan. The happy-seeming

Camilla she had known for a few days had gone away with the big wave and the disappearance of Fitz. She was like a ghost again. Although she had, like some of the other ladies, followed Vida's lead and removed the aubergine top layer of her skirt—such fabrics were crucial to maintaining the privacy between huts—and given up on wearing what was left of her slippers, still she wore layers of petticoat, and the fitted bodice of what had once been her dress.

"Where's she going?" Vida asked.

"We were right to build here—it's the highest, flattest ground—but she's taken it hard."

"Oh!" Vida was ashamed of her thoughtlessness. "Of course—the grave."

"Yes. It's close to where we buried her husband. She might seem like a hypocrite. But she loved him. Whatever games they played they all played; they were her family."

"Oh."

"Have you noticed her going off like that?"

"No . . ." But even as she said it she knew it was a lie, that in fact she had seen Camilla doing this at least twice before. "I'll follow," Vida said. "See where she goes."

It was not, Vida decided, that she was an *entirely* new person. She was still a little jealous of Camilla, afraid that her connection with Fitz was deeper, and more real, than Vida's own. But she knew that was absurd. And anyway, she thought that Fitz would have liked it if they were friends now.

As she moved through the jungle, the sounds of the camp dwindled—the children's cries, the constant susurrus of roofs being thatched—and the cawing of birds, the buzz of insects overwhelmed her ears. It was not until she had traveled a distance that she noticed how firmly she gripped the spear. For some moments she was lost. Then she saw the white splash of Camilla's petticoat, heard the sound of falling water. They were at the pool. The spray rose up, catching the bright midday light.

So, Camilla was only here to bathe, Vida thought. She had worried for nothing.

But as soon as Vida's shoulders relaxed, she saw that Camilla had no intention of stopping. She was climbing up the sheer, rocky side of the waterfall, where little green sprouts clung to small patches of soil. The way was steep, and Camilla used her hands to ascend. Vida's first thought was how scratched and dirty Camilla's hands would get, how ripped and ruined her petticoat. But then without thinking she followed, testing the ground as she went, never trusting her footing.

Despite her melancholy, Camilla set a determined pace, and by the time Vida reached the high ridge a sheen of sweat covered all her skin, and her chest was dry, desperate for breath. For a moment Vida had almost forgotten about the other woman. She'd had to concentrate while they scrambled upward and had stopped noticing much.

But now they emerged into the open air of a vertiginous height. On one side, the mountain rose up to the peak from which the stream trickled and grew into the waterfall. On the other, the ridge jutted in the direction of the open sea. Before them the little plateau curved and fell away to a verdant valley. For the first time, Vida saw the far side of the island—beyond the valley was more jungle, more hills, and another rocky pinnacle beyond which lay beaches and the same ocean—that watery plain that continued on in every direction.

"Wild, isn't it?" Camilla said.

Vida startled, surprised that Camilla had known she was being followed. She took a thoughtless step that sent pebbles cascading off into the nothing below.

"Careful," Camilla said. When Vida saw the play of her smile she knew that she had misinterpreted her old rival's mood.

"I was going to say the same thing to you," Vida whispered.

"Oh." Camilla leaned her head back from her body and assessed Vida. "I know what you thought. It's not that. We can't all be you, you know—daring and resourceful. But I know our situation is different now. There's no time for moping. Still, I loved him. I like coming up here, seeing this, and thinking how he would have loved it, too."

Vida wasn't sure whether Camilla was talking about

Carlton or Fitz, and for a moment of burning discomfort she tried very hard not to want to know. Then she realized it didn't matter. "Who wouldn't?" she whispered.

"Oh—plenty wouldn't. That Mrs. Brinkley person you're on the wrong side of, for one. She would have fainted away to see where we *really* are. But I like it."

"What's that way?" Vida asked, pointing toward the peak.

Camilla's eyes went in the direction that Vida had indicated, and when she looked back at her friend her own gaze shone with fear and wonder. "I don't know."

"Don't you want to know?"

"It's so high that way!"

"Yes, exactly—we'll be able to see *everything*."

They hesitated in nervous excitement, and then Vida put down her spear.

They went, Vida first and Camilla close behind, clinging to the vines until there was no more vegetation, until it was just rock and they had to use their hands as much as their feet to reach the peak. The air became cooler, their breath labored. In a little while they ran out of mountain. They were so high they might have been upon the throne of a goddess, the place where some pagan deity went to rest and observe her worshipers.

"I'm dizzy," Camilla whispered.

"Me too," Vida said. But she wasn't. The atmosphere had a different quality here—it was less dense with moisture, with salt; it had a coolness that she felt at the roots of her hair. Her heart was beating steady and clear as a church bell. She took Camilla's hand and said, "Don't worry."

"If you say so."

"Don't you think it was all worth it, just to see this?"

Camilla murmured uncertainly. But Vida thrilled to this rare vantage, to see all the world roll slowly down, down, to the shimmery carpet of the sea as it unfurled onward to infinity. "Should we go back?" Camilla asked.

Vida agreed that was probably best. But she hesitated. And in that moment of hesitation she noticed something she had not seen before.

In the grassy open space way below were a pack of dark, wild creatures chasing each other in circles, rutting and turning on fast, sturdy legs. *Pigs!* She could scarcely credit the existence of yet more life, just beyond the summit, but there it was.

"Come, please, if you like me at all," Camilla was saying as she little by little scaled backward down the mountain.

"I do," Vida replied gallantly, and followed her.

In fact she liked—no, loved—everyone and everything.

All the sprouts and weeds and pebbles and trees and birds and eggs and shells and grains of sand and flowery smells, and all the beings big and small, near and far, hideous and lovely, mean-hearted or kind, that had ever been.

And another notion was gladdening Vida's mind. She knew what that spear could be used for. She had the answer to Sal's question; she couldn't wait to tell him.

TWENTY-THREE

"Well, go on, guess what I saw," Vida said as she sank down beside Sal.

While she was gone he had woven the vines together into something like a basket. Otherwise, he was as he had been when she left—his long legs folded beneath him, his injury hidden as he sat beside the steadily burning embers. He was very Sal about this, and did not do as she commanded. He just glanced up at her with an expression both all-knowing and bent with amusement.

"I know a good place to put that, by the way."

"Oh?" He laid the trap down and leaned back on his arms.

"By the rock that is shaped like a big grayish, pinkish egg; the fish are always in frenzy there in the morning for some reason. Not the really big fish. Just, you know, those silver ones about the length of your arm."

"Then we will put it there," he replied easily.

"You're not going to guess?"

"The Queen of England."

"No."

"A troop of traveling circus acrobats."

"No."

"Circus *lions*?"

"Wild pigs!"

"What?" Sal said. Vida felt very warm and gratified to see his face, which never went very north or very south of perfect equatorial placidity, as it broke open in true surprise. "How many?" he asked.

"Twenty, maybe."

His smile was so beaming with private light that he looked away from her shyly, as though meeting her eyes with that sort of happy expression was more than either of them could bear.

"Well?" she demanded.

"Well what?"

"What are we going to do now?"

He brought his knees up, propped his elbows on them,

squinted at the waves. "I don't know . . . what should we do now?"

"About the pigs, I mean."

"Oh, well—you have what you need, don't you?"

The spear that she had spent all morning on was indeed still in her hand. "Well, but . . ." How curious that she had, in the course of the last few hours, stood at the top of a mountain and felt no real fear, and now, talking with Sal, before a gentle sea on a calm day when the wind just nudged meaningless little clouds from here to there, she should have the precise sensation of standing before a cliff.

It was like leaning out over a great height, not being told what to do—it sent a violent shudder up her spine, and made her feel helpless.

How baffling, how utterly irritating, how characteristically Sal, that he should continue to be such a difficult person, and never, not once, just do what she expected of him. It was perhaps on account of this whirl of emotion that she spoke without thinking. What came out of her mouth surprised her. "No," she said, "not all I need."

"Oh no?"

"Well, I mean, let's just say for instance that I *was* able to spear a wild pig—just for a joke, let's say I could do it—then how would I ever get it back here?"

"That's a good question."

Vida glanced where he was looking—out at the sleek gray back of a dolphin breaking the surface of the ocean. "I'd need help. Jack, I suppose. You're much too gimpy to be of any use."

"Yes," he said, his mouth bending downward in self-deprecation, "that makes sense."

"Even so, we couldn't carry it all the way back. There's a reason those hogs are on their side of the mountain. The ridge that separates us from them is high; there's no easy way around it that I can see."

"Is there nothing here that you could use?"

"*Must* you talk to me like some child about to take a grammar school test? Of course there is. Rope—we could haul our prey back. And the old tablecloth—we could wrap the thing, suspend it from a pole."

"That's a good idea."

"Oh come, you're not going to send me off on a hunt. Didn't Fitz specifically tell you to look after me while he was gone? Aren't I to be protected at all costs from such rough stuff?"

"I don't think Fitz knew who you were when he said that."

Vida was so surprised that Sal would speak thusly of the dead, not to mention the dead young man he'd served most of his life, that for a moment she could think of no reply.

"You don't have to go."

"Well, who would you send in my stead?"

"Jack and Brinkley, I suppose."

"But—" Her heart rebelled so furiously at this notion that for a few moments she had no vocabulary at all. The whole mission had been her doing—he couldn't just *give* it to somebody else.

"But?"

"Well, you see—it's my spear."

Sal grinned and she saw his gleaming, slightly askew teeth. "Then I guess it'll be you, won't it?"

Vida beamed.

"As the captain of this mission, I have a request."

"Anything."

Without a wince, Sal was on his feet. "I am pretty much healed, and I want to see what's on the other side. May I be your second in command?"

The afternoon had advanced some by the time Vida, with Sal close behind, found the surest path down the escarpment on the far side of the ridge that separated their beach and their jungle from the wide valley on the other side. Vida had wound all the rope that had washed up from the *Princess* (and was not strictly necessary for keeping their huts standing) around her waist. The pocketknife was tucked into this jerry-rigged belt, all of which made a curious fashion with her water-stained bloomers and undershirt—she could just imagine this getup as an illustration of some half woman, half beast in one of the more sensational newspapers—but all in all she was glad that she looked a little fearsome. She did ask herself, as her tough bare feet searched out solid ground for their descent, what madness had brought her here, to this moment of living. Then she remembered: it was Sal, goading her with his leading questions and smug grin.

"Sal?"

"Yes?"

"You're only *pretending* to let me be in charge, right?"

"And what would that gain me?"

Vida did not get a chance to answer, because just then the herd of pigs came dashing from a thicket of low bushes, their bodies arcing together to make one curved shape through the purplish grass. They were tusked, their hides a mottled brown. They were unlike any pig Vida had ever seen, and for a moment she was all tingly at the wonder of them and forgot what she'd come here to do.

How had they come to this remote place? How had they lived all this time?

She wanted to know the answers to all the mysteries of existence, to understand what higher purpose had brought her, or the pigs for that matter, or the waving grasses, or even the tiny bugs that harassed her sleep, here, to this place, into being at all. When she and Sal had set out she had been rather drunk on determination—she had wanted Sal, and all the others too, but really mostly Sal, to know what it was she was truly capable of. Now she wasn't sure if she was capable of anything.

A great bird soared above. A cloud passed over the sun, dimming the valley. Then it traveled on and all was bathed in gold again. Her heart was beating like a drum.

Then the herd returned, lifted the dust, came their way.

She wanted no harm to come to any living thing. But she knew the persistent hunger she felt, as did all the others who had survived the *Princess*. She saw the hollowness in the eyes of the children, saw how spindly their arms had become. The spear was heavy with purpose in her hand— she fixed the nearest of the pigs in her sights, and asked its forgiveness. Once upon a time she had stood at the margins of ballrooms and decided that the attention of a certain young man would be hers. So it was now. She lifted her arm, she put the power of all her days into the hurling of the spear. As if by magic it sailed, it hit, just where she knew it would—sinking through the back of the pig, down through its chest.

Sal whistled. She was sure he hadn't believed she'd be able to hit her mark, and she turned for the gratification of seeing him having to acknowledge he was wrong. But his head was bent, as though to honor the fallen animal.

The other pigs reared and howled. They circled their

injured member. Sal was at attention again—with his long, whip-like arms he hurled rocks one after another until the pigs disappeared back into the thicket.

A kind of madness whooshed through Vida. Every tiny part of her body was alive with unbearable power. The beat of her heart went on steadily, a little louder than before.

She seemed to ride above herself after that—she was aware that they tied up the pig in the tablecloth, that they carried the heavy body back up and down the mountain, that Sal's breath was even and calm, and that he matched her pace the whole time.

She was grateful for the way he allowed her silence.

The other survivors cheered and danced at the sight of their kill. They chanted her name in praise. She smiled at their celebrations but didn't know what to say. The sun was on its downward trajectory by then, and she was relieved by this, for everything was a little too much at just that moment—too bright, too cacophonous, too humid, too real.

She undid what remained of the rope around her waist, and, without thinking, walked out on the rocks. She leapt from one rock to the other, moving out along the peninsula until she was surrounded by the ocean. From the last rock she swooped, dove. Her arms pulled, propelling her body outward into the swelling water. At last, in the rhythm of the tide, she felt the enormous relief of being shrunken back to just herself. She was only Vida—not more, not less.

It was only then that she thought to tread water, wheel around, and look back.

At first it perplexed her how far the land was—how tiny the encampment had quite suddenly become. The swell lifted her up and pulled her down. She had the thought that she ought to be afraid. But before fear could grip her, she saw the darkness of a body moving through the waves. Sal reached her in another minute, and he too began to tread water.

"There's a mean current," he called over the spray.

"Oh?" she asked, as though it had nothing very much to do with her. Of course it had everything to do with her. The realization that he had risked his own safety was a tightness in her belly.

"We'll have to swim along the shore!" The usual knot of his hair had come undone, and he pushed it back from his face so that it hung wet and sleek behind his ears. She could see that he was out of breath—she might have noticed that she was out of breath, too, if she hadn't been feeling quite so manic and powerful. Without discussion they began to swim, side by side, parallel to the beach. They swam a long time, and eventually, when Sal gave the sign, they reached the rocks at the far end of the long beach, and began to carefully make their way back to the sand.

Even back on land the swaying of the ocean was still in her body. Her limbs felt heavy. Sal, indefatigable in the waves, moved slowly now, and as if in surrender fell against the sand and threw wide his arms. She lay down beside him without thinking. She could hear the rise and fall of his chest as his breath slowed. Only then did it occur to her that she had been listening to his breath all day.

What a scandal this would have been back home! She was dripping wet, glittery with sand, wearing bloomers that didn't even cover her knees, and an undershirt that left bare her shoulders, and she was brown as toast. But try as she might, she couldn't find any shame lurking in the back corners of her mind. He glanced at her, and she saw the stars in his dark eyes.

Where shame might have been there were other feelings. She felt giddy, and nervous, and pleased with everything. Her first instinct was to fill the quiet with nonsense—she wanted to tell him things she remembered, or hoped for, or point at some insignificant detail of the landscape. Yet no detail seemed particularly insignificant, and there was something in the quiet between them that was delicious and that she didn't want to disturb. She shifted her body onto its side, so that she faced him, supported her head on her fist, and they watched the sun on its evening sojourn.

"Have you ever noticed," he asked, when the sun was a melting half circle on the gleaming edge of the ocean, "that it never looks the same?"

"That's true," she said. Everything she had done that day vibrated under her skin. Her body was tired and peaceful.

"Come on," he said, clambering to his feet and offering his hand. "We'll miss the feast."

Once on her feet she waited for him to release her hand. But he didn't, and she found that she didn't want to either, as though to let go would mean letting go of that perfect moment, lying in the sand while the waves crashed in and out.

"Well?" she asked, when it had been much too long and the sensation of his palm against her palm was filling her belly with butterflies.

His eyes glistened in the twilight. "Well what?"

Once again she had the sense of a cliff, of an opportunity to say something that frightened her and that once said would be impossible to unsay. "Well," she said, dropping his hand. "Should we go back?"

"Yes." He looked away. "We should go back."

It pained her to release that moment of perfect contentedness. But somehow she felt that it would come and go and return again no matter what she did.

The smell of the fire, the wood smoke, reached them as they walked back toward the camp. For a minute or two there was nothing wrong in the world. Then she saw the flash of white in the woods—saw Camilla, watching from between the trees.

In her eyes, Vida saw what she must look like. Saw the horrifying impropriety that Vida had been blind to while she lay on the beach with Sal, but which was the atmosphere she had breathed all her life. When she saw Camilla's face, Vida remembered all the social codes she was currently breaking. And she remembered Fitz, who Camilla had loved, and who was not here now to see her being so familiar with Sal.

Even so, it was hard to take all those rules seriously here. That elaborate etiquette, those codes of behavior, seemed a game now. Even Dame Edna, whose profession was to record the doings of the highly civilized and elaborately dressed, didn't believe in those rules. Maybe, really, those rules were just a meager and unimaginative way to order one's days. For the first time, she wondered if she wasn't better off—if she wasn't a better person entirely—without any of those rules at all.

TWENTY-FOUR

For the rest of her years, Vida would remember this lesson: no garden, however Edenic, is immune to the wild weather of one's internal life.

In that brief interlude at the water's edge, she had been so at ease that she thought nothing could ever disturb her again. But within the hour, and only a beach's width away, that ease was like an experience a thousand years in the past. Around the big fire a throb of anxiety overtook her. The women looked askance, they said private things in each other's ears, and Vida's thoughts rushed on hurly-burly.

For a brief and heady moment she hadn't cared at all what anybody else thought. But just as fast she found out that she did, that it was not so easy to shake off a lifetime of conditioning.

She looked for Sal, but could not find him. Anyway, she knew that she should not go seeking his company just now. She should avoid suspicion.

Yet she was troubled; her skin crawled with their stares. And she wondered if it was because she had hunted, because she had killed. Or was it because she had been swimming alone with Sal (and what did that signify anyway)? There were so many ways in which she was bad, she felt a little crazed by them all. And had the others added something extra from their own imagination—had rumors begun already of something untoward between her and Fitzhugh's man?

Nothing happened! said the petulant child who rambled on and on in her head.

But who exactly was that child arguing with?

The smell of meat cooking was so strong, Vida felt sick and crept away from the fire.

In the night she was harassed by bad dreams.

In her dreams, she passed through the fine rooms of her glorious social career, wearing clean clothes, between the beautifully embellished skirts of the ladies who decorated the manicured, topiary-laden lawns of the leisure class. But when these ladies turned their faces on her, it was with the masks of tragedy hiding their real features. All of this was quite substantial and real. Then, in the next moment, it was slipping away through the trapdoors of her mind, and she was sweating on a mat on the ground, beside Eleanor, Miss Flynn, Sonja, and Sonja's children.

She pulled her bloomers and her shirt from where she hung them in the night to air out, and pulled them over her underthings, and went into the morning, which was still fresh and a little cool.

The memory of yesterday's swim disinclined her from her usual routine, and as she stood there, outside the huts where the other members of the camp snored and rested after their feast, she could not shake the foreboding of the dream.

Vida walked along the palms that cut through the jungle, to the pool at the base of the waterfall. After swimming in the ocean so often she was surprised by the stillness of that pool, how cool it was, and she swam under the spray of the falls, and emerged in the room demarcated by its watery curtain. She felt a little better in the noisy quiet of falling water. But when she swam back under and emerged, the heavy knot of her hair became waterlogged. Camilla was standing at the side of the pool.

Have you come to slander me to my face was what Vida wanted to say, but instead a very neutral "Are you here to bathe?" filled the air between them.

"No." Camilla shook her head for emphasis and worked

her hands together. Her petticoat covered the length of her legs, same as yesterday, and the purple bodice cinched the narrow of her waist. "I was looking for you."

Vida made circles with her arms through the greenish water. There was more light and warmth in the sky now, but she was still a little cold and wanted to climb onto the dry rocks. Yet she felt shy of Camilla suddenly. "Why?" she asked.

"Don't you want to get out?" Camilla asked.

"Yes."

Camilla offered her hand, and with surprising strength assisted Vida in clambering onto the rocks at the edge of the pool.

"Thank you," Vida said, when Camilla didn't seem likely to say anything, and all the stillness and low murmur of nature was contributing to a rather awkward creeping feeling that jittered Vida's toes.

"Isn't that funny," Camilla replied. "I was here to thank you."

Vida watched Camilla suspiciously. "Thank me?"

"Well, yes. You might have made me talk about Fitzhugh, when we were on the peak, and you didn't. You've been so kind and accepting of our . . . unusual history. I like that we both cared for him. Anyway, then you brought us food, real food!"

Vida smiled. A swell of pride came over her. "And here I thought you were here to shame me."

"Why would you ever think . . . ?"

"Last night, when I was coming back along the beach, I saw you, in the woods."

"Oh." Camilla laughed nervously. "Yes, I must have looked ghoulish there amongst the trees. I was there because you went off. I was terribly worried about you, swimming out in the current. I wanted to make sure you were all right. I guess I still want to make sure you're all right."

"Of course." Vida laughed too, and tried to lift the knot of her hair from the itching skin at the back of her neck. "I thought you were going to spread rumors about me."

Camilla's expression flashed with understanding. "I see what you thought. You . . . and Sal. No. No, no. I didn't think that you—well, you couldn't. In a hundred years I wouldn't think . . ." Her face was flushed red as beetroot, and Vida almost felt bad for her. She was so embarrassed she seemed to be having trouble finishing a sentence. "What I mean to say is, girls like us, we are trained too well. Trained to please others with our manners and appearance. It would go against everything to do something that didn't serve our husbands and fathers and brothers, to do something that might actually please us."

Vida's response was so quick it was a kind of instinct:

"You don't think I'd even be capable of a scandal? I don't mean to be rude, but *you* were."

"Yes. I suppose that's true. This would be different though. I can't say why exactly." Camilla lifted her chin and assessed her interlocutor. "Oh, what does it matter? We are here, they may never find us, do what pleases you."

Now Vida blushed at the implication of Camilla's words. She felt confused, and wanted to be light, free of weighty thoughts. "Would you do something for me?"

"Anything."

Vida lifted her clothes and took out the pocketknife that she had held on to since yesterday. "Would you cut my hair?"

"Oh no. I couldn't. Your hair? What if . . . what if . . ."

"You said yourself they may never find us. But it is a certainty that I will never get the knots out."

After a moment of hesitation, Camilla crouched behind Vida and pulled back the mess of hair. "Are you sure?"

No, Vida was not remotely sure. Her head swarmed with doubt. Her hair had been one of her best features, or so she had always believed, and its elaborate arrangement had been one of the main tricks she'd employed to distract from the inadequacies of her face. The weight of it seemed the thing that tethered her to the Earth. Without it she might float away, she might be hideous, she might not even be herself.

"I don't have to," Camilla said, as though she could hear the blood pumping in Vida's ears.

"Oh do it, just do it!" Vida almost screamed.

Then she felt the knife sawing through her braid. There was no going back now; she would never again have that particular skein of glossy hair. She squeezed her eyes shut and reminded herself that after everything—after being lost at sea, after losing the man she thought she'd marry—she could not cry over this girlish triviality.

When Camilla had finished, the tough tail that had once been her beautiful hair lay at her feet. She felt as though she had been relieved of an enormous burden. Her laughter, too, was sudden and light. She and Camilla linked arms, and walked back toward the camp together.

What exactly had been keeping her so bound all this time, it was hard to say. She had liked her elaborate clothes, and she had always been rather skillful at pushing the rules of behavior that did not suit her. But she felt free in a new way now. The wisps of pale brown hair were weightless on her head; her feet merely grazed the carpet of the jungle floor. All around her she heard the tiny shifting of leaves and insects, water and wind, the sigh of a world she had not known existed.

TWENTY-FIVE

In the afternoon, when she had already been awake a long time and accomplished much, Vida sat on the beach under a palm, her toes buried in sand and her attention quite fixed on the coconut that she was hollowing out for a rainwater-catching vessel. They could never have enough rainwater catchers. But, for the third time, she scraped too hard with the old metal implement, and the shell cracked, and with a whelp of frustration she threw the useless husk as far from her as possible.

"Idiot," she muttered, and threw down the rusted implement, too.

"Dear one," said Dame Edna, who had been quietly

sitting beside her, pressing bark between two flat stones for paper, "it's not the coconut, or that old shoehorn or whatever it is, that's giving you so much trouble."

"I don't think it was a shoehorn," Vida said.

"That was not my point. My point was to do with your vexation."

"My vexation?" It was true that for some days Vida had itched with a restless energy that she hardly knew what to do with. The camp was functioning well, yet her mind wandered and wondered; she could not find a moment of contentment. "What could be vexing me?"

"Oh, I don't know," said Dame Edna with that airy amusement that was her constant manner.

"I think I'll go for a walk," Vida said, and put the mystery implement back in the woven basket of all the other rusted metal bits that weren't quite anything but might someday be used for something.

"Be careful," the dame said indifferently, not glancing up as Vida passed by.

There was still plenty of time before they built the dinner fire. She might have asked Camilla to come with her. The camp now acknowledged them as particular friends— both were Farrar widows, in a sense, though of course they never said that sort of thing—or Dame Edna, who had asked her for all the details of the far side of the island, or

Peter, who was curious about the wild pigs. But, though she could scarcely admit it, it was Sal her mind kept wandering to. Sal's company she wanted.

And so it was Sal who came with her up the steep climb beside the waterfall and emerged onto the heights.

The last time they had come this way they had been preoccupied with whether or not they'd really be able to hunt a wild beast. They hadn't noticed much. The patterns of weather on the ocean, near and far, the glimmer of sun on waves, the clouds massing like mountain ranges in the distance in pretty pastel colors. She noticed all that this time. Here, in the midst of unspeakable grandeur, she felt thrilled from the tip of her nose to the nail on her pinkie toe by her sheer existence.

"Have you ever seen anything like it?" she asked Sal.

The sun was bright and they both had to shield their eyes and squint to see each other. His dark hair was restrained at the back of his head, but the breeze whipped a few strands across his face, the curve of his nose. His lashes were like the points of black stars. As always with Sal, there was a whole world in what he didn't say.

"You *have*?" she gasped, her voice light with wonder. Yet she felt an odd creep of disappointment, too.

"With Fitz, of course. We trekked the Himalayas and crossed the plains of Argentina and . . . I only mean to say that we have—that *I* have—stood on a few summits."

Vida wasn't sure why this should blunt the pleasure she took from the view.

"But I've never been here before."

"No," Vida said quietly. "And neither have I."

His smile overtook his face. "This is a good one."

"Is it?" She couldn't bring herself to smile back. "How would I know? Maybe this is a very average summit."

"Don't you remember what you told me in the dining room of the *Princess*?"

"No." Vida had to laugh at that. "Who can remember such things?"

"You told me that the adventures of young women are adventures of the heart—or of husband-hunting. And that it was enough for you to see the heights of the world through the eyes of the man you would marry."

"That does sound like something I'd say," she allowed, although the Vida who would have said it seemed very far away. "But of course I have no husband."

"And I have no other summit. Should we see what more is out there?"

They walked down into the valley, through the grasses, under trees that were entirely different from the trees on the other side of the ridge—trees that dripped purple flowers and disgorged bright birds—walked past streams and wooded pools. They saw shelled sea things that had been broken against the rocks, leaving gleaming piles of treasure.

The seabirds had dropped them to make their feast. On the far side of the island they found another cove, this one even more dramatic than the one where Fitzhugh had entertained her one night by moonlight.

"This place was a volcano once," he said.

"How can you be sure?" she asked.

"I can't. I've been to places in the world where they know there was a volcano because of the way the ash is compounded in the rock, and because of the lore of the people who live there. They're always shaped something like this. The island will have a high ridge and a valley, a cove cut open to the sea that long ago was burned by hot lava. My favorite place in the whole world is like that. An island in the Mediterranean. A giant volcano erupted there once, and wiped out a great civilization. We went there to rest after a trek in the Sahara, and I'd go down to the port at sunset and talk to the old fishermen bringing in their haul for the day. If Fitz hadn't needed to return to New York, I would have stayed there on that volcanic island a long time."

Vida shivered at the thought. "You don't think *this* island could erupt."

"Oh, no—that was long ago."

"How does a person know so much?" Vida wondered out loud.

Sal shrugged. "There is an eon of history in every pebble, if only you know how to interpret it."

"Sal," she said. The very sound of his name in her mouth made her shiver. She'd said his name so many times by that point. But it was hard to say now—there were so many things she wanted to ask him, and they all seemed very difficult to put into words. "Do you remember when you swam out to me? The night we got the pig, the night the current was strong?"

"Yes."

"And afterward, on the beach?"

"Yes."

She was blushing furiously with her own girlish stupidity. Why had she brought *that* up? It was because she couldn't stop thinking about it. She desperately wanted him to be thinking about it, too.

After a long pause, to her enormous relief, he said, "That was nice."

"Yes, wasn't it nice?" Her words were coming faster now, she didn't feel that she could control them, she was afraid she would say something too true. "I remember being so easy and full of good feelings."

"I was, too."

"Well then why didn't you—" She was out of breath suddenly, was having a hard time knowing what it was she was trying to say. "What I mean is—you might have tried . . ."

"Tried what?"

Vida's laugh was high, nervous, stupid sounding. What was that laugh? She didn't sound like herself at all. It seemed very urgent that he understand that was *not* her ordinary laugh. She would tell him. She opened her mouth to explain, but instead she heard herself say, in a clear and even voice, "To kiss me."

"Oh."

"That was very, very silly of me to say. Why would you want to kiss me?"

"It's not that I didn't want to."

A big breath filled the sail of her lungs and the surface of her eyes was suddenly wet with an emotion that she wasn't sure she knew the name of. "Then—why?"

"I wouldn't."

Vida scowled. It had been so easy to get Whiting, and Bill, and Theodore to kiss her—why should Sal be so difficult? "Am I that hideous?"

"No! No, it's just that I wouldn't kiss you if you didn't want me to. I know that girls like you, your reputation is so important. That if you do the wrong thing you're finished."

Vida studied him. "Don't you want me?" she whispered.

"I'd like to know what you want." The words sounded like an evasion, but the steady way he held her gaze felt like the opposite.

"How would I even know?" Vida had gone trampling

over everyone and everything to take what she thought she wanted, and it had only led to disaster. She was aware suddenly that they were a boy and girl standing on a beach where there was no evidence that people ever had been or ever would be. Just the two of them, in sun-bleached rags, like the only boy and girl on Earth. "I wasn't raised to know. Not really."

Sal's eyes creased. He smiled broadly. "Vida, you're the most remarkable person I've ever met. If you don't know what you want, it's because you haven't asked yourself."

Vida's brow flexed in confusion. "So much talking," she murmured.

The distance between them was about a foot, all of it wild with energy. She could hear his breath, smell his skin. Did she want to kiss him because they were alone on an island together, or because of the black crown of his eyelashes, or because he was mysterious, or because she felt so wonderfully large in his presence? It seemed very important to be sure. And because it seemed important to know for sure, to not be her usual impulsive self, she stepped sideways, away from him, and gazed across the low, damp beach, out across the flat expanse of ocean, and saw . . .

"What in the . . ." she murmured, squinted. There was a little black spot, like a fly on a landscape painting. A shape, way in the distance, like a toy ship on a duck pond.

While she stood alone with Sal, want had bloomed in

her like a wild flowering vine. It was still there; it pulled her like gravity.

But she was distracted from *that* wanting by a desperate curiosity regarding the ship-like thing, this evidence of people beyond this beach, this island. This odd proof that she and Sal were not the only two people on Earth.

And afterward, she would always wonder what might have been if she had not looked away.

"Is that a ship?" she said. Maybe it was a trick of the eye conjuring the thing she had hoped to see every day since their arrival. Then, when she was sure it was not a hallucination, she wondered if it might somehow pass—if it might not notice the island at all—if they might be forgotten twice.

"Yes," Sal said.

Their eyes met again, but the urgency now was of a different kind. They barely spoke as they hurried back up the ridge, along the edge of the island, the wind cold at their ears, both of them seeking each other's gaze, then glancing back to make sure the ship was still there, their stomachs tight and hard with the wretched possibility that it might pass and not know that they were here. That this could well be their only chance.

As they descended along the waterfall, their breathing became noisy and anxious, and they grasped for each other's hands to keep from falling.

"Hurry," she called to Sal. He was coming along behind, but not fast enough. When the camp was in view she became impatient and began to run. "Get the fire lit!" she cried. She was thinking that if they could get the fire going soon enough, they could light torches and climb to the heights and then surely someone on board would notice them, surely the ship would turn, and they would be rescued. This was all she could think of—and what she had recently wanted in the most deep and secret part of herself—or for that matter what was *worth* wanting—shrank in her mind. As she emerged from the jungle, she began to shout and swing her arms overhead. "Torches!" she cried. "Torches!"

But the others, those thirty and some people who had become her whole city, the only world, did not hear her.

Already they drifted from the huts, onto the rocks, down the beach, their mouths hanging open, their gaze intent upon the ship that was making a wide turn in the open ocean. It had drawn a circle around their island and was slowly but surely coming their way, the gray smog of the smokestacks drifting over the pinkening sky.

Vida's shoulders rose and fell. She was trembling all over with the scarcely to be believed possibility that they might be rescued. That they might be found. Within her rib cage was such a war of hope and despair. She didn't like the trailing gray smoke, and yet she feared the huge ship would dissipate into thin air. Her sun-brown legs went rigid. She braced for what was coming. The wind off the ocean lifted her hair, which had been chopped below the ears, and was now a strange amalgamation of strands, curls, knots, and little braids. It was not until the dinghy was coming into the cove, the silhouette of a man standing at the prow while the oars lifted and plunged into the waves, that she considered what a feral creature she must seem.

Like the others, she advanced toward the water with her gaze fixed on the seascape.

As soon as she began to wonder if it was him, she knew it was. Then she knew it more so. Then the golden certainty circled her head, firm as a tight-fitting crown. When the dinghy reached the shallow waters, he leapt out and came striding through the water, his dark pants soaked above the knee, the salt spray gleaming on his face. That same sculptured face she had seen in newspaper illustrations, in ballrooms, that she had imagined in her wedding photo. It was that same sand-colored hair rising above his forehead like a wind-shaped bluff, those blue eyes like a crystal glass of water held against a noon sky.

Fitz was here.

He was alive.

That it was really him was hard to believe. Yet she saw that it was true. The wet sand filled the space between her toes, the skin at the back of her knees itched, she felt crazy, like her head was a balloon that might go flying off into the upper atmosphere if her body let go of its string.

What should I do was a thought she heard, as though it had been asked by a passing stranger. There was nothing to do, nothing obvious, and in a moment she began to cry and laugh at the same time. All she had feared and hoped and dreaded since the night the ship sank rose up, overwhelmed her. Meanwhile Fitzhugh, the real and very alive Fitzhugh, strode through the clear azure waves, sank to his knees at the place where the waves broke and receded, and grasped her hands.

"You're alive," she managed to get out through the stream of hot tears that drenched her cheeks, the laughter that she couldn't manage to get under control.

"I gave you a scare," he observed.

"You're alive," she repeated witlessly.

"I'm sorry. You must have thought the worst. But Vida, Miss Vida Hazzard, I'm here now. I will never let you out of my sight again. I promise. I'm here, and I'm going to take you home and make you my wife."

Beyond him she could see the people in the dinghy bobbing on the water. There were four men sitting at their oars, they were the ones who would row them back to the big ship out in the open ocean. Vida gasped and gasped. Her face was wet with tears, but suddenly she couldn't cry any more. She managed to take a breath, to put a stop to her strange laughing.

"Can I bring you there?" he asked, indicating the ship. "Your mother and father are eager to see you."

For a moment she had no sense of the world. It was so hard to believe. Maybe she was afraid to believe. Yet it must be true what he said. They were all right, everything was all right, her mother and father had survived. Fitzhugh stood and faced her and she couldn't help herself, she needed someone to hold on to, to steady her shaking. She threw her arms around his neck, pressed her body against his chest for support, and whispered, "Thank you, oh thank you, oh thank you so much," into his ear.

PART FOUR

The Fate of the <u>Princess</u>
by Dame Edna Sackville

A concatenation of private rail cars has been
traveling cross-country rather more slowly than is
usual—they have had to cut their speed considerably
before entering a town, on account of the large
crowds that have gathered to welcome the survivors
of the sinking of the <u>Princess of the Pacific</u>, of which
I was famously one. This has been a heartening
experience for all of the survivors, who, as I have
expounded upon in my serialized account, suffered
a trial of body and spirit on a desert island in the
South Seas and were rescued only by the heroic
voyage and return of Fitzhugh Farrar, sole heir to
the Farrar Line after the tragic drowning of his older
brother. Our trip back to the mainland was upon the
grandest of the Farrar ships, which has recently been
rechristened the <u>Vida</u>.

However, several of the survivors have confided

to me privately that they will be glad to finally reach New York, where the Farrar family has put up all members of the island camp in the Waldorf-Astoria indefinitely. The ordeal on the island was of course exhausting, but that is nothing compared to being feted by crowds of thousands! What we all know, and few will acknowledge, is this, my dears: the crowds are particularly vociferous on account of the sweethearts whose union was sealed on the aforementioned island. As you have read in this account, the proposal was of a most dramatic and memorable nature. It is said, though they have been coy about a date, that Fitzhugh Farrar and Miss Vidalia Hazzard, who met as fellow passengers aboard the Princess and began their courtship in a faraway place of swaying palms, will be wed before the year is out. Keep reading this column to learn if this rumor can be credited. . . .

TWENTY-SIX

"What are those?" Vida asked, her palm pressed to the glass in the private salon of the Farrar ferry, which delivered its transcontinental-to-transatlantic passengers from the Pennsylvania Station in New Jersey to the docks of Manhattan, where they might take an evening's rest in one of the city's fine hotels before beginning their journey to Europe. That was her own destination—hers and Mother and Father's. They were all dressed in smart new suits for their first trip to New York City, Vida in a fitted high-necked jacket and skirt of cornflower blue—a shade she could not possibly have worn with her former complexion, but which was quite striking on her now—and a broad, beribboned hat; Mother and Father were in maroon and dark gray. Her life was just as it had been before the *Princess* (parties, dresses) except much grander, and much more talked about in newspapers.

Meanwhile the life she had led on the island had become dreamlike. She knew she had been there, but it did not seem quite real.

Except, sometimes—or maybe, really, if she was being frank with herself, several times an hour—she would close her eyes, and the smell of the ocean and the breeze against her neck and the salt from the sea sticking to her ankles were more tangible than this busy, safe world of railcars and fitting rooms and interviews and celebratory dances. She could almost hear Sal saying:

Look at the world, look at all this wonder, stay still and just look at it, what are you rushing for, what else do you need?

Then the life of parties and social columns seemed the illusion. She would be surprised when she opened her eyes and saw that it all went marching on. That more invitations arrived, and very interesting people sent notes seeking her friendship. There were so many appointments to be kept; it seemed the rest of her life had been planned out for her. That without a word from her, the whole trajectory of her story on this Earth had been written, described in print, heralded before it even took shape. And, all the while, various travel accommodations had been made in her name—she was moved inexorably toward a future she couldn't remember agreeing to. Another day, another place like this: a first-class salon on a train or boat, with all the tassels, crystal lamps, silken settees, and regularly circulating trays of tea or champagne. An aura of luxurious and perfumed quiet that enveloped her thoughts and made her tired.

"What are what?" Fitzhugh, who sat beside her on the sofa, one leg crossed over the other, looked up from his newspaper and glanced at the river. His appearance too had undergone a change—he wore a trim black jacket and chewed his bottom lip as he read the news. Her handsome fiancé, the one she'd dreamed of. Yes, the river was crowded with every kind of ship, skiff, or tug, and beyond the water traffic rose the high buildings and factories of a city unlike any Vida had yet witnessed.

But she had meant—as she had thought would be obvious—the long sheets of white on the blue-gray surface of the Hudson. She pointed: "Those."

"Ice floes," Fitzhugh said.

"I've never seen anything like it," she whispered. "Rivers don't freeze where I come from, they just keep running."

"This one keeps running, too, believe me. The Hudson is a great highway. It brings goods from New York Harbor to the Great Lakes. It must have been damn cold overnight, or those ice floes wouldn't survive with all the boats on the water."

"Isn't it strange?" She meant the feeling of the word in

her mouth. "Ice," she said, to taste this fantastical concept. On the island it had been hot, often intolerably hot. You would have thought she dreamed about ice all the time. But the opposite was true. She'd forgotten its existence. She was about to say this when she realized that it was Sal she wanted to say it to, not Fitz, and then she had tripped once again into a murky room of her consciousness where she felt helpless, and a little stupid, and most definitely ungrateful.

Shouldn't she just feel lucky? Lucky to be alive. To be rescued. To be engaged to the famous Fitzhugh Farrar.

But there were so many things she wanted to ask Sal, and he was always leaving rooms when she walked into them. She was always catching a glimpse of his back, and though she hoped that he would turn, that he would meet her eye, he never did. He would be gone again, and she would be one again with that helpless yearning feeling. The feeling that tugged at her, demanding to know what might have been. Then she'd wonder if she had made it all up—that Sal had wanted her, and she had wanted him. Maybe that was just a delusion caused by too much sun and salt water.

Surely yearning for something back on the island was delusional. What after all would have become of them if they hadn't been rescued? It would have been a nightmare, she reminded herself, not some blissful dream.

"Well, it's frozen water, I don't know if 'strange' is the word exactly. . . ." Fitzhugh folded up the paper and tossed it on the little teak side table. He smiled, put a hand on her shoulder. "Have you ever seen snow?"

"Oh yes, there's a lodge Mother and Father like in the winter. There's plenty of snow in California. But that sounds strange, too, now that you mention it."

"I'm sorry, I wasn't thinking. I've taken this trip a thousand times, but you've never seen the approach to the city. Should we go up to the observation deck?"

"Oh yes, can we?" Vida asked.

They crossed the salon, Vida trailing behind her fiancé, to the wingback chairs where Mother and Father sat, both reading the newspapers that had been delivered to them by servants in Farrar Line livery at the train station as their twenty-seven pieces of luggage were loaded on a wheeled cart to be delivered to the ferry. Having lost one suite of fine bags, Vida had thought this a little ridiculous. But Mother seemed to have learned the opposite lesson from the sinking of the *Princess*, and insisted upon bringing enough spare clothes for a lifetime. Vida had rolled her eyes, but Nora reminded her what a trial Mother had been through, that she should go easy.

"Oh, but do be careful," Mother said now, almost standing up as though to come along with them.

"I know that it will take some time for you to trust this," Fitzhugh said in his steady way, "but I will never let your daughter in harm's way ever again."

Mother smiled and lowered herself back into her seat, and Father patted Mother's knee. "Well, put a fur on, anyway," she said.

The air on the top deck of the ferry was sharp and exhilarating. Vida felt the cold under her cheekbones, behind her earlobes. This despite the fur she had dutifully draped over her shoulders. A city was coming into view—a city unlike any she'd ever seen. It went on and on forever, its forest of docks stretching off the coast of the place, the buildings that rose from its whole length, as far as she could see. She didn't know precisely what lay beyond that first line of cityscape, although she had somehow or other absorbed all the legends of the ladies and gentlemen and their carriage rides around Central Park and their fancy dress in the ballroom of Mrs. Astor and the way they watched each other from across the opera. As she stood, in the middle of a great river, on a ferry surrounded by other ferries, alongside the unattainable bachelor who had seemed the male version of her equally unattainable self, a curious feeling sprang spontaneously from the region of her breastbone, and it was so unnatural that it took her a moment to identify it: she was *nervous*.

"Do you think they'll like me?"

Fitzhugh was leaning against the rail, staring off at the city, and he laughed and glanced at her. "Who?"

"I don't know . . . New York, I guess. Your friends."

"What would make you worry about a thing like that?"

"I'm not worried, exactly. It's only that . . ." Vida's gloved hand floated involuntarily to the back of her neck, where Nora had done as good a job as she could with pins to make it look as though her shorn hair was swept up in some fashionable arrangement. "Well, you don't think it makes me less chic, to have my hair so short?"

Fitz's grin darted to one side. "Oh, Vida," he said, his voice changing, lowering—it was no longer the sure voice of the Farrar scion but something more private. "Is this because I've been a gentleman with you?"

His eyes went over her shoulder, determining who was around. But the other passengers were staring at the city growing larger before them, oblivious to the famous couple in their midst.

"When I was on that raft, in the storm, when the sea was all around me and we seemed certain to drown, I kept thinking of you, thinking of your lips, and I thought that if I could only steer her true, I'd survive and I'd be able to kiss you again." His gaze held hers, and his hand moved to her corseted waist as though to show her how much he'd thought about her body.

Her heart did a pirouette, thinking that he was about to kiss her again, here, in front of everyone.

Holding her waist he leaned in, let his lips hover at her ear. She was breathless, waiting, wondering what he would do. Then he placed a chaste kiss just slightly off the mark of her mouth, and returned to the position he'd been in before—elbows leaned casually against the rail—as though nothing had happened.

"I've been thinking about that a long time," he said, staring out at the river but smiling in a way that she felt was just for her.

Her heart was pounding, although she found herself curiously unable to reply in kind. Not truthfully. Which was odd—she had been the master of a lightly bent truth in the service of getting what she wanted. And getting a boy to kiss her so that he would want to go on kissing her, and thus have to make all the promises that might otherwise be withheld, had ever been her game. But the game did not thrill her as before, and without the game, the moment had lost some frisson. *Say something,* she admonished herself, but before she had a chance, Fitzhugh concluded their conversation.

"Don't worry—they are sure to be impressed by you."

Vida nodded and returned her gaze to the big city growing larger by the second—she was reminded of that long-ago day at the Embarcadero, of the sheer cliff of the *Princess,* of the jittery rush that was the beginning of a voyage, when a girl has a mission and something to prove. She wasn't sure what she wanted now.

Or, she wanted too much.

But something was different on this journey—she was different.

They knew she was coming, of course—she was betrothed to one of their own. But because of the ordeal of the survivors of the *Princess*, she had become rather legendary herself, and she was looking forward to showing them how impressive she was, too. She gripped the rail, and imagined the adventure that lay beyond those piers.

Tried to, anyway.

But that phrase of Fitzhugh's—"I've been thinking about that a long time"—echoed in her thoughts. Her heart clenched. She thought of kisses she had had, and kisses that never were. She wondered for the millionth time what would have happened on that beach the day they were rescued if she hadn't stepped away. If she and Sal had arrived there a little earlier, a little later. Was this her forever? Riding the machinery of the Farrar Company, being carried from one place to another, thoughts of what might have been never far behind.

TWENTY-SEVEN

"I can't wait for it to be over," Vida said in the direction of the three-part mirror, but really to Nora, who was just finishing with the little pearl buttons that went up the back of Vida's lilac satin gown. The neckline revealed a lot of neck and shoulder, the sleeves were airy poufs, the skirt was a mermaid's tail, and Vida had to acknowledge that neither she nor Nora had lost their touch in these matters.

Nora observed her in the mirror. "What part of it?"

From a suite in the Waldorf-Astoria, Vidalia Marin Hazzard, who had been famous in the picturesque backwater of a city where she had been born, had set about making herself a young woman to pay attention to in the hothouse of New York. This was a role she'd been born for. Now that she was on stage she found it was almost too easy. New Yorkers were very impressed by themselves and their city. But to her eyes it was much the same as anywhere—just bigger.

In short order she had become a regular at certain restaurants, tearooms, and dressmakers' shops. She learned to seem to watch a play or an opera while in fact noting from the corners of her eyes who was sitting with whom, and what they were wearing, and whether the particular set of their expression indicated that they felt on good terms with, or excluded by, fine society. She learned the system of streets—grid-like, except where they went all screwy and were laid down at curious, crooked angles—and how to argue with the driver of a hansom cab if he seemed likely to take advantage of her apparent newness. They could not all know that she was soon to be Mrs. Fitzhugh Farrar, of the shipping fortune Farrars, who lived in a Fifth Avenue palazzo that was staffed, on an uneventful day, by fifty-five (on the day of a function, twice that). Vida had come to know this house, too, which would be her house someday. Everything in that house was strenuously formal—the servants wore gloves, and so did the guests, who were announced by the second butler, even if it was just a little tea or something. Vida quickly discerned that a person could live there and, without any special effort, avoid other people who lived there, too. This was, as she admitted to herself and to Nora but to no one else, a relief. Mrs. William Farrar, mother of Fitz and the late Carlton, was a formidable woman, fearsome with her staff, unsmiling with her friends, a woman who traded favors, and whose favor was everywhere sought and rarely to be had. She was a legend, and Vida—who had always thought of herself as the sort of girl who would one day be a legendary hostess herself—*should* have liked her. But try as she might she could not persuade herself that she did.

This was unkind, she knew—Mrs. Farrar had lost her oldest child, and then learned that she would lose her second son in a different way. That she would lose him to a girl nobody had ever heard of. Winning her approval was the sort of campaign Vida used to enjoy. What a delight it was to be underestimated, and then to see the surprise in a person's face when they realized what you were *really* made of! But, at the end of November, when Vida had been a New Yorker of ten days (all of them absolutely snow-smothered and toe-numbing), she found herself in her fancy hotel dressing room being tied into her evening's finery by Nora and afflicted by a malady that she had been heretofore free of: boredom.

"What part are you hoping to be over soon?" Nora asked again.

That was perplexing, and Vida had to turn the question over for a moment or two. "The wedding, I guess."

"Well, it's only another week, you shall have your wish. But I feel I should at least mention that a wedding is usually only the beginning."

"Oh." This sounded true, but it also unsettled her stomach, so Vida babbled in another direction. "Do you remember that night I said, 'What's all this about another boat; I want to go to the party and laugh at all these people who are so easily impressed'? Can you believe that foolish whim got us here?"

"Yes and no," Nora replied easily, and went about busying herself with the strand of freshwater pearls that she had wound around Vida's coiffure to disguise that there wasn't especially much coif. This was Nora at her most irksome: not willing at all to engage Vida's fantasies, her attention set upon the mission at hand. "Here we are. What else can you say? Fitz's man sent up a note twenty minutes ago. I don't think you can keep him waiting any longer."

Vida entered the famous ballroom of Alva Vanderbilt, at Fifth Avenue and Fifty-second, on the arm of the young man she'd campaigned for and who was now hers. The place was a chateau on the outside. Inside it was alive with flowered vines and potted palms; the floors were of black and white marble, and the fireplace was supported by caryatids, and the roof was of carved oak, and all the staircases were massive and curving and may as well have led all the way to the sky. Vida wasn't such a student of interiors—none of the grandeur impressed her particularly. It was always what *happened* in fancy rooms that interested her. The house went on and on, room after room, each a little different but mostly just gleaming with golden accents and astoundingly high ceilings. This was the sort of victorious entrance that girls of social ambition dream about, and Vida—never unambitious herself—should have been giddy with her success. But she was consumed with the thought that everything looked just as she had imagined it would; that this famous place held no surprises.

The only moment when something did *not* look just as she had known it would was when she saw Alva Vanderbilt herself. She was sitting on a chaise surrounded by sycophants, and Vida realized in an instant that the grand dame was no longer the young woman of twenty who once hosted a fancy dress ball to open her house and prove to New York's high society that she was one of them. She was a dowager now, dressed impressively, but not at all in the latest style.

"She's so old-fashioned," said Vida.

"Oh, well, what does she have to prove?" Fitzhugh said, as though her indifference to the changing times was admirable.

But there was something mummified in her that frightened Vida, made it seem that she believed she could win against nature. Like the women on the island who had clung to their modesty, their propriety, their high-necked dresses and their rigid etiquette in the face of the unstoppable weather and the pull and push of the tide. Vida wanted to explain this to Fitz, and knew she couldn't. That she couldn't made her feel alone, even at the center of the swirl.

They advanced beyond this scene and through picture galleries and salons that smelled of cigar smoke—the sound of string music always reaching them faintly from just one room over—and Vida did as she knew she ought, and smiled without showing her teeth or seeming too eager. Vida tried to enjoy the appreciative glances in the direction of her dress—which really were very flattering—and the ripple of interest that followed wherever she went.

At the edge of the ballroom, they came across a couple that Fitzhugh seemed to know well. "This is Adele Jones," Fitz said of the woman, who was festooned in heaps of pale red chiffon. "We've summered together in Newport since we were children."

The men stepped a little away, and bent their polished heads together to confer over something important-seeming in private.

"Pleased to meet you," Vida said, and offered her hand in greeting.

Adele Jones appeared irritated to have been thus abandoned by her companion but she said, "I'm just charmed."

"I'd love to see Newport," Vida went on, undeterred by this minor cut.

"Oh, I'm sure you will. Though our rugged little coast is I'm sure nothing compared to what you've seen with your own eyes."

"How could it be? The island was a beautiful place. I was frightened often, and glad to be found, but you should have seen the view from the summit. The world went on and on, as though there were no people in it."

Adele's face puckered. "Is that a good thing?"

"I wouldn't have thought so." Vida could see that she had gone wrong somewhere. She had been guileless when she should have been alert to the layer beneath what was said aloud, and also the layer below that, and the layer below that again. She had forgotten how rivalrous women could be with each other in these kinds of rooms—how rivalrous *she* had once been. But she went on, determined to explain herself: "I was very in love with grand cities and civilized gatherings and all of that—but I must tell you, there is nothing quite as beautiful as the world with no building or road to mar it, the world brand new but also ancient, everything untouched by the busy agendas of people like us."

"You're too profound for me, dear," said Adele with a smile that was neither warm nor charmed. "But I can see that you've gotten quite a lot of sun. How will *that* look on your wedding day?"

Vida smiled more brightly and held Adele's gaze until Adele was shamed into looking away.

"Vida," said Fitz, turning back from Adele's husband, wearing an expression that began as a warm smile but was tense, alert to trouble, ready to change into something else at any moment. "Will you dance?"

"Oh, yes," Vida said, relieved to leave the conversation she had muddled somehow. She lifted her arms, and let her fiancé place his hands at her waist and wrist and move her backward, into a dance. "I don't think that woman liked me very much."

"I heard what she said. I love how you look. Anyway, she *will* like you. We went around together for a time, so she might take just slightly longer than everybody else to admire you as I do. But she will. They all will. Don't worry."

She was glad she wasn't the same girl as before—the kind who would puzzle over a slight all day and all night. It was easy now to move away from Adele Jones. Whatever she had against Vida didn't matter to Vida at all. She didn't have to play by those rules.

As they moved across the floor, through the rise and fall of bodies, their own frames lifting up off their toes and coming down to their heels as they turned and turned and turned to the music, she experienced that peculiar sensation, that coming back on shore after a long swim.

She missed that sensation—that rocking that was just a memory of being rocked by the sea. "I'm not worried," she said, and her lips parted in a smile that was not about this room, or this moment at all.

"Then what?"

"I was just thinking of this day when I swam out too far in a bad current and Sal followed me—he showed me how to swim along the shore until I was out of it. It might have been scary, but it wasn't. I was so pleasantly exhausted afterward, and it was as though I saw where I was for the first time. Where all of us are, I suppose. It was a good day."

"Vida."

"Oh, dear." She snapped back from the memory, and produced the high tinkling sound of her most effervescent laugh to put him at ease. Why had she revealed so much? Yet she had that crazed feeling, like standing at a cliff's edge with no desire to step back to safety. "Sal's your friend, I know—"

"Vida."

"There's nothing to confess, it's just that—"

"Vida!"

"But we *did* become close. In fact, I felt that—"

"Vida, enough!"

She was startled by the vehemence with which he cut her off. She couldn't think now what she had been about to say. She was confused, unsteady. The mania of the previous moment evaporated. Fitz glanced around, to see if anyone had noticed. But the room was noisy; everyone was a little drunk and consumed with their own business.

"Enough," Fitz said. He said it quietly, but with more force. Vida understood that he was forbidding her from saying more on the topic of Sal. "It impressed me very much how brave you were through the whole ordeal. But now that you are saved, now that we are to be married, you should put it in the past."

Vida felt stung by his vehemence. That he had so forcefully told her what to do. But she could put that away. She had to. She effected a cheery tone. "Yes! You're right, of course. Let's be married, let's have it all over with as soon as possible, and then we can go off with our bags, lightly packed, in search of the next summit."

"Summit?" When Fitz's brow folded up in confusion it had the strange and winning effect of making his eyes seem more blue than the moment before.

It made him look very handsome, and Vida smiled, thinking of how he would look in a little cabin on a remote peak in the Alps. She laughed again, more naturally this time. "Yes. Once the wedding is over you can resume your explorations, to new summits of all kinds, and I'll be with you, of course, to mend the mosquito netting and pick the wildflowers."

"Vida," Fitzhugh said as they reached the edge of the

dance floor. He led them through a doorframe and into a quiet hall.

"Why do you keep saying my name like that?"

"Like what?"

"Like I am a child that must be managed."

"I hardly think you are a child. But I do need you to listen carefully. And understand. I am the sole heir of the Farrar shipping concern, and it would be unseemly for me to risk my life adventuring all over the place. I am needed in New York, to oversee the business. My life is here now." He grasped her hands and met her eyes with an expression of urgent and—she couldn't help but think—humorless conviction. "Our life. You understand?"

"Yes," Vida repeated like a bright student, although the way he was staring at her made her feel rather like he were the man in charge of ticket sales for the Farrar Line and she was a customer being rushed into buying a first-class ticket she did not at all need. "Yes, I understand. I just feel a little faint."

"Do you need some air?"

"Yes—and to be alone for a minute." If she could be alone for a moment, could master herself, she could be the woman Fitz expected her to be. "I'll be back soon."

Fitz nodded, he smiled in his rakish way. "All right. Don't be gone long."

It took a great deal of maneuvering through crowds to find a place that offered fresh air and was not already populated by cigar smokers.

Then, as she was trying to find her way to the servants' quarters, to someplace private and quiet, she saw Sal, moving away from her down a hallway, like he was always moving away from her.

"Wait!" she called. She glanced behind her to make sure no one had heard, then she called out again, louder this time.

He paused reluctantly, as though realizing he couldn't escape. When he turned, his expression was serious—though a momentary smile flickered across his face when their eyes met. Then it was serious again, almost weary.

"What now?" he asked.

"I was just trying to find a quiet place not full of people shouting to be heard, with a little night air. Can you help me?"

His eyes searched the ceiling. "There are a hundred servants here who could help you better than I could."

Vida didn't think that was true. She wanted to say so, but knew she shouldn't. "Why do you keep running away from me?" she asked instead.

"Why?" He smiled again, but sadly this time. He glanced over her shoulder, then back at her. "I don't think you really need to be told why. I had a strong feeling for you. I can't have that feeling now. You're different. You aren't who I thought you were."

The clatter of metal platters falling somewhere close by startled Vida. She was aware of her surroundings—of the chandeliers, but also of the large staff. *I had a strong feeling,* Sal had said. She hadn't known he would be so direct. She wanted him to tell her everything. She was afraid, too. Her pulse raced. Anyone might have heard. "Shhh," she whispered. "Don't," she said. "You offend me. I'm not different. But that was a different place. We have to forget it."

"Yes." Sal gave her a curt little nod. "I know. That's why we should not talk."

He was gone before she could think better of what she had said. Then she was alone in the grand hall. Her throat pained her, but not as much as her heart. Her heart was a field of anguish. She held her belly, wishing she could tear all her frippery off her body.

TWENTY-EIGHT

"Oh, Vida darling, listen to what Dame Edna has written about you now," said Mother from her side of the breakfast table, which was topped with marble, and then with every imaginable pastry.

This mention of her name in the press did arouse a curiosity in Vida, but perhaps not with the naughty pride it might have before—a fact which she tried to tell herself was on account of the excess of champagne she'd imbibed last night. At the current moment Vida was spread across the chaise of the salon in their hotel suite, a cool compress on her forehead, trying her best not to think too much. The region behind her eyes was not at all right.

"Again?" said Father. "You'd think there were no other young women in New York."

"None who have survived a shipwreck and are about to be married!" Mother replied with probably more volume than the situation warranted (though it was entirely possible that was just Vida's impression, on account of the dull ache behind her eyes). "Anyway, she's our Vida—doesn't it please you to see her every utterance lauded in print?"

"Of course it does, dear," Father said, lifting his own paper as though to shield himself from his wife's vociferous defense. He used the opportunity to wink theatrically at his daughter, and add: "But I reserve the right to tease her about it."

"Oh Daddy, stop," Vida replied, and pressed the heels of her palms into her eye sockets.

"Anyway, she writes that you quite impressed that grand Mrs. Vanderbilt with your stories of building thatched roofs on the desert island."

"But not the story of how I hunted wild boar," Vida muttered, rolling onto her side and becoming quite intent upon the raised arabesque pattern of the yellow silk chaise.

"What's wrong with *her*?" Mother drolly sipped her tea.

And Father—Vida supposed—made a gesture that implied she'd been too free with the passing trays of champagne last night.

"Didn't you have fun?" Mother persisted.

It was getting a little silly, she knew—a little unbecoming of a girl who would be a wife by New Year—to be lying on a couch with her back to her parents, pouting over nothing. She mulled her mother's question seriously and said after a few silent moments: "I did . . . just not as much as I *thought* I'd have."

Her father, bless him, didn't laugh, but there was mockery in his voice when he replied, "The horror. Whatever shall we do?"

"Go shopping, probably."

"Yes, good idea, and put it on the Farrar account."

"You're terrible," said Mother, but in an adoring way, so that Vida knew she rather liked the idea.

Vida swung her legs to the floor and gave her silly parents as earnest a face as she could manage and clasped her hands together like she did when she was a little girl. "I always thought I was too big for our little world. That I belonged in ballrooms like last night. You know, the most storied ones. Do you think it's strange that I felt disappointed by that? That I feel disappointed by the whole thing?"

Before, her father had been directing his private asides her way, but now they were addressed to his wife. "What does she mean by 'the whole thing'?"

"Do you think she means what I think she means?"

"Yes—yes, I think she does."

"Vida, darling, Fitzhugh is the perfect match. If you're

313

disappointed by him, I'm afraid you're in the wrong way of life."

Vida had not seen her parents' faces so alarmed since they'd been on board the *Vida*, in those surreal hours where she remembered what a hot bath and an iced drink were like. They hadn't yet trusted their own eyes about their daughter's survival, and she had had to persuade them to let her go off on her own for even a quarter hour at a time. She had hoped in that quarter hour to somehow run into Sal, to see if he was feeling what she was feeling. But that had proved impossible, and meanwhile the machinery of engagement had moved on—it seemed a wedding planner had been hired by wireless, and she couldn't even remember saying yes. "But what if he's not?"

"Oh Vida, you were always like this, even when you were a little girl." Mother sighed from the depths of her being and took the grave step of folding and setting aside *The Daily Chimera*. "You always wanted so much. *Too* much. You will have to learn to be satisfied by someone, or something, and soon, or your life will be aimless, and you won't be anybody at all."

Well. That did sound bad. Vida, chastened, averted her gaze.

She might have taken this very sage-sounding advice as the gospel truth had the genteel little bell not dinged just then, and one of the head concierge's liveried minions appeared. "Pardon me," he said, tilting himself into the room.

"That's quite all right," Vida said, waving away his apologetic tone. "We are a small family of three—we welcome any distractions."

"Very good, mademoiselle. This came for you."

Vida glanced at the small box in the servant's hands, and experienced a strange twisting fear in her gut—what if it was from Fitzhugh, what if it was a beautiful piece of jewelry, and she didn't want to have to send it back, and then she would *have* to marry him? She wasn't even sure why this prospect should frighten her, but it held her oddly frozen between the doorway and the table where her parents watched her.

"Go on, Vida," her mother said, in the tone she had used to tell Vida to eat vegetables as a child. "Take it."

Vida reluctantly accepted the box into her hands. "Thank you," she said.

He dipped his head and retreated through the door.

It was then that she noticed that the box was plain brown—it was not from a fancy jeweler or one of the department stores on Ladies' Mile. She lifted the lid and saw the folded pocketknife, which once upon a time she had used to cut her hair.

"What is it?" Mother asked.

Vida couldn't explain everything it signified. "A blade," she said.

"Oh, no," said her mother. "Oh no, oh no. If you accept a blade as a wedding gift, it means the marriage will fail. Don't you know that?"

Vida was about to find her father's eyes, to share this disbelief in her mother's silly superstitions—that the gift of a knife could sever a relationship for real.

"Well," her father said amiably. "Is it a nice one?"

"Yes," Vida said. Her heart had begun to kick.

"What are you saying?" Her mother had gone pale. "You have to go, give it back immediately!"

"Yes," Vida whispered. The knife had reminded her of something, some true part of herself. She wanted to hold it, but she couldn't stand the idea of accepting it as a parting gift. "You're right."

"Go!" said her mother, worrying her hands.

"I'm wearing a nightgown," Vida protested. All of her wanted to go, wanted to chase after he who had left her the knife. But she was afraid; she was afraid of what that would mean.

"Well," said her mother. "Put a fur over it."

Vida did as she was told. She ran into the hall. "Wait!" she called.

The servant turned at the sound of her voice. "Yes?"

"Who brought this?"

"A young man who works for the Farrar Line."

"When?"

"Just now, mademoiselle."

"Take me to him now. It is of the utmost importance."

The fur coat did mostly obscure the peach frills of her nightgown, and she tried to look dignified as they rushed down the stairs. On the second-floor landing she caught a glimpse of herself—her hair waved, sun-bleached, curling at the chin, the frilly peach skirt of nightgown swishing over the little poufs at the toes of her house slippers, her face tawny as a desert cat. She did consider returning to her dressing room then, summoning Nora, putting on the uniform of smoothed dress and painted face before she did anything rash. But she was moved down the next flight, through the ornate lobby, by a shivery dread that if she did not catch Sal before he left, her whole life would veer in a terrible direction.

"There he is," the bellboy said.

She thanked him and rushed on through the hotel lobby.

"Sal!" she cried to the tall figure about to disappear through the double doors and onto the street. She hadn't meant to be so loud and desperate-sounding. The doormen were implacable, but other guests, loiterers, diners dressed for the grand tea room, glanced her way, and Vida wondered for a moment if she had made a mistake, if she wasn't drawing attention to herself, dressed as she was and rather out of control, if the man about to disappear onto the street wasn't even the one that she had been looking for. It was entirely possible that at this moment (and in every moment that came before) she was wrong about everything.

But then he turned.

It was him.

His hair was tucked up under his brimmed hat, and the light of the chandelier in the lobby reflected in his dark eyes, and his lips bent upward at the corners when he saw Vida and offered her his hand.

"Why did you give me that?" she asked, trying not to show quite so nakedly how happy it made her to see Sal again.

"Oh." The lopsided smile disappeared. "Have I offended you?"

She thrust the box forward. She didn't know what else to do. Emotion gusted through her, pushing her this way and that. And there he stood, infuriatingly, gorgeously placid. He was the same Sal: calm, amused, posing riddles, so that she stood exposed in all her wild feeling. "Did you give me this?" she demanded.

"Of course—didn't you see my note?"

Her cheeks were flushed. "No," she admitted.

"I just thought you should have it—you were so brave

on the island. We didn't talk like this then. But it could have been different. Worse. You showed everyone how to adapt to the place—I think that made the difference. I didn't think you could, but you proved me wrong. You have my—my—" For the first time, Vida saw Sal a little tongue-tied, and it made her heart drop. "You have my admiration," he concluded, finally, with effort. "I'm sorry I said you weren't who I thought you are. Now I know who you are, it's impossible for me to be around you and not allowed to talk to you all the time. That's what the note said. That—and some other things I thought you should know."

"Oh." Vida felt very childish, and drew the box back inside her coat. She itched to open it again, to read the note that Sal had written her. Then she thought of something else. "Are they staring?"

They stood facing each other only a few feet apart. Sal was wearing a navy cloth coat and simple hat, and his eyes were intent upon her. Then they lifted, surveyed all that was behind her in the lobby, and found her eyes again. "Yes."

"I shouldn't have been so loud. I'm sorry."

"That's all right."

"We should go."

"Where? I'd ask you to go for a walk, but your shoes . . ."

Vida put her hand on the elbow of the doorman who had been studiously pretending that he couldn't hear a word. "Would you get us a cab?"

"That's the sort of thing people talk about," Sal said.

"I didn't think you cared about such niceties," she answered, and in that meaningless phrase she knew she made her wishes plain.

A minute later they were situated in the back of a hansom jerking its way through traffic in the direction of Central Park.

Vida removed the box from her coat and put it on her lap. "Why did you give me this?"

"I just told you—"

"Now—why did you give it to me *now*?"

"Because I'm leaving."

"Don't be ridiculous, you can't *leave*."

"A few months ago," Sal said, "you didn't know I existed."

Vida swallowed hard. Her mouth was dry. She wanted to tell him how glad she was to know now. But instead her voice was cold, glib. "I didn't mean you should stay for me, of course. Fitz needs you."

Sal looked away from her. Outside the business of the world went on—men in suits, women in hats, trucks, deliveries, newspapers, their headlines shouted by children on corners. "He employed me as his assistant when he went on explorations, that's all," Sal replied. He sighed, released some bitterness into the winter air. "And there aren't going to be any more of those."

"He told you, too?"

Sal nodded and kept his attention fixed on the white drifts and dark buildings outside the little window of the cab.

"I'm sorry."

"It's all right. It couldn't have gone on forever."

"But you're sad, I can see it."

Sal shook his head at the passing scene, the droves of people in furs and dark hats, on sleds, on horseback. Then he turned back. Vida felt overwhelmed with gladness to see his curious, off-kilter smile. "Not because of that."

They had entered the park, and were jostled along its path by a pair of horses dressed in their own flannel coats. "I was thinking of you last night," she said. "I was remembering how when we came out of the ocean I could still feel the movement of the waves."

"Yes," Sal said. "I remember that too."

They sat in a comfortable silence as the carriage moved through the very manicured nature of the big park at the center of Manhattan. The trees were painted white by an early winter snowfall. Eventually the driver reversed course, and she knew they were heading back to the hotel, and Vida felt a strange grasping within, as though something very precious had disintegrated, become sand, and was slipping through the narrow of an hourglass; that if she didn't think of something very clever soon she would lose it without ever knowing what it was.

"Here we are," Sal said.

"You should take the cab back wherever you're going, and tell them to charge it to our suite."

"All right."

"All right then."

"It was nice knowing you."

"Yes." She could think of nothing suitable to the moment that was building inside her and taking on frightening force. "It was."

Sal was looking at her in his bemused way, and she suddenly felt very foolish.

"I'm sorry, I'm being very stupid. You're laughing at me. You don't know why I'm still here."

"No, I just want to remember you like this. In the morning, with no makeup, and your hair not brushed at all. Like you were there."

Vida's mouth formed around a response that she could not summon. She was thinking of that afternoon on the beach, of the moment just before the moment when she saw the little ship in the distance. Sal had said something to her. He had just said something that was really important. It had been lost in the excitement of what happened next, but she hadn't forgotten it. It was here now in her thoughts. He'd said that she was strong, and that if she didn't know what she wanted, then it was because she hadn't tried to know.

She asked herself—she asked, *What do I want?*

And then quite unexpectedly her fingers fluttered up, brushed his lips, his jaw, gently pinched his earlobe. The space between them shrank. A sharp winter breath filled her chest and her mouth found his mouth. For a moment he did not respond—yet she knew she had not made a mistake. Then he returned the pressure of her kiss, and she knew what it was to want and be wanted in equal measure.

The carriage was rocking to the gait of the horses and the uneven pavement of the city as they kissed. They kissed again, and his hand found her hair, and his nose brushed her nose. He sighed, his whole body seemed to sigh, and she felt the sigh move through her, too.

Then she heard the driver's hand on the door handle and she drew back as quickly as she could.

"Mademoiselle," said the driver.

Panic froze Vida's features. "When will I see you?" she asked. Already the driver was supporting her, was very nearly lifting her and placing her down on the street.

"Now you understand why I have to leave. I've already booked passage, for Friday night."

"That's the day after tomorrow."

"Yes."

She was trying to think of something sensible to say but her brain was uncooperative. "The night of the party."

"Yes."

"But," she said stupidly, desperately, "you *must* go to the party."

"I'll come, then, to say goodbye."

She could feel the eyes of the driver on her, and beyond him, the eyes of all the windows of all ten stories of the Waldorf-Astoria Hotel. Her clothes were loose but the rest of her life was constricting, was holding her tight, limiting her movements. "Well, in that case, I will look forward to seeing you there," she said in as impersonal a voice as she could manage, and curtsied as best she could, before retreating, under the golden awning, where she watched the carriage draw away from the hotel, its wheels finding the darkened grooves in the snow before disappearing into the uptown traffic.

TWENTY-NINE

Celebration to be held for the next Mrs. Farrar
by Dame Edna Sackville

This evening, at the house of Winthrop Farrar, the shipping magnate, and his wife, the former Isabella Carlton, a period of mourning for their elder son will end, and a period of celebration will begin. A party shall be held to formally announce the engagement of Fitzhugh, the younger son and now sole heir of the family concern, to Vidalia Hazzard, the daughter of a prominent San Francisco family and one of the survivors of a trial on a desert island which was covered in a thrilling, much celebrated four-part serial by this column. The fast set are all competing with one another to look their best. Not invited? Don't fret, I am—the bride-to-be is a particular friend of mine, and you can read all the details tomorrow in these pages.

Days of frantic and competing newspaper accounts had whipped up a frenzied public interest in the engagement party being thrown at the Farrar Palazzo on Fifth Avenue, with the unhappy result that deliveries had to be made through a difficult-to-part crowd, and many ill-starred oranges had rolled from crates carried aloft, been ground by sundry boot heels into two-days'-old snow. At dusk, a police detail arrived to clear a path for the guests to be carried over the slush at the gutters and to the mauve carpet that had been laid over the limestone steps to protect the elegant footwear of the members of New York's oldest and best families—eminent ladies and gentlemen who were also, in their own understated way, manic with curiosity about the event.

Vida drifted toward it, pulled on by the tide. Her mind thought only of Sal, of his breath and the words he had written to her and the way she felt when she was with him. But she could not figure out what do about that. There was no answer. So she allowed herself to be feted, to be dressed, to called upon and talked about.

Although the Farrars had sent one of their own carriages to fetch young Vida from the Waldorf-Astoria, she had observed from the hotel's second-story drawing room how the curious crowd had noted the intricate *F* and *L* design painted on its shiny side. How they mobbed the carriage and would not yield their place! She was shocked, and a little frightened, by how determined these strangers were for a sighting of the young woman from a faraway land who they had been following in the columns, and who had already gone through all the trials necessary to be transformed into an American princess. Vida, a little afraid of them and what they wanted from her, had asked the concierge to take her out the back way and put her in a plain hansom.

Now, waiting in line with the other carriages to arrive at the lowest step of that mauve carpet, Vida peered out. She knew she would not disappoint the crowd. She was wearing a Doucet gown of sky blue chiffon that was embellished all over with tiny specks of coral, and a delicate little white gold tiara nestled in her hair, and an enormous ermine. She had rouged her cheeks and darkened her lashes and brightened her eyes with little drops.

Every minute detail of her appearance met the requirements of fairy tales. She could win their love, she knew; but this masterful social coup, which she would once have delighted in, felt overwhelming now, like a rich dessert after a ten-course supper.

"You're not yourself," Nora observed from the seat across.

"No."

"Well, you *look* yourself."

Vida's eyes darted from the scene outside the carriage to Nora. "Not too suntanned?"

"Just the right amount to remind everyone of your exciting journey to this moment."

When the door of the cab was pulled back by a Farrar footman and the crowd saw who it was, they roared. The chanting of Vida's name startled a flock of birds perched on a nearby tree, and their dark silhouettes filled the violet sky. She was lifted by a footman, ferried in his arms over the slush and up the first few steps.

Upright and on her own two feet again, she felt the full brunt of the crowd's adulation. She saw the beaming faces of children and young women gazing at her, illuminated with the hope that she who had everything would bestow a little good luck on them. To her their energy seemed a slow, gentle wave, and she was sorry for her hesitating. The sweet bath washed over her, and she lifted her hands, wanting to offer something back in return. They were still calling her name, cheering for her, when another footman appeared on the top step. The Farrar machinery kept on, too fast for her to resist, and as though she were another piece of luggage being moved along, she was borne through the grand doorway and into another realm.

The foyer was paneled in dark mahogany and dense with the smell of hundreds of white mums in ormolu vases. After the grand steps of the Farrar mansion, this place had an odd hush, although she could hear the murmurs and music of a party already underway in the next rooms. Her coat was removed from her shoulders. She glanced back for Nora, but Nora was already being led down an unobtrusive little staircase to wherever the servants waited for their masters to be in need of them, and Vida herself was proceeding along a Persian runner, between the liveried sentries who stood stoically waiting for her to pass as she moved onward to the brilliant center of things.

And somewhere, in all of this, was Sal. He had promised her. She would see him, and then she would finally know what she should do.

The Farrar ballroom was speckled with chandelier light and packed with black frock coats and swirling gowns and the flash of eyes wanting to know who else had arrived, and whether or not their appearance was especially eye-catching or just your average, everyday sort of decadence. Vida knew precisely what they were thinking, for she had thought in much the same way for many years of her life. She wanted to survey a room of fine people dressed their absolute best, and feel her place atop the invisible hierarchy of coveted invitations and elegant possessions and incomparable taste. And for a moment her old self felt gratified by this confirmation of her ability to win the attention of anyone, anywhere that she pleased. That ripple of triumph to have all eyes on her and know how far she had risen.

The crowd parted for her, and she saw Fitzhugh, the shine of his hair catching the light, and the blue of his eyes a perfect match for her dress. Instinct propelled her. She smiled with a closed mouth and floated toward him. When she arrived at his side, his elbow hooked hers, and they began a slow rotation through the room. The moment with Adele Jones at the Vanderbilts' really was an aberration—she felt nothing but a warm, envious awe from the crowd now.

"Mother is thrilled that the press will be moving on from the sinking of the *Princess*," Fitzhugh said as, arm in arm, they moved from one grouping of old family friends to another.

"How could they not?" Vida replied with winning confidence. At just that moment she saw her future mother-in-law through the crowd, wearing spangled purple. She was in conversation with the Duke of Lemmon, and when she felt Vida's gaze, she tilted her head and met it with her own. For a moment the two women regarded each other across a sea of tulle. Then the elder lowered her lashes, and returned to Vida the same exact closed-mouth smile that Vida had just been bestowing on all the world.

A sense of clarity settled around Vida's temples. She knew she had the woman's respect now; that the grand Mrs. Winthrop Farrar would not turn away from Vida in subtle dismissal again. Unlike Vida's own parents, Mr. and Mr. Farrar read all the papers, and they surely knew that the discussions of the Farrar Line's stock price in the wake of the sinking of their newest ship on its maiden voyage were bad for business, and that having the Farrar name on the front page for another reason would be to all of their advantages. This revelation did not wound Vida. In fact it was the sort of coup that she had always delighted in. She wasn't worried about having Fitzhugh's true affection— if she didn't have it now, she would in time, as she always eventually won everybody over. Great hostesses had gotten their entrée into society in worse ways.

"You mustn't think—" Fitzhugh glanced at her, realizing what an unromantic thing he had said.

"I understand perfectly. Don't worry, I'm not so delicate as to be offended by the ways of the world."

"No." Fitzhugh winked at her, and she winked back, and for a moment she remembered the night they met, how she had watched him playing the game of society as well as she played it. How much she'd wanted to meet this male version of herself.

She remembered it all, as she might remember a story vividly told by someone else. She gazed at Fitzhugh, trying to see him anew. He had inherited his strong jaw and blue eyes from his mother, and it seemed to Vida a sure sign of what he would become. Not daring, but shrewd; a man who could read a room and play it to his advantage. Well, Vida reminded herself, that was who she was, too. Unsentimental, ambitious. Yet she could not escape the sense that she had set her eyes on a great prize, and that it was disappointing that it should be so easily won.

Every inch of the room was encrusted in something gold-colored, or in polished wood, or strung up with velvet, or painted in oils. And yet it felt small to Vida, and very cramped. There were so many people between her and a door, and she had a sudden desperate need for a wide-open space and a view of the world from a solitary height.

Who was she? Sal had seemed to know, but he was nowhere to be seen now, and anyway he had never been inclined to tell her how to act or who she ought to be.

"Where's Sal?" she asked.

"Sal?"

"He said he was leaving tonight—I wanted to say goodbye." She wasn't sure if Fitz's long expression was because she had reminded him of the loss of his friend, or because he suspected what Sal meant to her. Or because he already knew. "We spent a lot of time on that island," she said quickly. "We were friends, too."

"Of course. Well, ask the butler—but he's probably gone already. That's Sal's way. He doesn't like good-byes. He just likes to be gone."

"Gone?" Vida wasn't in control of her face.

She wasn't sure how she left Fitz.

Crossing that room was like fording a wide river.

There were so many people in the way, and she needed badly to get past them, around them. But everyone wanted to take her hand and whisper a blessing. She was half-mad during the eon it took her to find the butler. Then she wasted yet more precious minutes trying to convince him that she really did want to see Sal—*that* Sal—and that yes, it must be now.

Now. Her mind was wild; she was so flushed. Time kept ticking away and she wanted to tell everyone now, now—she must see him now. Why, why had she not acted till now?

In the lower levels of the house, in the servants' quarters, she could hear all the stamping and talking above. After so many days so congested with events, with things, with shopping and learning new names and new streets, she was grateful for the relative quiet. She would have traded the world hammering at the ceiling above to have one more minute in the cab with Sal.

To know what would have happened if they had gone on kissing.

What the next kiss would have been like, and the one after that.

To know what might have been on the island if they had never been rescued.

"What, *Sal*?" said the housekeeper, emerging from her office and glancing sidelong at Vida's ornate dress. The butler was with her, and Vida felt sorry for interrupting what might be their one moment of rest all day. "But he left hours ago."

How could she explain? She couldn't. She just let her emotions be obvious on her face. "Please," she said. "Please help me. I have to find him."

The housekeeper's eyes rolled to meet the butler's. They seemed to converse without words. Then he nodded at her, she sighed as though she had seen it all before, and they hustled Vida into a plain cloth coat, and then into one of the cabs waiting at the side door, telling the driver to make haste to the Farrar pier.

THIRTY

"Careful, miss!" cried the stevedore as she rushed by him. "The dock is icy."

"Thank you," Vida called back. But she was heedless. Her cheeks flared pink in the cold air. The pier was crowded, but the scene looked puny and insignificant under the endless night. The white haze of previous days had cleared. She could see the stars—they were fewer, strewn in a different pattern, than the stars over the island. Yet those pinpricks in the curtain of the sky seemed to whisper of a vast and unknown world. "Wait," she called back to the stevedore, "where is the Farrar pier?"

"Third from the far end, miss!"

She tried not to run. But she couldn't help herself. She

felt exactly like a romantic heroine in her fine dress and a plain coat, moving as fast as she could through crates and pyramids of trunks to catch the ship before it departed. She could picture herself just how Sal would see her when he spotted her from the top deck.

She would be breathless, and he would have stars in his eyes.

He would be waiting for her to come, and she would appear at just the right moment.

And whether their second kiss would happen as soon as they found each other, or would be weeks in coming, was just another mystery sweetening on her tongue.

This picture was so vivid in her mind that she did not at first believe what she saw beyond the Farrar kiosk.

On the black water of the Hudson with its shimmery ice floes was the transatlantic steamer, trailing its wake of churning white foam, still large but growing smaller by the second. Her heart was pounding crazily. How badly she wanted to be on that ship, and how impossible it was to cross the water and reach it. Vida felt too broken by this impossibility to weep. She wanted to cross that freezing water that now separated her from Sal, but couldn't. She wanted to drown in it.

She had been lucky in so many ways. Above all, she had been lucky enough to meet her true self. And she had abandoned that person for a world of gowns and parties she did not even like. Vida would have traded any treasure in the world to have Sal's gaze on her, to feel his fingertips brush over her hair, down her neck. But that was gone—that was all gone now.

As she returned along the pier she saw nothing, heard nothing.

All she felt was her own fury at being unable to go back in time, to make it so that she had arrived earlier. When she arrived on the street she wasn't sure of her own name or address, she was heedless of who saw her, who witnessed her in this state, who might understand what she was up to and spread stories of her badness. So it took her a long time to realize it was her name that a woman was calling.

"Vida, darling!"

Then her focus became sharp, and she saw Camilla in the open doorframe of a waiting cab. Whereas previously her heart had pounded wildly, now it was quiet as the moon. Vida remembered Camilla watching her on the island. Could Vida still trust her as she had then?

"Don't worry," Camilla said as she arrived at Vida's side. "Nobody knows I came."

"How did you know where to find me?"

Camilla lowered herself from the carriage, and lifted her skirts up so as to not muddy them in the slush, and came to Vida. "I saw you leaving the ballroom," she said, and gathered a fistful of Vida's skirt, and put it in Vida's hand, so that her hemline would also be protected as they made their way back into the waiting cab. "And I recognized the wildness in your eyes. Mr. Hess, the butler, told me where you were going. He used to protect my secrets, too."

"Oh."

"Come on, it's a big party, no one will have noticed that you were missing."

"You don't think so?"

"All women get overwhelmed at parties that are held in their honor. It would be strange if you *didn't* go off to be with your maid and have some sherry to fortify you for the rest of the night."

"Is that how it always is?"

"Of course not. There's much stronger stuff than sherry." Camilla smiled wanly. "Once you're married you'll find out about that. I'll help you. Don't worry."

That wasn't what Vida had meant to ask about, but she felt too blown apart to make any sense. They did not speak again. Camilla took Vida's hand in hers, and Vida knew from the warmth of her grasp that Camilla wasn't going to tell the Farrars where Vida had gone. Camilla knew exactly what to do—which side door to tell the driver to stop at, how to navigate the warren of servants' stairs, so that they arrived back in the great ballroom of the Farrar mansion as if from a little reprieve on the terrace.

Although Vida felt that she had just traveled a vast distance, nothing here had changed.

How long had she been gone? So much had happened. Yet here everything was as it had been. Except maybe there were more people crowding the dance floor, and their talk was louder, and the excitement had reached a manic pitch.

"Give a little wave to Fitz and Mother so they notice you," Camilla whispered in her ear. "And let's go to the ladies' lounge and have some brandy so you can get your wits back."

Vida lifted her hand in the direction of her fiancé and allowed herself to be led.

The brandy stung her mouth and snapped her back to this place. To the rose-flocked wallpaper, the statuary and lamps, the footstools and cut flowers of the ladies' lounge.

"What is this all for?" Vida said. It seemed like a dream.

"Don't ask questions like that, they will drive you mad."

"You're right. I know you're right. The girl I used to be would never ask nonsense questions like that."

"Good. It's good you're talking that way. Here, have some more," Camilla said, lifting the cut-glass bottle to refill the crystal tumbler in Vida's hand. "Don't worry, you'll forget."

"So you did know, when you saw us on the island?"

"I haven't the faintest idea what you're talking about."

"Please don't be coy with me."

Camilla's beautiful face was blank as a page.

"Please," Vida repeated pathetically.

Camilla sighed and looked at her hands. "I didn't know then. It was all so strange there. It was the expression on your face in the ballroom tonight. I knew that face," Camilla's eyes found Vida's, "because I often wore it myself."

"Because you were torn between two men."

"Yes."

"You were in love with one man, and married to another."

"Yes, something like that." Camilla removed the tumbler of brandy from Vida's unsteady hand. "Your heart is frantic now. I can see its flutters through your dress. But these passionate impulses, they go away. Today I would trade anything to have my husband back, though he never thrilled me the way—the way the . . . other did."

"But what if it doesn't?" Vida whispered. "What if the happiest I will ever be was on that beach? What if this feeling I have for Sal doesn't ever really go away—what if it just withers and dies from neglect?"

"Then I suppose you had better go find him. But Vida, I know you. I see who you are, what you want. Isn't it this—a very grand life, tours of Europe, new clothes every season, belonging to that rarefied company who decides who eats at the best tables, who is invited into the finest rooms, and who isn't?"

"Well, yes," Vida sighed. That *had* been what she wanted. When Camilla put it that way it seemed ridiculous to disavow an old and long-held dream for something that had already sailed so easily into and out of her grasp.

"Good," said Camilla. "Now drink this up and let's go down."

Vida did as she was told. When she stood up she was dizzy and the room dazzled her with the stars that exploded in her field of vision, and she was glad of Camilla's support as she moved into the hallway. "But Sal. On the island we were . . . we could have . . . I felt that . . . what I mean to say is, what if I love him? What if I love Sal? What if that was real love?"

"Hush," Camilla said.

There, suddenly, and then passing very close in the other direction, was Dame Edna Sackville. *Where did she come from?* Vida wondered. Then she felt the keenness of the gossip's gaze, it was blinding, and saw the emerald of her gown, so reminiscent of another, long-ago party. When Vida saw it she remembered the way Dame Edna had described her in the column—the glamorous Miss

Hazzard—and she straightened up and tried to look the part.

But her heart wasn't in it. She felt hollow inside and couldn't move her face at all; Camilla had to nudge her back in the direction of her fiancé.

THIRTY-ONE

For the second time that week, Vida woke up shaky all over. There was a piercing, throbbing feeling somewhere in the region behind and just south of her smooth forehead. When she moved too quickly her stomach lurched and she knew she must not do that again. In the not-so-distant past, she had experienced days of dehydration and hunger, sunburn, and the innumerable agonies of living mostly outside without any suitable footwear. The combination of the feeling behind her forehead and the complaints of her stomach was, without qualification, much, much worse.

She had only herself to blame.

After she and Camilla returned to the ballroom, there had been champagne, and after the champagne had come burgundy, and after burgundy there had been champagne again. The waiters had made it easy, but it was undoubtedly she who had accepted. Just as Camilla had promised, no one else noticed her despair. But still, she had wanted to be anywhere else. Champagne had, briefly, taken her somewhere else.

That throb behind her eyeballs blunted her memory—she was sure that there were some things she didn't remember at all. And yet other scenes rose in her mind, vivid and shaming.

Scenes of her too-loud laughter, her too-exuberant dancing, scenes of her gossiping spitefully with whomever had gossip worth hearing.

Someone had laid out the morning papers beside a carafe of water and a silver urn of strong tea. But why say "someone"? That *someone* was Nora, of course—Vida just didn't like thinking of how Nora must have had to help her out of her dress, how Nora must have seen her so pathetic and awful. Vida had been rescued at sea, so she knew what it was to be saved, and yet it was nothing compared to the gratitude she felt regarding Nora's circumspect kindness this morning.

With a teacup and saucer carefully cradled in one hand, Vida lifted the pile of newspapers and placed them on the coverlet. The front page of the *New York Star* had run an illustrated picture of her dancing with Fitz, and though she looked a little more gay than she supposed was strictly appropriate, the pen-and-ink version of herself did seem to be having fun, and wasn't that her job as the newest member of the Farrar empire, to distract from other troubles by seeming fun?

The Daily Chimera was beneath the *Star*, and Vida's breath stopped momentarily when she saw the little gold-edged notecard.

For Miss Vida Hazzard
Compliments of Dame Edna Sackville

She didn't know why it should seem ominous, so she shooed away her foreboding. The picture on this front page was also of her, though it was a portrait that had been done back in San Francisco, and there was something about her likeness that was unmistakably not *quite* as chic as it would have been if it had been done in New York. She drank more tea, thinking everything would be better again soon, and she opened to the page where her story would be told.

She read that page's headline with a detached curiosity: *Secret Island Liaison of Farrar Fiancée!*

Such was the pitiful malfunctioning of her brain that she had to think another moment before concluding that *she* was the fiancée in question; that the liaison was a speculative one to do with Sal and not with Fitzhugh; and that Fitzhugh was the one she was engaged to be married to.

She herself was Vida—she didn't think it could hurt to just remind herself of that point for clarity's sake, given the fragile state of her poor mind.

Then she reminded herself to breathe. Breathing was awfully important.

Her eyes skimmed the article, which had no details of a liaison, and was entirely based on a few words overheard in a ladies' lounge. Words that Vida herself had said, she knew, but which had been twisted around suggestively so that it sounded like much more had happened than actually had. Dame Edna was a genius at suggesting carnality without ever saying anything very straightforward.

When Vida reached the last sentence, she refolded the newspaper and put it aside.

Then she saw that the notecard had a note scribbled on its back side.

Dear Vida,

I'm sorry we won't be allies. I did have such high hope for your social career. But things being as they are, I can see that you are going to deprive me of my big wedding story, and I had to get ahead of my competitors. You'll understand.

I wish you luck, whatever you do.
D.E.S.

The cold-bloodedness of it was shocking, but also rather bracing. Vida put aside the papers and the note and the tea. Her hands functioned well; her mind was becoming nimble again. She turned toward the nearest mirror to have a look at herself. Oddly, a smile was spreading across her face.

Vida was led by a waiter through the empty private dining room on the third floor of the Waldorf-Astoria. The walls were lined with portraits of men in double-breasted suits with drooping walrus mustaches and a glint in the eye that signified, to Vida anyway, their ability to win and hoard great wealth. Otherwise everything in this place was the same mahogany color. A beam of sunset came through the far window, and this seemed wrong, somehow. Sun did not belong in this place where men smoked cigars and spoke of industry. She was glad she had worn a new suit in a dark shade of blue—fitted to her small body, but not too showy.

When he heard her approach, Fitz glanced up from the papers spread before him.

His face was drawn and sad. His eyes were tired. She had an instinct to go and comfort him, but sensed she should wait to be asked to sit down.

"You've seen the papers."

Fitzhugh's fingers drummed the table. He took in her expression, and then he glanced at the window. "In a moment, my family's public relations man will be joining us, and we will discuss how exactly we'll go about refuting this false story, and what sort of retribution is suitable for Dame Edna. He'll want to know if Dame Edna seemed a little daffy on the island? If she drank too much seawater perhaps? But first, I want to know *how* not true it is."

"Excuse me?" Vida was still thinking about the prospect of retribution, wondering what was meant by that, and hadn't quite understood the subtlety of Fitzhugh's question.

"You say it's not true, and I believe you," he said evenly. "But Sal is my friend. He was before he quit abruptly and went off, anyway. I can see he was fond of you. I want to know—is there any truth to the story?"

Vida's throat ached and she had to lower her eyes to the floor. She couldn't quite bring herself to answer, so she just swung her head in a way that wasn't quite an affirmation or a denial.

"In what way *is* it true?" Fitz persisted.

Vida's eyes were wet. She steeled herself, met Fitz's narrowed gaze. "It wasn't a 'liaison.' He never touched me on the island. It wasn't like that. We became close, that's all, and after a while without meaning to I found that I wanted to be around him more than anything else."

"And what do you want now?"

The truth tumbled out of her. She wasn't sure she could have dissembled now if she wanted to. "The same thing," she said.

Fitz folded his hands before him on the table. He seemed very tired, and Vida wondered if he didn't want her to retreat from the room, and from the city, as quickly and soundlessly as possible. But that wasn't it. He inhaled deeply, and she remembered his old trick of inflating himself, of making his body and his presence larger than it was in any literal, physical sense. "A marriage is long, and much of it is a kind of business arrangement. Together you build a public front behind which a home is maintained and wealth is accumulated. One of the reasons I so liked you was that you seemed to understand that. We can fix this, Miss Hazzard. The public relations man is very good, and he thinks Dame Edna has overplayed her hand one too many times. The people adore you, he says, and a sympathetic portrait in other newspapers will right things, and the overall good for the Farrar firm of having a wedding in the papers at a time like this cannot be ignored, regardless of whether it carries a slight whiff of scandal or not. But I do really care for you, Vida. If I am sounding overly practical, that is because I am now in charge of my family business. I am not the younger son anymore. But I care for you, and it matters to me what is in your heart. So I will ask you again, what do you want?"

"I'm sorry, Fitz," she said. "I want the same thing as I wanted before."

Fitz looked away from her and very slowly took one of the papers in front of him, flipped it, and put it facedown on another pile.

She waited for him to say something, and when he didn't, she asked in as strong a voice as she could manage: "Do you know where he has gone?"

The face that lifted toward hers was entirely unfamiliar to her. There was an anger in his blue eyes that she had never seen before, and the "No" that he pronounced, before looking away from her again, cut her more than a string of shouted obscenities would have. As Vida turned away from him, she felt weighed down with all she had so suddenly lost.

But as she walked to the doorway she became lighter with every step. Perhaps it was only that she had set down an enormous burden in that room. As she left it and arrived in the hall she felt so weightless she thought she might actually lift off the carpet and take flight. She could hear her heart again; it had been beating steadily all this time. The elevator doors opened and she went in.

THIRTY-TWO

In the days that followed, Vida shed other poundage. She gave away all but one trunk's worth of her new clothes to Nora. She said her goodbyes to Camilla, and suggested that Nora be hired immediately as her lady's maid. But Nora said she had been keeping company with Jack, who she'd gotten to know on their cross-country journey, and that Jack was sailing away soon, and that they couldn't stand to be apart—she was going to take a position on his new ship and be his wife. So Vida packed her own trunk with some clothes and personal effects and the little knife that Sal had given her, the blade that reminded her who she was and what she really wanted.

The legend of Vida Hazzard—that plucky and brilliant

girl from San Francisco who had survived the open ocean and a desert island, who had very nearly made the match of the century and then been quite publicly ruined—began to change, too. At first the crowds outside the hotel were even more rabid. The calls from other reporters were unceasing. A publisher offered her a heap of money for her memoirs; a theater producer insisted her story must be brought to the stage. But when neither she, nor her parents, nor Nora, nor Camilla responded to these entreaties, or to the gathered crowds, the interest began to fizzle. Public attention returned instead to Fitzhugh, who was said to have been seen around town in the company of Adele Jones.

That did smart a little.

The Vida who liked to get what she set out for, who had gone to great lengths to win that which she was told she could not have, became alert again, did think over what she would have to do to take back her prize. But she went on a long walk and waited for her desire for a grand life to come again. It didn't. Instead, some new desire led her to a bookstore on Broadway, where she purchased several travel guides to the Mediterranean region, as well as a history of the ancient world, and another one that told the stories of several prominent volcanoes.

On the day she set off Mother's lip trembled, but she was brave and didn't cry.

Father smiled—it was a sad smile, but mixed with a kind of grudging, adoring pride.

"I'll write all the time," Vida promised.

"Good," her mother said, and held her close awhile. "I hope you will be very happy."

"I think I will," she said.

"I only ever wanted you to be happy," Mother went on, not letting go. Vida had always thought her parents were a little silly, but they surprised her now—they seemed to understand that Vida was seeking something true, and to want that for their only daughter. "You always wanted so much. I thought getting you as much as possible would make you happy forever."

"I thought so, too. But maybe what I wanted all that time was less."

How much less was only really apparent in the simple cabin that she occupied by herself with the contents of her one trunk and the books that she had purchased on the long solitary walk that she had taken down the wilds of Broadway. But with less, she found, you can see and feel so much more.

With less, she might for instance find herself alone on the top deck of a steamer crossing the Atlantic at dawn and understand that one does not dwell in the busy cities of men, but on the great curve of the watery Earth. She might feel, in some deep and ancient corner of her mind, the true romance of the ocean. She might find in some dusty old books she had acquired almost by accident, on a day when she was looking for something else, clues to where she is going, and how she will search out what she truly wants.

She might discover, too, that journeys are always longer and more arduous than what one has carefully planned. That a girl will sometimes find herself in shabby port cities, with only second-rate hotels. That she will despair of ever finding the right port. She will be brought to tears over how difficult it is to order the right dinner in a language she doesn't speak, and this will be made all the worse by the knowledge that she is being conspicuously ridiculous. But then she might also learn that second-rate hotels have their own charms, that there are far worse fates than being ridiculous, and that every port can teach a girl a little more how to be oneself in the world.

And as she travels she will acquire a kind of easy certainty.

She will begin to be sure, without knowing exactly how it will happen.

Maybe she will find Sal on his Mediterranean island, maybe she won't.

Some deep confidence of the heart begins to tell her own story.

EPILOGUE

Maybe it happens like this . . .

Vida's ferry arrives at dusk at a rather dusty port. Representatives from the little hotels in the village built into the high cliffs appear, enthusiastic in their pleas that she choose their establishment over the others. Donkeys decorated in colorful tassels and pom-poms carry her luggage up the steep path. She asks if there has been another American in the village, but the people at the port, unaccustomed to an accent like hers, shrug in confusion, evade the question. She looks around. No, there is no American in the crowd, no tall boy in plain clothing.

She thinks, as everyone on any voyage of true consequence thinks from time to time, that she has made a terrible mistake. She wishes herself transported home, and consoles herself that she will have a night in a hotel room and a good breakfast in the morning and she will write a cheery postcard that she almost believes and then she will book passage back the way she came.

For some girls that might be the end of the adventure.

For some it might even be the right choice.

But Vida remains, as always, determined. She has come a great distance already.

On the island she had learned to be especially observant of the way waves break against rocks. She listens now to the sounds of the sea. She glances toward the end of the docks, wonders if there might be another little dock just around the outcropping. And so she goes on, takes the simple plank walkway that bends around the outcropping, and there she finds another cove with a smaller port, where the fishermen bring their boats in to avoid the big ships at the big port. The fishermen are hauling their nets, spreading their catch on the pier, shouting to each other in a language she can't understand at all.

And then she sees him.

He's sitting on a lone chair outside a simple restaurant, with a week-old American newspaper that he isn't really reading folded up in his lap.

And he looks back, not surprised at all, and says, "How did you find me?"

ACKNOWLEDGMENTS

This book was mostly a smooth sail, and that's all due to my wonderful editors. Thank you to the great Sara Shandler. Thank you to the brilliant Alice Jerman. Thanks to my friends at Alloy who have been marvelous collaborators for a long time now: Josh Bank, Joelle Hobeika, Hayley Wagreich, Romy Golan, Les Morgenstein, and the rest of the team. Thanks to Erica Sussman, Alexandra Rakaczki, Clare Vaughn, Christina MacDonald, and everyone at Harper. Thank you Joe Veltre and Tori Eskue and everyone at Gersh. Thanks to Adrienne Miller, Ryan Hawke, Hannah Tinti, Darin Strauss, Anne Heltzel, Jessie Gaynor for readerly and writerly support. Thanks to everyone I've learned from in teacher land: Julia Fierro,

Michele Filgate, Alisson Wood, and Leah Johnson, among many other inspiring colleagues. And thank you to Marty McLoughlin—without you, none of it is possible.

"I remembered," she says. "The story you told me about the island with the volcano."

And he beams as though this were the sweetest thing a girl has ever done for him. "Will you sit?" he asks. "If you sit here, you'll hear the locals shouting the most unbelievable profanities."

So she sits, and undoes the buttons of her dress at the wrist. In a little while her hand and his find each other as they watch the fishermen go about their business and listen to their cursing so that the first words she comes to know in that foreign tongue are the ones a proper girl isn't allowed to say. She puts the ferry schedule on the table between her and Sal, so that Sal knows it is there. The sun going down makes all the world look made of gold. Neither of them can stop smiling. Neither Vida nor Sal knows when they will leave, or where they will go, or what sort of people they will become, only that they will be traveling on to the next island together.